INTO THE DARKNESS

MITCH TANNER BOOK TWO

L.T. RYAN

LIQUID MIND MEDIA, LLC

ltryan70@gmail.com

http://LTRyan.com

https://www.facebook.com/JackNobleBooks

ACKNOWLEDGMENTS

Special thanks to Amy, Barbara, Caryn, Karen, Marty, Melissa, and Pati.

CHAPTER ONE

He sought refuge under the canopy of the centuries-old live oak. The leaves couldn't stop all the rain, though. Thin and fat, drops passed through unscathed and pelted the top of his head. Wet, matted hair clung to his forehead. The Spanish moss hung low under the weight of the storm, whipping sideways in the gusts.

Thunder cracked and lightning lit up the land as it scratched down from the heavens and clawed up from hell to meet somewhere in the middle, revealing a sky the color of a week-old corpse.

The living avoided the graveyard tonight. Most other places, in fact. Few were crazy enough to be out in this kind of weather. Samantha might be Category Three by the time she hit the border of Georgia and South Carolina. Savannah would get nailed, but Charleston would see far worse.

He didn't care.

Though the living refused to go near the graveyard, the souls of his victims were out to play.

In all, five of the women he'd murdered — although if one were to ask him, he'd say they were liberated — were buried in the ground here. More than any other local graveyard. Of course, thirteen of them between the two port cities were still missing. The bodies of those ditched at sea had not yet washed ashore. And no one had come upon the women he'd dumped deep in the low country woods.

Nor had they connected those from his travels throughout the country.

Through the hammering rain he saw their translucent souls dancing, free and naked, relishing every time lighting and thunder ripped apart the silence and darkness.

As much as he fed on the energy, even he had his limits. After an hour of playing with the dead, he stopped to visit Lucille. He stood in front of her tombstone for several minutes. Like the other graves, he didn't need light to know what was written there.

The police wanted him badly enough that they devoted a team of detectives to finding him, and he had lived unnoticed, right under their noses, for years.

Until they caught him.

It all started with a visit to Lucille, years ago.

"Lucille," he said. "Even in death, you're such a bitch. It was all because of you."

He dropped to his knees. With his eyes closed, he ran his hands through the damp grass, allowing each blade to choose a path on either side of a finger. Though cold, he imagined the liquid to be fresh blood pouring from his victim. A new one, perhaps. It had been so long that memories of those he had killed did little to excite him.

Except for one woman. The one who had bled on this very same spot. He'd stabbed her one time shy of enough. If only he'd plunged his blade once more, deeper, twisting and cutting and tearing until she faded, things would have been different. He would have been allowed to continue carrying out his work. Ridding the area of the dark-haired whores who pervaded the streets and squares.

He could have carried his mission further across the country. More connections would have been made. He wanted to add to the five men who now helped to achieve his goal. His vision. His dream.

The wind died down to a breeze. The voices of the trees quieted. A lull in the storm engulfed him.

He lifted his hands from the earth, brought them to his face, and wiped the blood of the ghosts on himself. He smelled it. Tasted it. The coppery sensation sliding down his throat felt so real. His hands and fingers tingled. Something stirred in his stomach. A feeling that hadn't been there in months. Excited at the prospects of killing, his erect penis pressed hard against his zipper.

Tonight, he would not discriminate. There was no time to plan.

He began his retreat as the storm resumed, leaving trails in the mud as he struggled to maintain footing while he descended the small hill to the road leading away from the cemetery. The deserted street offered no refuge from the torrential downpour. Why would anyone visit the graveyard or anywhere else tonight? The storm was the reason he felt safe coming out of hiding.

Fifteen minutes later he walked along Skidaway against the wind toward the river. The streets were deserted and dark. He saw no traffic lights, street lamps, or house lights. The power had gone out. Preemptively, he presumed. Those lazy bastards didn't want to work during a hurricane. He was the only one with that kind of work ethic.

A car turned from East Anderson Street. The headlights caught him in a spot where he had no cover. The driver flashed hi-beams. He continued walking forward. The car cut across the street and slowed to a stop in front of him. He shielded his eyes from the rain as the driver's window descended, revealing a twenty-something brunette and her three companions. They were similar in looks, but none as perfect as the woman driving.

"You shouldn't be out here," she said. "Hurricane is going to hit soon."

"Got caught at the cemetery," he said, altering his accent and offering a slight smile. "Came all the way out from Kansas to see it."

The woman looked back at her friend in the passenger seat. They kept their voices low, making it impossible for him to determine what had been said. They looked like the kind of intelligent women who presented the type of challenge he enjoyed. But they would pull away without him. He was sure of it.

"Where are you staying?" She smiled while squinting against a heavy wind gust. "We'll give you a ride there."

He placed his hands on the windowsill and leaned forward so he wouldn't have to shout against the noise of the storm. "Stupidly, I got off the bus and walked right down here. Figured I'd be able to find a room somewhere along the river."

"You'll never find a place now."

He looked up into the rain, stood with his hands out, and shook his head. "I know, I know. You must think I'm the biggest idiot in the city, right?"

"Pretty much." The woman bit her lip as she looked him up and down.

There was nothing menacing about him. He went out of his way to make sure of it. Clean cut, short hair, polo shirts, tan chinos. His face was always clean-shaven. Fingernails manicured. Neat and simple looking. His frame belied his strength. Wiry, but not overly muscular. Plenty strong enough to do the job, though.

She gestured toward the back door. "Get in. You can stay with us. It's not the nicest place, but we've got a great couch."

"You sure it's wise to invite a stranger to stay in your house?"

Her grin widened. "Something tells me you're a safe bet. Now get in."

The rear driver's side door popped open. He saw the two women there scooting along the bench seat to allow him room to sit. He adjusted his bag so it was on his outside shoulder.

The night wouldn't be as fun if they discovered the knife and handgun it contained.

All four women introduced themselves. But he only remembered Alice, the woman driving. He told them his name was Rick Harrison. A lie. He then wove a tale of growing up on a farm, then leaving home for the Army — special forces, of course — only to wash out because of a broken leg that hadn't healed properly. It had acted up again tonight while he fought the wind and rain.

By the time they reached the women's home on the other side of Forsythe Park, the women had let their guard down completely in front of the guy they perceived to be an idiot who came to Savannah in the middle of a hurricane with no place to stay.

Perfection achieved. Almost.

They stayed up for another hour or so, drinking wine and warm beer. Talking and even a little flirting. He heard their stories. In one ear, out the other. He didn't care what made them tick, what their life dreams were. Those dreams would end tonight. Only his dream could carry on.

He wished them all goodnight on their final night as they slipped down the hallway to turn in. He made note of which door each went into, then took thirty minutes to clear his mind. Meditation, it'll help you achieve your goals!

CHAPTER TWO

Two of the women bunked in the same room. He had to be quick about killing them. He hated being quick. A cock-roach deserved a quick death. Not a woman. For she was a play thing in her final minutes.

He stuck a pillow over the first woman's face, both hands over her nose and mouth until she stopped squirming. Her muffled cries for help barely reached his ears. Then, using the same pillow, he smothered the other woman's face, but only to stop her screams from drifting out of the room. He took his knife and used it to cut her shirt from the bottom up. She railed against him. The blade sliced into the flesh of her abdomen.

"Damn you," he whispered as he cut her neck. Stupid whore. Covered him in blood. He couldn't surprise Alice like he had planned. He pulled the pillow off the dead woman's face. Her opened eyes glistened. "All you had to do was play along for a few minutes."

The floorboards creaked in the hallway outside the room. He stopped and leaned back against the wall. At the end of the corridor there were two doors. But he found himself unable to recall which one led to which woman. The whore's rebellion had thrown him off. Enter the wrong room, and everything was ruined. He'd have to kill Alice right away instead of playing with her first.

What a shame.

Alice tantalized him in all the right ways.

He continued down the hallway, walking close to the trim. It helped to reduce squeaking. He stopped at the end of the corridor between two doors. One to the right. One to the left. The house exhaled a steady hum, while wind and rain battered its shell. He closed his eyes, absorbed the sounds, and held his knife out.

"Oh, show me the way, my steeled companion," he whispered.

When he looked down, the knife pointed to the left.

Of course, the door with the seashell sign hanging from a bent nail. Alice's room. She had said she grew up on the beach in Florida before attending the Savannah College of Art and Design.

SCAD, he thought. What a silly name.

He opened the door on the right. It smelled floral. Overly so. And it was hot. A sheet covered the woman. As he neared, he noticed how tightly wrapped it was around her ass. She mumbled something indecipherable as she drew one knee up. He stepped into the room, spun in a half circle, and shut the door, holding the knob tight to the right to prevent the latch from clicking while he turned the lock.

At the side of the bed, he clawed for her face, but found her hair. He traced his fingertips along her body toward the foot of the bed. Felt the dip in her lower back. The shapeliness of her ass. His preference for her to be on her back diminished. The stomach would be even better. He wedged his fingers into the crease where her thighs met.

She tensed. Her leg snapped back and her thighs pressed tight together.

He snatched her pillow, wrapped it around her face. As he straddled her back, he tied the ends of the pillowcase together. She thrashed underneath him, but all it did was arouse him. He worked his hands along her arms until each gripped a wrist. He wrenched them back until they touched. The pillow muffled her choking sobs. He held her arms in place with one hand, and grabbed the bedsheet with the other, which he used to tie her wrists together. She continued to thrash, her back pressing against his testicles. He went still, closed his eyes, cocked his head and listened.

Her moans melted into the howling wind and pelting raindrops. There was no way they slipped past the door. The door which he'd shut. The door which he'd locked.

He had time to get some of the vitriol out of his system.

Alice would appreciate that.

Using his knee, he wedged her thighs apart. She twisted and bucked, but couldn't force him away. He tore her panties down the middle. But then the sensations that stirred in the graveyard, and yet again while she fought underneath him, were no longer present.

As much as he wanted the release so that he would be in control when he went to Alice, that would not be the case.

"Shit. You stupid, stupid bitch. What's wrong with you?"

He hopped off the bed. The woman rolled over and retreated to the corner. The pillow slipped down, revealing her darkened eyes, nose and mouth. She could have screamed, but she didn't. Instead, she whined breathlessly.

"Please, don't."

Using the sheet he snatched off the floor, he wiped her friend's blood off his blade. Then he lunged forward and gagged her with the bloodied sheet. With her arms bound behind her, she could do nothing other than kick to defend herself. Not an easy feat with his weight bearing down on her thighs.

He rose up, one hand behind her head, pulling tight on her neck. The other holding the knife in front of his crotch, inches from her throat.

One way or another, he'd have his release.

And so he stabbed her over thirty times. The blade penetrated her face, neck, chest, abdomen and thighs.

He left her to bleed out, the knife buried deep in her stomach. The doorknob on the other side of the hallway felt cold against his flushed skin. He gripped it. Turned it. Cracked the door. Felt a rush of cold air that smelled like lavender wash over him.

"Hello, Alice," he said in his country accent. "I thought we might talk for a while."

She rolled over. Her form cut through the darkness as she sat up. She switched on a flashlight aimed at herself. He could see from her exposed breasts and erect nipples that she was happy he'd entered her room.

"I was hoping you'd join me," she said.

"I know you were, Alice." His voice had changed. He was no longer the unassuming man caught in the storm. He was the man they wished they'd never run into. He was Novak. "But this night is not going to go as you expected."

CHAPTER THREE

I'd been awake for an hour by the time the alarm on my cell phone started blaring. I reached over my daughter Ella Kate's slumbering body and silenced the horrid device. Her hair was pulled back into a ponytail, the ends draped over my shoulder. She lay still, trapped inside a linen burrito made of sheets and a comforter. She'd managed to steal them all during the night. Didn't matter much to me. It was late September, and the nighttime temperature was cool enough I could leave the windows open without freezing or overheating myself to death. Probably wasn't a good idea to let her sleep in the same bed, but our lives had been turned upside down and right side over.

If it kept us both sane, then so be it.

It was five a.m. Too early for the sun to be up. Too early for me to be up. But I had no choice, even while suspended from work. I'd slept for three hours, if that. That'd been the case the past couple of nights. Impending doom, I supposed.

My hearing with Chief Warren was scheduled for today at

nine-thirty. I faced a lengthy suspension for assaulting another detective.

Assault, my ass.

If the guy was half as tough as he acted, a single punch wouldn't have taken him down.

They'd likely bring up a string of other infractions that had been swept under the bureaucratic rug and kept there until they needed to use them in an effort to keep me away from the job for as long as they were legally allowed. Maybe even longer.

Huff — my boss — wouldn't do much to help. He couldn't. He hadn't been in middle management long enough to be able to put up and win a fight with Chief Warren.

My sole hope rested with the case my partner, Sam Foster, and I had blown wide-open a week or so earlier. If it weren't for us, Beans Holland and Debbie Walker would be dead. Two young kids who had been in my ex Lana's fourth grade class.

In the same school that Ella Kate attended.

Horrible to think what could have happened.

Now, you'd think the fact we rescued those kids would be helpful for my case. If only. I had a feeling it'd come back to bite me in the ass. I pissed off a lot of people. Broke a lot of rules. Hell, I'd do it again, too, if it meant bringing those children home.

My phone erupted in song again — some tune they'd called *Soft Morning Rhapsody*. I flipped the phone over and traced the slider to turn the alarm off. Ella hadn't noticed. Oh, to sleep like that. I kissed her cool cheek, rose, and proceeded to the bathroom and hopped in the shower. After drying off, I stepped into my gray suit pants and pulled a white cotton t-shirt on. It looked fresh and bright in the mirror. No stains. I slipped my button-up over it, letting it hang open. I'd throw on the jacket and tie at the last minute. Hell, right outside Huff's office suited me fine.

Ella Kate sat up as I opened the bathroom door. She stretched her little arms over her head and belted out a dramatic yawn. Her mouth must've twisted in seven directions.

"Morning, Daddy."

"Hello, angel," I said, leaning over and kissing her forehead.

"Why are you up so early?"

"Got a meeting."

"At work?"

I nodded, avoiding eye contact. "Come on, let's get you ready to see your grandmother."

She freed herself from the tangled web of sheets and hopped off the bed. "I can get ready myself."

I leaned back against the wall to allow her space to pass, smiling as she blew by and marched right out of the room. When I saw her again she had on a pair of jeans with hearts made from gems running down the leg and a t-shirt adorned with the cast of *My Little Pony*.

How long until she'd outgrow such things?

How much had Robbie outgrown since we last saw him?

I hadn't seen my son since my ex-wife, Marissa, left with him in the middle of the night more than a year ago. A few days ago, I received a postcard in the mail from him. Looked to be sent from Denver. It provided the first clue as to their location since they had disappeared.

An hour later, Ella had eaten and I'd caffeinated myself to the point where I could drive. She stood there with her Teddy, aptly named Doggie, and a pink backpack. I loaded her into the Boss — my 1969 Boss 429 Mustang — and we made the short drive over to Momma's house. The roads were empty and still slick from the shower that'd blown through a few hours before. Faint orange sky peeked over the cluttered horizon.

Momma stood at the front door with a mug of steaming coffee.

She shuffled Ella into the living room, turned on the TV, and then pestered me with questions.

"Have you heard anything about which way they're leaning?"

"No, Momma, I haven't. I've told you before these things are tight-lipped. The chief has a file on me that's two-inches thick. At least."

"And another five inches thick that shows him all the good things you've done." She fanned herself with her hand. "The people you've helped. The cases you've solved. You and Sam are the only good cops left, Mitch."

"Maybe I should bring you along to lobby for me."

She rolled her eyes and shook her head. "Always making jokes. What are you going to do if they fire you?"

I glanced around the kitchen. "You got an extra room here, right?"

"For Ella. You'll be sleeping in the doghouse out back."

"Yeah, well, that might be too nice for me."

"That's right. It is. So don't you come back here without your job intact. Got it?"

I shot her a smile, hoping it would instill some false confidence in her. Judging by the look on her face, it didn't do the trick.

"Anyway," I said a few moments later, "I've gotta get going. Sam's meeting me for breakfast. Said he's got some info from Huff about what the chief might hit me with. Could help knowing in advance. You know? Get a defense going in my head."

"You said you hadn't heard anything."

"I hadn't. I'm about to. If I have a few minutes, I'll call."

She ushered me toward the front door. "Give my love to Sam. And be sure to remind him how lucky his mother is she doesn't have to deal with her son getting into trouble all the time."

Sam the Angel. Yeah, right.

Standing on the stoop in the cool air with the sun peeking over the house on the other side of the street, I felt like a teenager again. Sam and I had been friends since high school. Not so much in the years before that. But even back when we were teenagers, it was me getting us into most of the trouble.

And this time I hoped Sam had something that would help bail me out.

Again.

CHAPTER FOUR

The diner was small, loud, a bit dirty, and had the rudest waitstaff I'd ever encountered. In all seventy-three times I'd eaten there. Why subject myself to such a hostile environment? They served the best scrapple west of Center City. The way I saw it, the grime on the floor added a bit of flavor to the food.

We sat there for five minutes without speaking. Sam stared out the window at the parking lot. His eyes only moved when someone entering or leaving the building walked past. Didn't take a mind reader to figure out he had nothing good to say.

Our waitress returned with our food. She set Sam's plate in front of me, and mine in front of him. She failed to refill my coffee, too. But she broke up the monotony, and for that I was grateful.

"So what's new?" I asked after shoveling down an egg and half my scrapple.

Sam shrugged and took a sip of orange juice. "Got a new case yesterday. Murder-suicide. He was eighty-three, she was seventy-four. We already got into her email, and it turns out she was cheating on him with her personal trainer. Guess how old he was?"

The image in my head wasn't pretty. "Ninety-two?"

Laughing, he shook his head. "Twenty-six."

"Get the hell outta here."

"Serious as shit, man. The husband was loaded. He, uh, had something to do with inventing a revolutionary heart valve replacement thing, or something like that. So it seems the young buck got wind of this, you know, through casual conversation with the wife. After a while, he and the old lady started forming a plan to get rid of the husband and take his fortune."

"Can't imagine what would've happened to her after that."

He shrugged. "Her money, so as long as she didn't marry him. He'd have to do whatever she wanted, I guess."

"But the husband found out and put an end to all of it."

Sam nodded, then scooped a pile of pancake into his mouth.

"You said we." I folded my arms over my chest. "Who'd they team you up with?"

He stopped chewing and held my gaze for a moment. A few seconds later, after he'd swallowed, Sam said, "You remember Morris?"

"Rings a bell, I suppose."

"Kid who transferred into Robbery a few months ago from a district on the other side of town."

"Yeah, yeah. I know him. That's who you're working with now?"

Sam nodded.

"They're giving him a little exposure to our world while I'm out, huh?"

Sam's eyes shifted left. It was only for a second. But that was a second too long. I knew it. He knew it. So he said, "No, he's making a permanent move."

"Shit." I balled my napkin up and tossed it on my plate. It rolled into a puddle of leftover egg yolk and stopped.

"Look, I'm not saying this is set in stone. You might get lucky in there today. Maybe Huff will fight for you."

I laughed. "Huff ain't doin' shit. You know he's got no pull. Chief Warren will slap him down if he so much as lifts one ass cheek to fart."

The conversation went to that place where conversations go to die. We sat there, silent, Sam staring out the window again. The waitress came by. Looked annoyed. Set a fresh glass of OJ in front of Sam and took my quarter-full mug away without asking if I was done.

"Anyway," I said, watching our waitress retreat into the kitchen. "What's your gut tell you on this case you're working?"

"Seems pretty cut and dry."

"You think the young buck had anything to do with it?"

"We're bringing him in today for questioning. But really, what'd he have to gain by killing both of them? And we don't have proof he was acting with the old lady when it came to taking down her old man." Sam wiped his mouth, then added, "Yet. But so far, the emails we've found implicated her. Once we can get access to his computer, we'll know more."

Interesting case, I thought. The kind I would have sunk my teeth into. Plain as day the personal trainer had some involvement in the plan to take out the husband. Maybe he was there to do it and something happened. The old lady chickened out, threatened to go to the cops. Sam needed to ask the right questions. Morris had to ask the right follow-ups. If things were going to travel down the wrong alley, it'd happen there. Hell of a case to break in an FNG.

"So what exactly have you heard about my hearing?" I asked.

Sam's lips thinned and his face tightened. "It's not good. Chief

Warren wants to use this latest incident to fire you. It's not enough, of course. But I hear his plan is to devote a full-time employee to going through every single case you ever worked, with me, and before me, all the way back to your newbie days. They're gonna try to find every possible mistake, slip-up, code violation you ever made. They'll take every single complaint ever filed against you. Doesn't matter if it was from a jaywalker from back when you worked downtown. Whatever happens today, just be ready to face the fact it might get worse. Once they have all that shit together, they'll have another hearing. And that's when Warren's gonna drop the hammer."

"Well, that figures. Chief's had a hard-on for me five years, at least." I grabbed a frigid, sweating glass of water. Tiny remains of ice bobbed along the top. "Guess I can count on my vacation lasting a little longer."

"Sorry, Mitch."

"Not your fault."

"They came to me. Interviewed me for four hours. I said every positive thing I could about you."

"So you're saying you talked for about three seconds, then ran out of stuff to say."

Sam laughed. "Pretty much. Someone had to, right?"

"Well, you're not the dumbass that knocked Fairchild out inside the office."

He slid his plate to the side and leaned forward, forearms crossing half the table. "I know the guy deserved it. But, Mitch, you gotta learn to control yourself. You might lose your job. What next? I mean, you already lost your wi–" Sam stopped himself.

I looked away. Said nothing. I felt the full effect of what he didn't say.

"Maybe you can negotiate with them," he said after a few awkward seconds.

"How?" I asked.

"Therapy."

"Are you kidding me?"

"You've got an anger problem, man." Sam leaned back and tilted his head to the left. "Look at you. You're getting pissed off at me right now."

"Are we through here?" I didn't want to spend another minute inside.

"Consider it, man. Might be the thing that allows you to keep your job."

CHAPTER FIVE

The meeting took place in Huff's office and not one of the bland meeting rooms. Surprised the hell out of me. Chief Warren looked pissed that this was his second time at our humble office in less than a month. Didn't help my case that both times were because of me. Every few seconds he'd brush some lint off his jacket or straighten his shirt. Huff drummed his calloused fingertips on the arms of the pleather chair. His stare remained fixed anywhere but on me.

I assumed the posture of a Buddhist monk, still and calm, my shoulders held high and pulled back. At least I looked in control on the outside. That wasn't the case on the inside. It didn't matter what I said, or how I defended myself. The decision had been made. The meeting was nothing more than a formality.

When the time came, I pleaded my case. My entire defense boiled down to the fact that Fairchild was an asshole. And I said as much.

"Detective Tanner," Chief Warren said. "In all my years in the department, I've never encountered a cop as off-kilter and arrogant as you. And I think that in itself says something. In my opinion, the city of Philadelphia would be better off if you were no longer a member of its police force."

"You know my record," I said. "I'll grant you my methods might be a bit unorthodox at times, but dammit, I get the job done."

Warren looked down at me. "And how does sending another detective to the hospital get the job done? Tell me how taking a man out of work for two weeks because his jaw was wired shut helps anyone around here, or the citizens who count on us. Christ, you know how understaffed we are to begin with."

"So why are you so hellbent on making me take a seat, Chief?"

Huff cleared his throat. "Tanner—"

"I'm not done, Lieutenant," Warren said, slicing sideways through the air with his hand. "Detective, I've got two people looking for any loophole they can find to get you kicked out of the department. And I'm not stopping there. We're scouring every case you've ever worked, and every call or report filed against you. So help me, I'm not only going to fire you, I'm going to put your ass in jail."

My old friend anger made a triumphant return. I sprung out of my chair, finger aimed at Warren.

"You wouldn't manage to hang on to that cushy job of yours if it wasn't for cops like me who get the damn job done. What was your record when you were out there? Huh? Whatever it was, I bet you didn't get to where you are now by being a damn choir boy." I paused a beat. "Or maybe you did. That's it, right? You've been a damn ass kisser since your first day on the job. Apparently, it doesn't stop when you get to the top, because now your lips reek of the toilets in City Hall."

"Detective Tanner!" Warren stepped forward. Veins popped like snakes on his neck and the sides of his forehead.

"Whoa! Whoa!" Huff lurched up and darted around his desk. He popped me in the chest with one hand, and Warren with the other. Drove both of us backward. I slammed into the glass wall. "Sit your ass down, Tanner."

"Yeah," Warren said. "Listen to your lieutenant, Detective, while he's still your boss."

"And you shut the hell up, Warren. You know damn well you were baiting Tanner."

Holy shit! Huff actually had a set, and they just dropped.

It appeared as though Warren didn't know whether to slap Huff or obey his command. The chief stood there like a dog trying to decide if he'd get the treat if he sat this time. Huff's face and posture remained stoic. I would've never imagined this from him.

It felt like the temperature had climbed twenty degrees inside Huff's office. Heavy breathing mingled with the constant drone of the HVAC system. The other two men engaged in a stare-off. Felt like they'd forgotten I was in there, too.

Finally, Huff lowered his outstretched arms. Tension eased from his face. "Chief, step outside with me."

On his way out, Warren shot me an icy stare that caused an involuntary clenching of my chest and arms. A sheen of sweat coated his forehead. His cheeks still burned red. Looked like his veins were going to pop right out from his skin. Huff had stepped in at the right time. A few more minutes, Warren might've stroked out on us. What was protocol if that happened? Would they hand me my badge and let me get back to work?

I waited two minutes before moving. First thing I did was look out at the hallway. Huff and Warren had slipped out of sight, leaving a view of the drab wall. Turning, I faced the homicide room. Everyone had cleared out, no doubt at the sound of my outburst, leaving behind a bunch of cluttered desks and sports coats draped over the backs of uncomfortable office chairs.

I pulled out my cell and checked my emails. A few new spam messages, but nothing else. No texts, either. Maybe all the other detectives already knew the outcome. Best guess, Huff told them to be gone. But what if they'd all turned on me, leaving Sam as my only friend in the room? Could I really blame them? By this point, they all must have started wondering who's next. Piss off Tanner and he'll belt ya.

I stared at the wall behind Huff's desk for a few more minutes. The guy was not one to decorate, so to pass the time, I pulled up ESPN's website and glanced over the headlines. Not even the upcoming Eagles versus Cowboys game could get my blood going as much as the encounter with Warren.

I stood again and turned toward the office. At least they hadn't disturbed my desk. Yet. It was covered in its signature clutter. All except for around the monitor, where two pictures stood. Ella Kate and Robbie. And staring at those two tiny faces, my mind locked in on one single thought.

There was hope for me yet.

CHAPTER SIX

Huff pushed open the door into his office wearing the look of a doctor about to tell a family their father didn't survive the heart attack. His eyes were cast downward and his gaze shifted from his desk to my feet. Slowly it inched upward. Our stares met, and he looked away.

"Just give it to me, Huff."

He was shaking his head as he sat down behind his desk.

"I fought for you, Tanner. I really did."

Now, if Huff had told me that a day ago, I'd have called bullshit on him. But after seeing the way he took command during our meeting, and the way he put Chief Warren in his place, I believed him.

"Appreciate that, Huff." I turned my head and glanced into the detectives' room. Still empty. "So, what's the damage? Two weeks? A month?"

He placed both fists, balled up so tight his fingertips were white, on his desk calendar. He stared at a spot in between them.

"Huff?"

"It's indefinite, Tanner." He let out a grating sigh.

"You're kidding me, right?"

He leaned back in his chair. It rocked back and then bounced forward. Huff steepled his hands together over his protruding stomach. The space between the buttons above and below his belly button opened. Stray hairs poked out.

"Warren's serious about this shit," Huff said. "And there's nothing else I can do. If you want to fight this, turn to your FOP rep and see what they recommend."

"Christ, all the trouble I caused them. The union probably wants me off the force as bad as Warren."

"You don't know that. Besides, doesn't matter what they think of you. Their only interest is doing what's right by cops. They'll take up for you."

I leaned back, letting my head rest against the cool glass separating Huff's office from the detectives' room. The feeling spread to my forehead and down to the base of my neck.

"Any questions?" Huff asked.

"Not really," I said. "I know the rules."

"I know you do. Don't break them. I'm serious, Tanner. You step out of line while on suspension, it'll give Warren all the ammo he needs. Only thing that saved your ass with the kids was the fact that you saved them. That's why he's digging for something else. No one would take kindly to you being busted down 'cause of that situation. We all know you did what you had to do."

I stood and pulled open the door to the room. Huff rose behind me. His chair collided with the wall. He bumped his leg into the corner of his desk and cursed.

"Sure you wanna escort me to my desk?" I said. "Might end up on workman's comp."

"Shut up, wise ass. Gotta make sure you don't take any files home."

"Think I'm gonna work for free?"

"If your head's in a case, I know you will."

I smirked. "You know me better than I thought."

He shrugged. "Take everything you think you might want."

I picked up the pictures of my kids. Held them to my chest. I felt like if I brought them home, I was admitting defeat. Perhaps, in more ways than one. I reached to set them back down.

"Tanner." Huff put his hand on my shoulder. "This might be your only chance. Warren gets his way, I guarantee you, he's not letting you back in here to get your stuff."

I knew his words were laden with truth. I reached across the desktop, grabbed my pen, a blank notebook, and the pictures of my kids. The department could keep everything else.

As I walked away, Huff said, "That all?"

I said nothing.

He raced across the floor toward me. The double tap of his hard soles echoed throughout the room.

"I think I know the way out," I said.

"I gotta walk with you," he said. "That's the rules, Tanner. That's all."

Sighing, I pulled the door open and stepped into the hallway. Sam was leaning against the opposite wall, chin on his chest, toothpick protruding from his closed mouth. He looked up at me. I gave him a quick shake of my head. He nodded in response. Nothing more had to be said.

"Huff, order Sam to show me out."

"What?" Huff said.

"You heard me."

"Fine," Huff said. "But you two do anything stupid, Sam will be in as much trouble as you."

We left Huff behind and took the quickest route out of the building. My car remained where I had parked it, perhaps for the last time in the detective lot. Bits of gravel were kicked up and skated across the asphalt as we walked over to the Boss.

I grabbed the hot handle and opened the door, leaving it open to let the air get out. It had warmed up since I went inside the station, and the sun shone directly onto the windshield.

"You getting paid?" Sam asked.

I shrugged. "Didn't ask."

"What?"

"You know I don't do this for the money. Got enough in that fund from the settlement after Dad's death."

"Yeah, I know. I also know you don't like touching that money."

"Just want to have it around for the kids. They're the ones really missing out. Think about it, they get to go their whole lives without seeing his rough side."

"Wish I hadn't." Sam smiled. "You gonna be all right?"

"Suppose so."

"What'll you do?"

"Hang out with the kid, I guess. Maybe take a trip or two. Pray like hell Warren's people don't uncover anything I've forgotten about."

"You think the stuff you remember is any better?"

Shrugging, I said, "At least I can come up with a counter argument relatively quickly. Anything I don't recall, who knows. I'm too direct to be considered the world's best bullshitter."

"Got that right."

"Title would go to you, anyway."

Sam laughed. So did I.

"I got a friend in Warren's office," Sam said, his face serious. "I'll ask her to keep her ears open. Maybe she can get involved and help make a few things disappear."

"Why would she do that?"

"Maybe she owes me."

"Maybe, huh?"

He shrugged. Sam kept a few things close to the vest, and I didn't pry when he did. He'd let me know if I needed to.

"I don't know about that, partner," I said. "I'm a sinking ship. Best not to add any more passengers."

I slipped behind the wheel of the Boss and closed the door. Sam knocked on the window. I rolled it down.

"Want me to come over tonight?" he asked.

"Better call first. Make sure I'm in the mood."

He nodded with a wink and then headed back inside. I twisted the key in the ignition. The Boss's 429 roared to life. I idled for a few seconds, then pulled out of the parking lot.

Perhaps for the last time.

CHAPTER SEVEN

I drove until the gas needle hovered above E. Along the way, I passed the entrance to my ex Lana's neighborhood. It wasn't what you would call on the way to Momma's house. I must've driven there subconsciously. Didn't realize it until I saw the street sign. I braked hard and whipped the wheel, cutting across the divide and in front of a couple of shocked oncoming drivers who blared their horns at me.

I wasn't sure what had become of Lana after she'd been arrested for her involvement in those kids' abduction. Did the judge offer her bail? Had she been able to post it? No clue. Don't care, don't wanna know.

Her car sat in the driveway, about halfway between the street and garage. A thin layer of dirt and a little mold covered the white exterior. Guess that was the case with most white cars that sat for too long in one place. The front blinds were drawn and the curtains parted. I took that to mean she had posted bond and was home, maybe on a house arrest-type deal. Not like she had anywhere else to go. No school would ever hire her again, assuming she managed to escape significant jail time.

To think, I thought I might marry the woman someday.

As Momma would say, I can read a criminal like an open book, but women were a mystery to me. Never could pick the right one. I thought I had a winner in Marissa. That didn't turn out so well, either.

I turned in the cul-de-sac and covered the side of my face as I powered past the house on the way out. Not sure what the point was. The Boss was a pretty recognizable car. At the end of the street, I stopped and reached for Robbie's postcard. My fingers traced the letters written by Robbie's hand, pausing on the postmark.

Denver.

Could it be that easy?

Doubtful. Marissa, for all her faults, was a good cop's wife. She was smart, with a memory like a sponge. She saw the world through similar colored lenses as me. She listened well. Perhaps too well. I divulged thoughts and facts to her that I know she kept locked in a vault in her mind. She'd know better than to let Robbie mail off that postcard from a city they were living in. The way I saw it, that left three options.

They were leaving Denver when he mailed it. Or they had made a trip there, perhaps from someplace nearby. Or he had done it when she wasn't looking.

Either way Denver would hold a clue. And now that I had some time off, I'd head out there and see what turned up.

As I got back on track to Momma's house, I thought of the other person I knew in Denver. Bridget Dinapoli. We had struck something up between us while working on the Beans and Debbie case together. I know they say cops and FBI don't mix, but there was something about the woman I couldn't shake. While the case ultimately got me suspended, Bridget received a promotion to the Denver field office. I'd mulled over calling her the moment I spotted the postmark on Robbie's note. The only reason I hadn't was I feared she *would* help. I didn't want her putting her career at risk for me.

But if I was going to be out there, well, it couldn't hurt to reach out to her.

An old faded red Ford Galaxy occupied most of Momma's driveway. I drove past, and pulled next to the curb, got out and walked up behind the car. It had local tags. The black interior was in perfect shape. I doubted the car had anywhere close to a hundred thousand miles on it. The steering wheel was wrapped in camouflage. Black Rosary beads hung from the rearview mirror.

I continued to the side entrance, leading to the kitchen. The door was locked. I rapped on it. The floor shook and the louvered glass rattled as my mother walked over and unlocked the door.

"How'd it go?" Her eyebrows were arched high into her forehead and her mouth hung open in anticipation.

"Not so well," I said.

She exhaled with a sigh. Her breath smelled like bacon and coffee.

"Come on in," she said, pulling the door open.

"Who's here?"

"Father Reyes stopped by. We've been praying for you."

I stopped and looked at her. "This a new thing for you?"

"What?"

"Church?"

"You'd know I was going regularly again if you stopped by more often."

"I'm here almost every day."

"Yeah, to drop Ella off. When's the last time you came in and had a cup of coffee with me?"

"Not now, Momma. Not with the day I'm having." I looked over and saw the priest standing near the fridge.

He nodded and smiled.

"Father," I said.

"Mitch," he said. "Hope you're well. Haven't seen you at Mass in a while."

"Yeah, well, no offense, but I'm a bit pissed at God at the moment. Having your kid stolen in the middle of the night can do that to you."

His smile dimmed, but didn't fade. If he were in my interrogation room I'd classify him as arrogant. "I might be able to help you with these feelings, Mitch. You should come by my office one of these days."

"I'll take that into consideration, Father." I turned to my mother. "Can we talk for a minute?"

"Sure," she said.

"Alone," I said.

"What? Oh, yeah." She walked over to the priest. "Father Reyes, would you mind waiting in the living room?"

He waved at me, then disappeared. The floor vibrated with every step he took.

"What is it?" Momma said.

"I'm thinking about getting away for a couple days."

She narrowed her eyes, waiting for the follow up.

"And I was hoping you could watch Ella for me."

"Sure, but where are you going?"

I shrugged, said nothing.

"I'm not going to do it if you won't tell me."

"Haven't decided yet."

She grabbed my forearm and bit down with her fake nails. "Do you know something about where Robbie is?"

I tipped my head, lowered my voice even more. "I might have a lead."

She inhaled sharply and sat down in one of her retro looking red vinyl-covered kitchen chairs. The seat groaned as she shifted to get comfortable.

"Take as long as you need, Mitch," she said. "I'm serious. Ella will be fine here. And if I need a break, the girl next door is an excellent sitter."

"She's at school now?"

Momma nodded.

"Give her a kiss for me and tell her I'll be back as soon as I can."

"You're not gonna say goodbye?"

"It's best I get going now."

I left Momma's, drove home, and parked the Boss in the garage. As I ate a quick lunch I noticed how hollow the house felt. Where four people had once been a happy, young family, nothing remained but tortured fragments of our souls. I shook the feelings aside over a beer and then changed into jeans, a grey pullover, and threw on some hiking boots. I packed a bag with a couple changes of clothing.

Fifteen minutes later, the cab pulled up to take me to the airport.

Less than an hour later, I stood in front of the ticket counter. I wasn't going to Denver. Not yet, at least. Why? Because I couldn't get it out of my head that Marissa was screwing with me, hoping I'd waste my time looking for her in the mile-high city.

So I purchased a ticket and boarded a plane bound for Savannah, Georgia, where my old friend Cassie lived. If anyone could help me find my son, it was her.

CHAPTER EIGHT

A half-dozen pissed off toddlers surrounded me on the flight. Their parents seemed oblivious to the racket they were making. I suppose at some point you just have to say screw it. Nothing can be done anyway. But damn, pass the headphones.

The incessant crying and screaming had the effect of making the flight seem much longer than the hour and a half we were actually in the air, robbing me of my planned thinking time. I was out of my seat almost a second after the wheels touched down. The flight crew cast scowling glances in my direction, mostly because other passengers were following my lead. I was lucky they didn't have me detained for inciting a mob.

I made my way through the hot and humid jetway and exited into the waiting area for gate 15, the last in the airport's single terminal. Aside from a young couple seated in the corner, the gate was empty. A wide walkway stretched past the other fourteen gates. Half were packed, sending their overflow into the available seats of the other gates.

On the first level I rented a mid-sized sedan from a guy who looked like a squirrel wearing glasses. When I told him I wasn't sure where I was staying, he scribbled a name on his pad, tore off a sheet of paper and handed it to me. Said it was his grandmother, and he knew for a fact her downstairs apartment was available for at least a month. Then he called her to let her know I'd be inquiring about it. After listening to the rest of his corporate spiel, I headed out into the heat and found my ride. The engine choked to life the way an abused rental car does. The AC spit out air reeking of a hundred different passengers this year alone. But it was cold. And after a crowded flight, that was good enough for me. The steady stream of air dried my forehead, leaving it chilled.

I had my cell's contact list open. My thumb hovered over Cassie's number. We'd been in contact recently while I was working the Beans and Debbie Walker kidnapping case. Bridget Dinapoli and I had flown down to Savannah during the investigation and met with Cassie. And now that I was returning so soon, how would she react? Cassie was a hard woman to read. I'd sat across the table from some damn hardened criminals who were easier to pick apart than her.

Eventually I swiped the list away and called the number on the torn piece of notebook paper. An old woman answered, excited, and told me she'd been waiting by the phone for my call. After a bit of back and forth, I agreed to rent her downstairs apartment for a week.

It took close to twenty minutes to reach the house situated on E. Jones Street, about a block from Lafayette Square and the cathedral. The heat smacked me in the face as I stepped out of the car. The air smelled of coffee. I turned into the breeze and spotted four people sitting around a bistro table with mugs in front of them. Locals, I presumed. Who else would sit outside drinking coffee in ninety-degree weather?

Piano music drifted out of the open windows of the house. I

climbed the old concrete stairs and rapped my knuckles hard against the door. The melody stopped. The old lady's footsteps banged closer. The door whipped open and she looked up at me, smiling. Her face was pale and wrinkled. Her hair silver and curled. She exuded a high level of energy and confidence. The smell coming from inside the house was a mixture of potpourri and burgers.

"Mr. Tanner, I presume." Her smile broadened, looking a lot less like a squirrel than her grandson, and extended her hand toward me. "Call me Betty."

"Yes, ma'am." I entered through the vacant spot where she had stood. "I've got your check right here."

"Just put it on the bureau over there." She turned and headed down the hall. "I'll get your key."

I stood by the doorway, scanning the layout. Everything in the place looked at least as old as her. She came back and tossed the key at me, then walked past me onto the front landing. I followed her down to a doorway hidden underneath the stairs. Musty air rushed past as I opened the door. I swear I saw mold spores smiling at me. She gave me a quick tour of the apartment, which ran the length and width of the house. Wasn't much, just a couple of rooms. Plenty enough for me.

"If there's anything you need, Mr. Tanner, you let me know. I'm here most of the time." She eyed me as I dropped my things on the couch. "You know the most interesting thing about Savannah?"

I remained motionless for a moment, recalling any facts I'd learned along the way. Nothing sprung to mind, so I shrugged.

"There are about five thousand more single women than men in this city," she said. "Those odds are in your favor."

I smiled and said, "I'll keep that in mind."

"I eat dinner at six in the afternoon every single day. Don't be late if you plan on joining me."

With that, she exited the apartment. Sunlight knifed across the floor for a moment then vanished as the door fell shut. I had a pang of guilt, something telling me I should've gone to see Cassie first. Every second I wasted was an opportunity for Robbie to slip further away.

So why hadn't I gone? What was holding me back?

That was easy to answer.

Fear.

CHAPTER NINE

A new plaything. It had been so long since he brought a new plaything to the cellar. There was that woman in the other cell, but she was already there. In fact, Novak wasn't sure how she'd arrived. Had he blacked out again? Sometimes, when it had been too long, the experience was simply too much for him to handle and he lost all concept of space and time.

Killing the three women in Alice's house would tide him over for a bit. Keeping Alice around would help him go even longer. She could keep him satisfied.

He pushed her door open and stood in the doorway, a slight smile on his lips. She lay on the bed, her back to him, knees tucked up to her chest. Her panties hugged her ass so perfectly.

"Hello, Alice," he said.

She turned her head far enough to see him out of the corner of her eye.

"You've got nothing to say?"

She looked away again.

Novak entered the room and walked over to the bed. He

placed his knee on the edge and shifted his weight toward it. The mattress dipped toward him, turning her body slightly. She covered her breast with her hand, but part of her nipple poked out. Novak leaned in further.

"You can say anything you want, Alice. Don't fear me."

How could she not? After what he'd done? He hoped she realized that wasn't him in the house. No, that wasn't entirely true. That was a different version of him. And, as he had told her earlier, if she didn't want to see that version again, she had better start engaging him.

"Can I get you anything?" he asked.

She rolled over onto her back, covering her chest with both arms folded over. "Water. Please, I need water."

Novak lowered his face toward hers and kissed her cheek. "Anything for you, my dear."

She bit down on her bottom lip and tried not to cry, but it didn't work. Novak almost felt sorry for her. Poor thing. She didn't ask for this.

Shut up! She sure as hell did when she invited you into her car.

He had a point. Why on earth those women thought it was a good idea to stop and help him was one of the world's great mysteries.

Novak left the room and headed back upstairs. He grabbed a cold bottle of water, unscrewed the cap and set the bottle down on the counter next to a stack of dirty dishes. He looked at them in disgust. Better to throw them away and buy new ones than wash them all. He searched the cabinet for the small vial of powder. It was further back than he remembered, and on its side. His fingers brushed against it, and it rolled further away.

"Son of a bitch!"

He grabbed a chair and stepped up on the seat, putting him eye level with the shelf. The vial had rolled all the way to the back.

He reached his arm in past the elbow. The chair teetered and he spread his base to counter the effect and keep it steady.

Novak popped the lid off the vial as he stepped down. He pushed the chair out of the way, and sprinkled some of the powder into the water bottle.

"Here you go, Alice," he said, reentering the room.

She remained on her back, but had given up covering her breasts. He tried not to stare. It would be impolite, right? She propped up on her elbows and snatched the bottle from his hands. He couldn't help but watch as her breasts wiggled side to side. Alice sucked down the contents of the bottle in less than ten seconds. Water dripped down her chin, onto her chest, finding the groove between her breasts.

"It's good, yeah?" he said.

Her eyes widened, her mouth dropped open, and she fell back against the mattress. She wouldn't respond to his question. She couldn't, not after what he'd just mixed into her water.

"And now we have fun."

CHAPTER TEN

I took all of five minutes to relax before working my way along a roundabout path over to Cassie's place, much to the chagrin of the rental car's GPS. The well-maintained garden squares in the city, which gave Savannah an old-world European flair, gave way to a short jaunt through the ghetto and eventually what most would call the 'burbs. A few landmarks later, I cruised past her house. Aside from the grass being a little overgrown, it looked the same as it had a few weeks ago when I visited with Bridget Dinapoli.

Would Cassie be the same? I had no doubt she would. She had a seriousness about her that wasn't always present in folks these days. Everyone's a damn comedian. At the same time, you could see right through her. She felt the pain of those she aided. It grabbed hold of her psyche and squeezed until she settled the spirits who pestered her.

I idled in front of the house for a few moments, staring across the green stretch of wavering grass blades leading to the door. The blinds parted for a moment. White gave way to black. I couldn't see her, but it was almost as though she spoke to me.

Quit dallying about, Detective.

I was halfway up the drive when the front door creaked open and the screen door jutted outward. Cassie stepped onto the porch. Her dark hair was pulled back, with a few dark strands hanging down and curling under her jaw, framing her face. She tucked the left side behind her ear, smiled at me.

"Surprised?" I called out.

She lowered her head a tad and shrugged.

"Of course you're not," I said. "Impossible to surprise a psychic."

"You know I don't like being called that," she said.

I held my hands up in mock surrender. "Only messin' with you, Cassie."

We stood on the porch, a couple weathered boards apart. The smell coming through the door reminded me of a farmhouse. Pumpkin spice, or something like that. I guess you could achieve the same effect at Starbucks, if you were so inclined. It was that time of year, after all.

"What brings you here, Mitch?"

"So you didn't know I was coming?"

"Didn't say that."

"So you did, then."

"And I didn't say that." That smile played on her lips again.

I dug my fingertips into my pocket where they came to rest on the weathered edge of the postcard containing Robbie's note. For a moment, it felt as though he was reaching out and wrapping his little hand around my index finger.

"Mitch?" Cassie shuffled forward a step and placed her hand on my arm. It felt hotter than it should have.

Reluctantly, I pulled my hand out of my pocket and gestured toward the door. "Can we go in?"

I followed Cassie through the entrance and down a dim hallway that led to the kitchen. The chair scraped across the floor as I pulled it away from the table. Cassie spent a minute at the coffeemaker. The machine started gurgling, and soon the smell of a fresh brew overtook the pumpkin spice.

She pulled a chair out and sat facing me. Her gaze traveled up and down, finally settling on mine.

"What's in your pocket?" she asked.

I hadn't realized my hand had traveled back to the note. I pulled it out, holding tight with both hands, and stared at the lettering on the front. My ex or another adult had obviously written the address, but Robbie had written my name. I traced the large M and T with my thumb. After a moment, I cleared my throat.

"It's from Robbie," I said. "Got it a few days after my last visit, after we rescued those kids."

Cassie nodded and took a moment or two to compose her thoughts into words. She was like a therapist at times, at least when she wasn't beseeched by the voices that demanded her help.

I interrupted her before she had a chance to speak. "I know you can't promise anything. And it's probably tougher than what you are used to, with him being alive." I diverted my eyes toward the coffeemaker. Could I be so sure of that fact? "But if there's any chance you can pick up on something, I...I need to know, Cassie. I need to know where my son is."

Her hand fell upon mine, fingertips gliding over my knuckles. She traced the remnants of the cut I sustained from knocking out Fairchild. I fixed my stare on her delicate fingers as they slid off mine and settled on the postcard. She tugged slightly on the end nearest her. I released my grip. In that instant, her demeanor changed. Her brows furrowed, creating a crinkle that started at the bridge of her nose and traveled up to the middle of her forehead. Her breathing grew erratic, and her eyes dampened.

"Shit," I muttered.

She looked up, shaking her head. "It's not...It's something else. I can't quite..." She let go of the postcard and jolted to her feet. "Something's wrong."

I remained silent, watching her back up until she hit the counter next to the stainless sink. The purr of the house fan billowing down from an overhead vent drowned out a slight buzzing in my ears.

And then it sounded as though two rifle blasts echoed down the hallway. It broke whatever trance Cassie had entered. She walked past me, out of the room and toward the front door to see who had knocked.

CHAPTER ELEVEN

The cadence of their speech gave them away even before I managed to decipher what it was they were saying. There was a rhythm to the way they spoke that I was all too familiar with. There was also a familiarity in Cassie's tone that indicated she knew the visitors.

And she wasn't pleased to see them.

I waited at the table for a few minutes, catching bits and pieces of the conversation. After Cassie's third request for the men to leave, and their subsequent refusal, I walked down the hallway with hard and deliberate steps and made my presence known.

The sunlight hit the men from the right, casting shadows across half their faces. They were roughly late thirties to early forties, about the same height as one another, but one was darker and stockier. His face was unshaven with about a week's growth. He had a brooding look. The other was his complete opposite. Fair, clean-cut, light hair with a perfect part on the left side.

The two men made no effort to conceal their movements as they reached for their pistols after spotting me. Neither drew their piece. They surveyed the potential enemy inside Cassie's house with a look of bewilderment. I guessed in all of their visits to her home, there had never been another man present.

Cassie was well aware they had spotted me. She swept her hand in front of the men. "You can put those away. He's a friend of mine."

"You don't have any friends," the dark, stocky guy said.

"You don't know everything about me." Cassie glanced over her shoulder. There was something reassuring about the way she looked at me. "Detective Tanner, come meet Detectives Pennington and Cervantes of the Savannah-Chatham Police Department."

"Pennington," the fair one said, reaching his hand past Cassie. "Don't mind Cervantes. He's got case-brain, and we're working a rough one. Anyway, you're a detective? Where from?"

I grabbed his hand, matching the strong grip. "Philly. Uh, Philadelphia."

Cervantes said, "Bit out of your jurisdiction down here, ain't you, Tanner?"

"Why's that? This is a personal visit. Cassie is my friend." I pulled free from Pennington's grasp and placed my hand on Cassie's shoulder. "She's not just someone I use when I can't figure out what the hell I'm doing."

Cervantes puffed up like he was preparing to strike. Pennington, perhaps knowing his partner well enough to see what was about to go down, stuck his arm out and pushed the stocky man back.

"Listen, Tanner," Pennington said. "We're not trying to be rude or condescending. We're a brotherhood, right?" He flashed a quick smile that was both rude and condescending. "We need to speak to Cassie about a case we're working on. So, we're gonna need you to leave for a while. Maybe head down to the river for a bit. Whatever. Just head out for a while, and call before coming back."

"I've done nothing wrong here," I said. "I'm not going no damn where."

The men glanced at each other. Cervantes said, "Then we'll take Cassie down to the station. You try to follow along, we'll have you arrested. Then you can spend the rest of your vacation in our nicest cell."

I had no misgivings about the condition of that cell. They likely planned to stick me in the drunk tank and forget to let me leave. Ever wonder how long it takes to adjust to the smell of puke, piss and shit? I didn't have any desire to find out while in Savannah.

Cassie turned and spread her arms, creating additional distance between the detectives and me. She stared at me for a moment, then at them. "I'm not going anywhere. Neither is Detective Tanner. He and I have worked together numerous times. He's a pro, and I trust him. And if things are bad enough that you need to drag me into the investigation, then I don't think another experienced investigator is going to hurt."

Cervantes cursed and reached his arm through the doorway as though he were going to drag her out of the house. I started to place myself between them. Pennington did the same.

"Cerv, that's enough."

His partner backed down.

"Cassie, it doesn't work that way," Pennington said. "We can't just—"

"Then you won't have my support this time." She grabbed the edge of the door and swung it shut on the detectives.

We stood there for fifteen seconds. Silent. Beads of sweat dripped from my hairline, down my forehead. There was no airflow in the entry hallway. It seemed to amplify the late summer heat. The muffled voices of the two men rose and fell. One argued louder than the other. Cervantes, of course. He was pissed, and it was bringing his accent out, the one he obviously strived to keep under wraps while working.

The doorbell chime cut through the still air. Cassie looked at me, a wry smile on her face. She pulled the door open. Only Pennington stood there. Cervantes was at the end of the driveway, hustling toward their sedan.

"Ready to play by my rules?"

CHAPTER TWELVE

I was surprised when Cervantes emerged from the car carrying a briefcase. I thought for sure he was done with us. Apparently not. He trotted across the yard and stepped into the house behind his partner. They both avoided eye contact with me. In fact, it looked like they wanted to spit on me. The disdain was etched deep into their faces.

And I can't say I blamed them. We detectives are a territorial breed. Throw two opposing gumshoes in a ring together and you had better be prepared to clean up a mess. In this case, if the tables were turned, I'd have walked. Their need for Cassie's help must've been fierce if it got them to swallow this much pride.

"Come on, Mitch," Cassie said, gesturing toward the hallway.

I followed her into the kitchen. The detectives' hard-soled shoes slapped the old pine hardwoods and echoed down the corridor. I grabbed a chair and slid it a few feet away from the table. I wanted a bit of distance between me and them.

"Coffee?" Cassie said. "It's fresh."

Cervantes shook his head while thumbing open the briefcase's latches.

"Thanks, I'll take a cup," Pennington said.

Cassie poured some into a mug, then set it on the table in front of him. The ensuing silent lull lasted almost a minute. All eyes focused on the manila folder, and the fragments of papers and photos spilling out from the side, the top one revealing the unmistakable sight of a blood-stained sheet.

"So, what is it?" Cassie asked. "Lost child? Runaway mom?"

Cervantes' dark eyes bore into her. He shook his head, said nothing.

"Murder," she said calmly.

"Triple homicide," Pennington said.

"I haven't heard anything about that," she said. "When did it happen?"

"Night of the storm," Pennington said.

"Two weeks ago?" Cassie crossed her arms.

"That's right."

"And it's local?"

"Yup."

"How come I didn't hear about this?"

"We've kept it under wraps, but we all know that's not going to last forever."

Cassie shot me a glance. It wasn't common for a triple-homicide to remain sequestered for so long. Someone would have leaked something to the media. Hell, they knew before most cops did when something like this happened. Nosy neighbors, and all that.

She asked the question we both wondered.

"Why?"

The two detectives stared at the folder. I could only imagine the brutal story the pictures within told. It can be hard enough to kill one person, let alone three.

Pennington cleared his throat. "Three women died in that house that night. But there were four there."

I said, "Is she a suspect?"

Pennington made eye contact briefly. "Not judging by the condition of her room."

"She's missing," Cassie said.

The men nodded, their gazes traveling toward the table.

"And you want me to determine whether she's dead or alive."

"We know she left alive." Pennington flipped open the folder. There were pages of notes, which he cast aside. He rifled through the series of photos of bloodied and battered bodies, three young women whose futures were stolen. Hopes, dreams, spouses, children all orphaned that night. The carnage on the floors and walls showed just how much rage the murderer had pent up inside. He held nothing back. Well, almost nothing, since it seemed he took a victim with him.

Pennington set a photo on the table and angled it so the bottom pointed toward Cassie. I leaned over her shoulder and studied it. It was taken near an exiting door. There were two distinct sets of bloodied footprints on the floor. One in shoes, the other bare feet with what appeared to be high arches.

"She walked out," I said.

"That's right," Pennington said.

"An accomplice?"

"About ten feet back there are two lines, like someone had been dragged. Whether it was her, we can't be sure, but at the point the lines stop, the barefoot prints start. At this time, we're treating it like a missing person. From what we've gathered from the families, these women had been close since their freshman year at SCAD.

Two of them, one of the murdered and our missing person, had gone to school together since second grade. Best friends. Planned on starting a design business together after graduation."

"Yeah," I said. "Well, you and I both know how those relationships can break down."

"Sex, money, power." Pennington scattered a few photos across the table. "I'm guessing money and power had nothing to do with this one."

"Three dead women, one missing?" I said. "This guy is all about power."

Cervantes backed up in his chair, dragging the legs across Cassie's tile floor, causing a screeching as loud as a banshee. I imagined trenches an inch deep being dug.

"You got a problem with us, Big City? You think we don't know how to do our jobs?"

"Cerv."

"No, forget that, *Penn*. Big City here thinks we're just some dumb hick cops. Don't know what the fuck we're doing down here. Christ, what the hell we even talking about this in front of him for?"

"Look," Pennington said. "If Cassie vouches for him, then—"

"Damn you, Penn." Cervantes jumped out of his chair and headed toward the front door. He stopped and looked back at Cassie, his stubby index finger aimed at me. "We'll be back for you in the morning for a walk-through of the crime scene. He better be gone."

"Don't worry, man," I said. "I'm booking my flight out soon enough."

The front door opened and then slammed shut with enough force to rattle the wall. A framed cross-stitch that said, "I Know the Voices Aren't Real, But They Have Some Really Great Ideas!" shook and ended up off-center.

Pennington rose and said, "Again, sorry about him. He gets worked up. Kinda has a chip on his shoulder."

"You sure it ain't a boulder?"

Pennington smiled. "Cassie, we'll see you tomorrow. And Detective—"

I threw up my hands. "Don't worry about me, man. I got no desire to stick around where I'm not wanted."

Pennington nodded with his lips pressed tight, and followed his partner outside.

After a few seconds, I glanced over at Cassie. Her eyes were fixed on the table where a single picture remained. It was of an empty bed with bloodstained sheets. One pillow on the floor, the other against the wall. A pink and blue bra in the middle of it all.

"Make sure you check the dresser," I said.

"What?"

I pointed at the picture. "The dresser drawer is open. Maybe she left, I dunno, a psychic imprint on it, or something like that."

Cassie smiled at me like I was a child telling her that the clouds were made of cotton candy.

"I'll do that, Mitch. And if I forget, you can remind me."

CHAPTER THIRTEEN

"What do you mean, 'remind you'?" I said.

"You're going with me."

"I'd rather bathe in rubbing alcohol after dancing with a porcupine."

"That doesn't sound fun."

"Neither does being around a jackass that calls me 'Big City' all the time."

She laughed, a rare occurrence for Cassie. It almost looked unnatural. At the same time, it gave her a light, airy look that made her even more attractive.

"What?"

"Nothing." She regained her mental balance. A moment later, she added, "I know he's a bit much, but he's a good cop, Mitch. Once you start working together, you'll see that."

"No, I won't, because there won't be any working together. They don't want me there, and I don't want to get involved. I've had enough of these in my day. You know what a case like this can do to you."

Her hand went to her chest as her gaze drifted toward the ceiling. "I do. You know I do."

I reached over, wrapped my hand around her wrist. "Sorry, Cassie. I know you feel this as much, if not more than we do."

"So humor me and stay." Her gaze intensified. She wasn't pleading with me as much as allowing me to feel how deeply she wanted me there.

I rose and walked past her. "I don't think I can."

"You have to."

"Why?" I grabbed the top of the trim surrounding the doorway to the hallway, digging my fingertips in as I stretched my shoulders.

"I caught something from the postcard."

I felt like my stomach dropped into my scrotum and my heart rose into my throat. I tried to speak, but ended up sounding like a baby seal.

"It wasn't enough for me to pinpoint anything precisely," she said. "And now, with this other case, and what I'm feeling, I don't know if I can get it back. At least, not until this is resolved. This case is... How do I put it? Taking over my mind. And I need your help, Mitch. If you help me, the sooner we find this girl, the sooner I can help you locate your son."

I didn't know how to react. It felt like she was extorting me, and it pissed me off. But the look in her eyes revealed pain and sorrow and the desire to help me. I felt it deep within my own being. I wondered about the world that surrounded her. The one the rest of us weren't privy to. Don't for a minute think I was jealous of her gift. Not for a second. There's no way I could handle all that contact—whatever it was—and the responsibility that came with it.

I lingered there, my arms stretched out and my head resting against my right bicep. It had to have been years since the last coat of paint was applied to the trim, but it smelled strong. There were traces of dark still visible underneath the white that she, or the previous owner, had used.

Cassie looked away from me. Shallow breaths and a constant drumming of her fingertips against the tabletop indicated she was anxious for an answer. Was there any but the obvious? If I had any chance of finding my boy, I needed Cassie's help. And time mattered. The sooner she had the case resolved, the sooner she could assist me. The decision was made the moment I decided to fly down to Savannah.

"All right, Cassie. I'll stay."

Through the chaos of the detectives' visit, Robbie's postcard had remained on the table where Cassie had dropped it. She stared at the writing, her hand shaped like a claw, perched halfway between it and her body.

She glanced up at me. Her eyes misted over. "You know what can happen when I pick that up, right?"

I nodded, slowly, understanding what she meant. "If that's the case, I need to know. One way or another, I need to know. Every fiber of being in my body tells me my son is alive and waiting for me to show up and take him away from the insanity that is his mother. But if that's not the case, if something has happened to him, I will hunt her down along with anyone associated with harming him and end them."

It appeared as though Cassie had to will herself to touch the postcard again. She grabbed it by the corner and pulled it close to her. She didn't read it. Didn't have to, I supposed. With her eyes closed, she felt it, ran the tips of her fingers across the front and the back. Her touch was drawn to the spot where he signed his name.

This went on for a solid five minutes. Not a word was spoken. The house took on a life of its own. The vents spewed cold air, speaking in some hushed language that perhaps Cassie understood. Hell, what did I know? I still had trouble believing anything was actually happening when she went into her trance. If it weren't for the results, I'd have laughed in her face.

"It's faint, Mitch."

The sound of her voice lulled me from a false state of serenity.

"I'm getting something," she said. "But still unsure of what, where, or who."

I rose from my chair, securing the postcard and stuffing it back in my pocket.

"Then I suppose we should both get a good night's rest so we can figure out what happened to that girl as soon as possible."

CHAPTER FOURTEEN

I had spent a couple of hours driving around before returning to my rental apartment. There was something about the lowlands at sunset. I pulled to the curb. All the windows in the old lady's place were dark. Asleep, I figured. And why not. It was after ten p.m. She had no need to be up past that. The city was reserved at this time of night for the freaks, partiers, college kids, and the folks waiting around the block for a scoop or two of ice cream from Leopold's.

Sleep was not easily attained, but once under, I was out until my alarm went off at five-thirty a.m. After a quick shower and shave, I threw on a pair of dark jeans and a grey button-up shirt and was out the door.

The old woman threw hers open about the same time. Had she been waiting for me?

"Coffee, Mr. Tanner?"

"I would, ma'am, but I'm kinda in a rush this morning."

"Please ignore anything you might have heard last night."

I stopped and glanced back at her. Her smile betrayed her

narrowed eyes and tight-knit eyebrows. Even the wrinkles in her forehead thinned out. What did her words mean? Were they as simple as what she stated?

The smile faded. "Well, you just knock if you're around for dinner."

"Yes, ma'am. I will."

The street was empty. Quiet. No sounds of a saxophone from a nearby square. The freaks and partiers and college kids had retired hours ago. The wind tore through the late autumn leaves, spinning them up and down the street. Sounded like a dozen joggers rushing past.

I grabbed a cup of coffee and then drove straight to Cassie's. The sun crested over her roof, shaking off the morning chill in the air. Clouds turned from silver to blaze orange. I headed up the driveway to avoid the heavy coating of dew on the grass.

Cassie opened the door, waved, then backed into the darkened hallway. The smell of bacon hit me before I reached the porch. By the time I stepped foot in the kitchen, she had a plate of bacon and eggs on the table with a steaming mug of coffee next to it. I practically responded like a dog.

"They are going to meet us here in half an hour," she said. "I already warned them that you'd be around. Go ahead and eat up."

She didn't have to tell me twice. I scarfed the food, had another five strips of bacon, and downed two mugs before the detectives arrived.

We met them outside. There were minimal greetings between the detectives and me. Their interactions with Cassie were subdued as well. Too somber a morning for anything more. This wasn't about any of us and we all knew it. Faces were long and drawn with the thought of what was ahead. I had a feeling I'd regret eating before the walk-through.

Cassie rode with me in the rental. Each of us made lame

attempts at conversation that quickly died while we followed the detectives. After twenty minutes or so, Pennington pulled their sedan over in front of a small house with a fence that wrapped around the entire property. Doors opened. Shoes hit the ground. We were still a block away. Cassie sat with her eyes closed.

In a cracked, breathy voice, she said, "This is the place."

I idled in the middle of the road. "I'm not a psychic and I could've told you that."

She turned her head toward me, slowly opening her eyes, the look on her face indicating she did not find my comment amusing.

Pennington stood at the front of his car, directing me to pull in front of them. After parking the rental, we convened at their trunk. The lid was popped open. Inside were a black and two blue milk crates filled with various items. Pennington tossed us each a pair of booties and gloves. I would have preferred the shotgun he had tucked in there, too.

"I don't need to go over the instructions with you, do I, Tanner?"

I blew a puff of air into each glove in preparation of donning them. "I think I got it."

"Follow me, then." Pennington waved over his shoulder and led us to the crime scene.

Cervantes had already entered. His shadow lingered in the doorway while we approached. It vanished before we stepped off the sidewalk. Why did he want to get ahead of us? I dove down the rabbit hole as we crossed the yard. Cervantes knew his partner. Knew Pennington's tendencies. The things the man would miss. He didn't know me, though. What if there was something in the house he didn't want me to notice?

He was waiting near the back wall of the room when we entered. His gaze drifted from me to Cassie, where it remained for a few seconds too long. His expression was neutral, making it difficult to gauge his intentions.

"Everything good?" Pennington asked.

"Yeah," Cervantes said, keeping his focus on Cassie. "No one's been in here. Looks like forensics finished up, and managed to do so without destroying anything." He nodded slightly, then added, "We figured keeping the scene as true as possible might help you, Cassie."

"I solved a ten-year-old murder for you when all we had was a fragment of bone and two small squares of fabric from a red-checked flannel shirt," she said. "I don't think it matters."

"Whatever." Cervantes turned and left the room in the direction of the kitchen, muttering something under his breath.

"It's a tough house to be in," Pennington said. "Even for us vets. Know what I mean?"

"That I do," I said. Didn't matter how many times you saw the sights. Each case had the ability to affect you in a new and even more disturbing way. Sure, we joked while in groups, attempting to stifle our true thoughts and feelings. But you can't escape demons. They have a way of lingering and overstaying their welcome. Even the ones that don't belong to you. Sometimes especially so.

"You feeling anything?" Pennington asked Cassie.

She reached out and traced her fingertips along the wall. Up as high as she could. Down to the chair rail. She dug into the groove and walked forward.

I followed Pennington to the kitchen. Bloody footprints staggered across the linoleum. Two distinct sets, for sure. One barefoot. With the benefit of sunlight, I looked back and saw how they approached from the hall Cassie had disappeared down. There, the person owning the size twelves walked while the other had been dragged, leaving a crimson trail in their wake. Had it been her blood dripping down her legs, or the blood of another that she'd been pulled through?

The sink looked undisturbed. White. Not a stain on it. Odd, I thought. The guy didn't bother to wash off in it. He wouldn't have taken the time to clean up the mess there and not the rest of the place.

"Was the sink like that from the beginning?" I asked.

Pennington nodded. "He was in a hurry to get out of here, not wash off. Pretty big risk."

"Guess he figured if he got pulled over the bloody girl in the backseat would give it away." I walked over to the sink, stared out the case window above. Cervantes stood in the back corner of the yard, smoking a cigarette. He let the smoke slip out of his mouth and nose. Looked like a deranged bull in a cartoon. Was he always this anti-social? I was about to ask Pennington when something pulled me back.

The sound of Cassie's hurried footsteps echoed off the walls. I spun around. She stood in front of the hallway, pale, gasping for breath. I rushed toward her. Pennington did too.

CHAPTER FIFTEEN

Cassie squinted her eyes against the brightened room, struggling with the constricted feeling throughout her body. It felt as though the sun had come down and engulfed her. Mitch rushed over from his position in front of the sink, reaching for a holster and pistol that weren't there. Pennington pulled his handgun and wove past Cassie. The man's cologne overwhelmed her, bringing her the rest of the way back to reality. She glanced over her shoulder and saw him blocking her from whatever he thought might be at the other end of the hallway. His physical presence could do nothing to stop it.

"What's wrong?" Mitch said.

"It's okay." She squeezed his forearm.

Mitch leaned back, his head quivering slightly as though he were trying to shake free of whatever thoughts had been there.

"It's okay, Mitch. I just need to be alone."

"What?" he said.

Pennington, having seen Cassie like this before, backed off and holstered his weapon. He walked to the back door. "We can go, Tanner."

Cassie reached for Mitch's arm again, tracing her fingers gently against his bare skin. They'd worked together several times over the years, but mostly from a distance. He'd never seen her up close when pushed this far on an investigation.

"I've got something here," she said. "I need to be alone now to get the most out of it. I'll be outside when it's over. Okay?"

Mitch mumbled his acceptance and took a few steps back. His intense stare made her cheeks burn.

"Please," she said. "Go, or I'll lose it."

Mitch turned away and walked out the kitchen door. Pennington looked back, his face tight, and nodded as he let the screen door fall shut.

The room went silent for a moment. Then the hushed tones returned. The voice wasn't clear, but she presumed it to be singular. If there were multiple spirits, it would be difficult to understand any single one of them, but not due to lack of volume. When there were two or more, it could sound like Sunday dinner at grandma's house, with everyone trying to yell over each other, vying for attention while they recounted their stories from the past week.

Cassie tread carefully down the hall, avoiding the crimson stains on the floor when possible. A dried river of blood streaked the wall, about waist-high. Tributaries stretched to the floor.

The voice grew louder, but no more discernible. She likened it to playing an album in reverse. A patch of light washed over the floor and faded a second later. She stopped at the first darkened doorway and peeked into the room. A burst of white light exploded from somewhere within, blinding her. Though the room was vacant, she saw the woman who had occupied it the night of the storm. Her naked body lay half on the bed. Her left fingertips grazed the floor. Her blonde hair was colored red.

"Is that you?" Cassie asked.

"NO!"

The force of the voice drove Cassie backward. Her head slammed into the door trim. She winced as pain radiated across her skull. But she didn't scream out. Doing so might drive the spirit away.

Weaving her fingers through her hair to rub away the dull ache, Cassie staggered back through the opening and swept the room with her gaze. The unmade bed told the story of the woman's last moments. But the vision was gone.

"Here," the voice said.

Cassie backed out of the room and walked to the end of the narrow corridor. The light from the main room of the house barely illuminated the space where she stood, glinting off the door handles. There were three more bedrooms remaining, one to the front of her, and one on either side.

"Right," the voice said.

Cassie reached out. The skin on her arm prickled as she wrapped her hand around the ice-cold knob.

"Open," the voice said.

She turned the handle, taking a deep breath to steady herself for whatever sight lingered on the other side of the door. The stench hit first. It had been present throughout the house, but not as intense as the putrid smell of death in this room. As far as she could tell, the others didn't notice it.

The woman was on the bed, holding her hands over her face. The blue of her eyes stood out from behind spread fingers. "Why did he do this to me?" Her voice was clear now, thick with a southern Georgia drawl. "Why did he try to shred me into pieces?" Blood seeped from behind the woman's hands and ran down her arms. It dripped off and disappeared into the void.

"Who did this?" Cassie asked. "Can you show me?"

"It was so dark." Her voice waned.

"Stay with me. Please. I need you to stay with me. Try to remember."

"Alice," she said. "Alice made it out alive. But only 'cause he took her."

"Do you know where?"

The woman reached out with her left arm, revealing a gaping hole in her face. A chunk of her cheek hung on by a thread of skin. She aimed her finger across the hall.

Cassie turned and stared at the opposite door.

"Alice," the woman said.

Cassie spun back around, but the woman had vanished.

"Hello?" she said.

No response.

"Are you still here?"

No response.

Cassie leaned forward and placed her hand over a splotch of dried blood on the bedsheets. She heard a whisper, but nothing else. The young woman had slipped into the same void as her blood and tears.

Cassie left the room, pulling the door shut behind her. It stuck against the warped frame and then clicked closed when she pulled harder. She reached out to the right, dragging her fingertips across rough paint, then brought her hand forward and grabbed the knob to what she presumed was Alice's room. Another flash of light overtook her vision. Soon it was replaced with the image of a man in his early twenties, dark hair and eyes, and a perpetual growth of scarce stubble on his chin and cheeks.

A whisper blew past like a soft breeze on a spring day. It sounded like it said, "Seth."

The vision faded. The darkened door took its place. Cassie turned the handle and pushed the door open. There were clothes on the floor. A dresser overturned. The bed was stripped. The sheets were not in sight. They had been taken by forensics for further processing. Whatever had happened in the room, the investigators believed it would help identify the man that had murdered the women and taken Alice in the midst of the storm.

"Alice," Cassie said. "If you can hear me, it means one of two things: Either you're dead, or something in this room still holds enough energy that your spirit is attached. If the latter's the case, and you can point me to the object, it'll help us as we search for you. There's a lot of us working on getting you back, girl. You've even got a cop from Philadelphia here to help. He's a good one, too. So come on, show me, Alice. Show me."

The soft rumble of a distant truck passed. The room fell silent. The entire house was like a corpse. No fan pulling in and pushing air through. No electricity to keep the pulse going.

Cassie closed her eyes, stepped forward, turned in a circle. She stood still for thirty silent seconds. She opened her eyes and scanned the room. A picture on the floor stood out to her. Cassie scooped it up and saw a photo of four women. It looked recent, but the edges had already started curling. She recognized one of the women as the spirit who had opened up to her. She was also able to spot the blonde from the other room.

And there was Alice.

"This is it," Cassie said. "I'm taking this with me, Alice. Stay calm. Stay strong. We'll be there soon."

CHAPTER SIXTEEN

I leaned against the siding a couple feet from the back door. The calendar said October, but no one told Savannah. It had to be close to ninety degrees and at least that in humidity. The sun blared down. Clouds gathered in the western corner of the sky threatening an afternoon shower. Nearby, someone had started their grill or smoker. The charred remains of their last meal filled the air.

Pennington and Cervantes stood at the other end of the shallow yard. They spoke in hushed tones meant only for their ears. No matter how hard I tried, I couldn't pick up what they were saying. Guess they wanted it that way. They took turns glancing in my direction. Was it me, or were they as apprehensive for Cassie to emerge from the house as I was?

A half-minute passed. Pennington crossed the grass. The odor of his partner's cigarette clung to him.

"What do you make of this, Tanner?"

"The crime? Hell, you didn't give me much chance to look around."

"We value your input, but there has to be a line." He looked back at his coughing partner.

"That's only gonna get worse the longer he smokes."

"Don't think he cares." Pennington's smile faded as he turned his head toward me. "Anyway, I meant Cassie."

"What about her?"

"What do you think of her *gift*?"

I took a deep breath before answering. This was one of those questions that he'd use to segregate me into one of two types of people. "You worked with her much?"

He nodded. "Since it happened."

"And by 'it,' you mean...."

"Yes."

I'd long since been familiar with how Cassie came into her gift. "So, then, you've seen some shit you just can't explain when it comes to her, right?"

"You could say that." He stuffed his fidgety hands inside his pants pockets. "You, too?"

"Look, all I know is that I've been at a dead end more than once, and something Cassie has said put me back on the right track. Now, I'm not saying she had the exact answer to the question. She hasn't always said the gardener did it with his spade and would have gotten away with it, too, if it wasn't for the meddling psychic. Follow me?"

"Yeah, of course," Pennington said. "She has a way of dropping a clue sometimes that I never would have spotted."

"Right."

He sucked in a long breath of air and shook his head. "Still, though, I can't help but believe it's all bullshit."

For a moment there I thought that Pennington and I could have been great partners. "I feel like an ass anytime I ask her questions about how she does what she does, what she sees...."

He smiled. "Glad I'm not the only one."

I followed his gaze to the back door. Maybe Cassie would finish sooner with both of us staring at it. "What about your partner over there?"

"Oh, yeah, for sure. He eats it up, man. It's part of his culture. Ingrained, right? He grew up with village witches, that kind of shit."

"Where's he from?"

Pennington started to answer, but both of us lost focus as Cassie pulled the door open. She stepped into the sunlight, pale, a sheen of light sweat across her forehead.

"Well?" Pennington moved to within a foot of her.

"Alice?"

He waved with two fingers to his partner. "What about her, Cassie?"

"She's alive." She bit her lip, then added, "Well, she was after that night."

"Anyone else?" he asked.

"One of the girls was butchered pretty badly. Stabbed repeatedly. Her face was carved up."

Cervantes moved forward and swatted Pennington's arm. Pennington backed him up a couple of feet.

"Give her some space," he said.

"Thank you," Cassie said.

"Did you see who did it?" Cervantes asked.

"I did see a male, but it was when I touched a doorknob. I didn't, you know, actually see him killing anyone."

Pennington said, "Do you remember his face?"

She nodded, releasing strands of hair which she quickly tucked behind her ears.

They went silent. The two men stared at Cassie. She glanced at the grass in an effort to avoid their stares, or maybe to pick up on something else. I breathed in the hot air and waited to hear their next move.

"Let's go back to the precinct," Pennington said. "Got some pictures you can look through. If none of those work, we'll get a sketch artist to meet you at your place."

"Sounds good." She looked up at me. "You coming along?"

"I—"

"He's not invited to the desk," Cervantes said.

"That's what you call it?" I said. "The desk? That's cute."

"You want cute?" He pushed past Pennington and grabbed my shirt. The son of a bitch was fast.

I wrapped my left arm around his right, then jerked it up and back. He grunted and let go of my shirt. I took a few steps back, fists up, ready to go. Pennington wedged himself into the middle and shoved both of us further apart.

"Go on," he shouted. "Go back to the car, Cerv. We can't accomplish anything with that schoolyard shit."

Cervantes threw up his hands in disgust. He hopped the fence and disappeared around the side of the house. Their sedan's V-8 roared to life. The car door slammed shut.

"Maybe we should pick this up at my house," Cassie said. "Prevent whatever turf war he's perceived is going with Mitch."

"That's probably a good idea," Pennington said. "And, Tanner, I'm sorry about my partner. I'll have a talk with him. We're all in this together, right?"

"Be sure to tell him he puts his hands on me again, I'll break his arm in three places."

"Mitch," Cassie said.

"No, Cassie," Pennington said. "It's okay. I'd feel the same way if I was in Philly and someone treated me like this."

After a few long breaths my pulse and breathing steadied.

Wasn't quite at normal levels, but the tense shakes exited through my fingertips.

"Let's say two hours. Should be enough time for Cerv to cool off." Pennington cut through the house to lock up.

Cassie wanted to remain outside. Perhaps she'd seen enough in there. We found the gate and made our way to the front yard. The rental car stood alone now. The detectives were gone and I finally had calmed all the way down.

I turned to crack a joke about Cervantes, but stopped mid-word at the sight of Cassie lying on the ground.

CHAPTER SEVENTEEN

I rushed over to Cassie and knelt at her side. She was staring up at me, but it was as though she looked right through me.

"Cassie?"

She didn't respond. Her eyes were unblinking.

"Is she okay?"

I looked back and saw a woman in her seventies wearing a green track suit standing on the sidewalk. Her Shih Tzu had its head cocked to the side.

"Should I call the ambulance?" the woman asked.

I waved her off and redirected my attention to Cassie. I put my hand on her cheek and turned her face toward me. "Can you hear me?"

She slammed her eyelids shut, shook her head, and mumbled something. Her body went rigid. She shook violently for about ten seconds. And then it was over. She sunk into the grass like she'd fallen asleep.

"Cassie? Come on, what's going on?"

The old woman said, "I'm calling the ambulance now."

"Just let her be," I said. "I'm a cop. I got this."

The old woman cursed at me and dragged her barking dog away. It stood with its legs locked. I turned to yell at it but noticed it wasn't looking at me or Cassie. It was focused on something else. What did it see that I couldn't?

"Mitch?" Cassie placed her frigid hand on mine. Her flushed cheeks stood out on her pasty face. The color spread in the next few seconds. "What happened?"

"You tell me. One minute we're walking and the next you're flat on your back staring up at the sky." I pulled her up to a sitting position. "Did you see something?"

Her eyes misted over as she shook her head. "I don't know. Don't remember a thing. I blacked out."

This wasn't the place to press her for answers. A few neighbors had gathered across the street. The woman and her dog joined them. The beast had stopped its racket. Whatever haunted Cassie had fled.

"All right, well, let's get you home." I pulled Cassie to her feet and helped her to the car. We drove straight to her house. Both our cell phones rang several times along the way. Neither of us answered or bothered to check who had called.

I half-expected to see Pennington and Cervantes waiting for us at her house to make another attempt at dragging her down to the station. The street in front was deserted. No one waited on the porch. I canvased the area, sweeping my gaze across the windows of the surrounding houses. No one lingered in the shadows. Business as usual, it seemed.

We headed inside. Cassie retreated to her room, saying she'd be good to go after an hour or so of rest. Fine by me. I headed into the kitchen, poured out the stale coffee, and started a fresh pot. Over the next ninety minutes I drank three cups and caught up on all the latest football news. It was a good week to be away since my

Eagles were on a bye. All I needed was for the Cowboys to lose and at least I'd be somewhat happy.

It had been Sam who had called while Cassie and I were driving back to her house. He hadn't left a message, and wasn't picking up now. Did he have something new regarding my suspension? It would be like Huff to have Sam relay it to me.

I was on the phone with Momma checking up on Ella Kate when Cassie entered the kitchen. She'd changed into a pair of pink gym shorts and a white tank top. In the years I'd known her, I couldn't recall ever seeing her bare arms or legs. The scars from her attack were visible, peeking out from the fabric clinging to her breasts. I must've let my eyes linger a second too long, because she folded her arms across her chest to cover up. I glanced up. Her cheeks were red, but she forced a smile.

"Sorry, I forgot you were here. I should've covered up better."

"Hey, it's your house. Do what you want. I'm not really complaining."

"Mitch...." She looked flustered for a second. "I should change anyway. Those two will be here soon. Cervantes always ogles me, and I don't want to give him any more imagery than I have to."

"Yeah, I wouldn't want that guy walking around thinking about me."

"He already is, except in your case, he's thinking of ways he can get rid of you." A smile played at the corner of her lips. "Or pound your face into the concrete."

"Spirits tell you that?"

She smiled and shrugged and then left the room. I leaned over to watch her walk down the hall. A few minutes later she returned wearing dark jeans and a black sweater.

"It's still almost ninety degrees out, you know," I said.

"I'm comfortable."

"You must've been freezing before. Every time you've touched me, it felt like ice formed on my skin."

She rolled her eyes as she grabbed my empty mug off the table. I caught a hint of Moroccan oil as her hair spilled over her shoulder. "The coffee's fresh?"

"Made it while you were napping."

She grabbed a second mug, filled both, and returned to the table. The next fifteen minutes were spent in an oddly comfortable silence. I checked my phone a couple times, finding nothing new, while Cassie flipped through the pages of a local *Savannah Living* magazine. Live oaks dripping with Spanish moss adorned the cover.

The knock at the door we'd been waiting on finally arrived. I waited in the kitchen while she attended to the guests. She returned with Pennington close behind. He nodded as he shrugged off his sport coat. It caught on his pistol's handle. After he freed it, he draped the coat over a chair and sat down.

"Where's the brooder?" I asked.

Pennington flashed a grin. Looked like he bleached his teeth. They were the brightest thing in the room. "Sent him home for the afternoon. His kids got a Fall Ball baseball tournament. Cerv was pretty broken up that he couldn't coach the team. It's pretty much his only way of connecting with his boys. But our case load is too damn heavy what with the budget cuts that've stripped our department bare. I'm sure you can relate."

I gave him a nod and mulled over what he'd said. Maybe I wasn't giving Cervantes enough of a chance. Perhaps this was why Cervantes was so on edge with me. Maybe he was like that with everyone these days. Overworked and underpaid rarely made for a content worker. Throw a stranger into the mix on a high-profile case, and fireworks could erupt.

Pennington unzipped a leather binder and continued. "Not

like we need him for this right here. Our dear Cassie is the star of the show for now."

"Coffee, Detective?" she said.

"I already drank two pots today. Any more and I'll be running naked through the Squares at two a.m."

"Make sure it's not the one in front of my rental."

Pennington chuckled. "You can guarantee it will be." His demeanor changed as he set the binder on the table.

Cassie remained by the counter. Her gaze drifted from the detective to the folder Pennington had pulled from his binder. It contained pictures. Not of crime scenes, but of men. Which men, I wondered. A random sampling, some with connections to the four women who lived at the house, possible suspects, and a few unconnected, just to test her?

"Cassie," Pennington said. "You ready for this?"

CHAPTER EIGHTEEN

Cassie bit her bottom lip, looking more vulnerable than at any time in the past. That included earlier today when she lay passed out in front of the house. She glanced up at me. I tried to offer a reassuring smile. She glanced away.

"Not to rush you," Pennington said, "but there's a woman out there, hopefully still alive. The sooner you help us narrow down suspects, the sooner we can get her back to her family."

Cassie extended a hand, palm facing us, to silence him. "No pressure," she whispered.

"My bad." Pennington leaned forward, turned the folder and shifted it in front of the empty seat.

Cassie pulled out a chair and slid into it. I caught another distracting whiff of her hair. She opened the folder and spent ten seconds staring at the first photo. In all, it looked like there were a dozen, give or take. Without a word, she flipped the picture over and set it to the side. Over the next two minutes, she moved through six more pictures, her eyes locked on those of the potential suspects. They were homogeneous in nature, those men. White guys. Closely cropped hair. Scraggly stubble on their jaws. Looked like young punks to me. Every year it seemed I said that more and more, though. If I had to guess, these were all connected to the women by romantic relationships.

The next picture seemed to pique her interest more than the previous ones. The guy was older, with dark, receding hair. His forehead was wrinkled. Looked like a career criminal to me, thrown in to throw her off.

"Something about this guy," Cassie said. "I don't think it has anything to do with this case, but there's something there."

Pennington scrawled something into his notebook as Cassie moved through two more pictures, giving them the same scrutiny as the others.

Then on the second to last, her expression changed and the color left her cheeks.

"What is it?" I asked.

"This guy," she said, tapping her finger on his forehead. "I saw him while we were at the house."

"What'd you see?" Pennington asked.

"His face." She waved her fingers in front of her. "It was just there, and it wasn't a positive feeling."

Pennington set his pen down. "Did you ever get a glimpse of the murder?"

"Not in the way you think. And certainly not with a face attached. I saw him—" Cassie lifted the photo "—when I went to Alice's room."

Pennington leaned toward the picture. I presumed he was taking note of the serial number as he scribbled something into his notebook.

"Who is he?" Cassie asked.

"Alice's boyfriend," Pennington said. "Ex or estranged, possibly."

"So you think there's a motive here?" I said.

"To hurt Alice?" he said. "Maybe. To kill the others, I'm not so sure."

"Already questioned him?"

Pennington nodded.

"And you think he knows something?"

"I think he's hiding something." Pennington dropped his pencil and wrapped his hands around the back of his head. "He was very apprehensive, sweating like a damn pig. Contradicted himself seven or eight times. Had no alibi for the night of the murder, other than he'd hunkered down in his apartment due to the storm. No one could vouch for that, of course."

"Sometimes no one can," I said.

Pennington lifted an eyebrow. "Suppose so. Anyway, he remains a person of interest."

"You got any others?"

He stopped short of saying yes. "Look, Tanner, I'm fine with you coming along and helping out. You might spot something we missed, or put two and two together when we're banging our heads trying to solve one plus three. But at some point, I gotta cut you out. And I think that point is when we start talking about additional suspects. I don't want to taint the investigation, and I don't want to put ideas into Cassie's head. That's by her request, as I'm sure you know, having worked with her in the past."

All valid points. Hell, I wouldn't have allowed him this far into an investigation. I wished he hadn't brought me along, though. I felt invested now, and that's a bitch of a problem.

"You need to talk to him again," Cassie said. "There's a question you need to ask."

"What?" Pennington said.

Cassie tilted her head back until her neck rested on the chair. Her hair hung in thick strands, past the seat. She whispered something as she reached out and placed her palm over the face in the picture.

"Where were you?" she said almost imperceptibly. "You weren't in your apartment. Where were you?"

I glanced over at Pennington. He looked as confused as I felt.

The moment ended with Cassie leaning forward again. "He couldn't have been at his apartment."

"Why not?" Pennington said.

"He'd rented it out for the week," she said.

"Where was he staying?"

"Makes sense he would have been staying with his girlfriend, right?" I said.

"Only they were broken up, or on a break, something like that. Things weren't on an even keel, as he put it."

"All right," I said. "So where, then?"

We both stared at Cassie, waiting for her to deliver the answer. She shrugged. "Got me, guys. You'll have to question him again to get to the bottom of that."

"Okay," Pennington said. "We'll locate him asap and hit him with this. Any way you think we can verify that?"

"The internet." I spun my cell phone. "Plenty of home sharing sites out there for people who don't like staying at hotels. In some cases, people rent out the place they live in, able to secure their mortgage payment in exchange for a week on someone else's couch."

"Good point, Tanner. I'll jump on that, too." He grabbed the photo and set it to the side. "What about the last photo?"

It was another older guy. He looked a lot like the first one. Judging by the look on Cassie's face, she seemed to think so, too. I glanced at Pennington in time to see him craning forward a bit. His fingers danced on the table. His gaze darted between the picture and Cassie. He was definitely waiting for confirmation on something.

She turned over the stack of discarded photos and rifled through them until she found the other picture. Side by side, there was no doubt the two men were related in some way.

"What's this?" she asked.

"You tell me," Pennington said.

"Kind of like the first one, he's got some baggage, but I can't see how it's related to this."

"Fair enough." Pennington rose and shrugged his coat on. "If anything else pops into your head, you let me know."

Cassie stood and started toward the hallway. "I want to go back to the house tomorrow."

"I'll arrange it." Pennington gathered his things and tucked them into the binder. "I can see myself out."

I followed Pennington to the door to see if there was anything he had to get off his chest, but didn't want to say around Cassie. He never looked back. What was the deal with the two older men?

When I returned to the kitchen, Cassie remained in the same seat. She stared through narrowed eyes at the table where the photos had been.

"What's up?"

She didn't look up at me. "Maybe there is something there."

"Where?"

"With those two men. The older ones. Looked like brothers."

"You think you've seen them before?"

"Anything's possible, Mitch." She wiped the edge of her hand across the table as though sweeping the images away. "I could've run into them at a gas station once or twice. It's not so much the way they look, as it is a feeling." She paused for a deep breath. The air whistled as she exhaled. "I can't really explain it." She looked up and smiled. "Why am I telling you that? You already know."

"I think I'm gonna get going. I've gotta digest all this, and I'm sure you do, too."

"You coming along tomorrow?"

"Wouldn't miss it." I squeezed her shoulder as I passed. "And hopefully your detective friends don't mind."

"I'll tell them I'm done if they give you trouble. Seems to be working so far."

"That it does."

CHAPTER NINETEEN

He stacked the dishes next to the sink without rinsing them. Truth be told, only one needed to be cleaned off. His. The bitch didn't bother to eat any of the pizza he'd picked up for them. He even went so far as to light candles and let her out of her cell. She just sat there after the shackles were removed. It took the threat of a knife in her stomach to get her to look at him.

Some guests were that rude.

Had he erred in keeping Alice alive? The confidence that brimmed in her the night of the storm was a distant memory now. She put up less of a fight than a perch. The only wounds on him were those that came from him punching the wall in frustration. He looked down at the dark yellow skin on his knuckles. Next time he'd make sure to miss the stud.

Perhaps a drink would help. He grabbed a bottle of wine and two red solo cups. The cap twisted off with ease. He tossed it into the sink. There'd be no need for it again. The two of them could down the bottle easily. She'd be dying of thirst. He'd intentionally withheld water from her all day.

He blew out two of the candles, dimming the room further. Shadows danced about. Always the gentleman, he rapped on her cell door and waited. A few seconds passed without a response. "I've brought something special for you, Alice."

Her apprehension bled through the crack beneath the door. He wished he could suck the air out of the room to lift her from her bed quicker. In fact, why hadn't she moved? It was her first free time without the shackles. Surely she'd be itching to stretch her legs.

He took a few steps back. His hands carrying the cups and wine lowered to his side. What had he left in the room? Normally nothing was available they could use as weapons. But had he made a mistake this time? Was she forcing his hand, inviting him in to get close to her, and then *WHAM!* She'd smack him across the head with a tire iron.

He laughed at the thought and told himself, "Don't let your mind get the better of you." He filled each cup halfway, set the bottle on the table and went back to Alice's door. There was no point using his manners again. He pushed the door open and entered.

She looked up at him, tears in her eyes, arms wrapped over her bare breasts.

"You see, I didn't even have to unlock it, Alice. All this time, you could have come out. Now, I know you were having a rude moment. I'm willing to overlook that if you'll share in a glass of wine with me."

She glanced at the red solo cup he held toward her.

"I know, I know. It's not really a glass." He pushed his lips out and glanced upward. A silly face meant to disarm her a little. "I can't trust you with one of those yet. Do you know what you can do with a wine glass once you break the bottom off the stem?"

She scooted back, tucking her legs under.

"No, of course you don't. You're sweet, Alice. Not full of malice." He chuckled softly. "Here, take this chalice. Together we can storm the palace." He set the cup on the floor in front of her and waited to see if she'd pick it up. "There's nothing mixed in there or anything like that. I don't play those games. If I want something, I'll take it. I don't need to drug you first."

She closed her eyes and lowered her chin to her chest.

"Suit yourself." He exited the room to grab the wine bottle, then returned. She hadn't moved. He squatted in front of her and poured another splash in his glass. Swirling the liquid, he stuck his nose in the opening and inhaled. "It really is a nice Merlot. You should try it."

She pulled back from his touch as he reached for her chin.

"Now, now," he said, smoothing her hair. She had nowhere to go. They both knew it. He downed his wine in a single gulp. He reached for her chin again. This time she didn't resist. Her head tilted back, lips in full view. He leaned in and kissed her. The wine was on his lips and tongue. She'd taste it. Oh yes, she'd get a nice mouthful. He did all the work, of course. Might as well have stuck a dead fish tail in his mouth. He pulled back and smiled at her. "Was that so bad?"

He took her non-response as an approval.

"I'm going to retire for the evening, but first, I'm leaving you with something."

She flinched as he reached out to set his cup next to hers. Then he emptied the bottle into both cups, rose, and left Alice alone with the alcohol. Maybe it'd chill her out. Convince her to trust him a little.

Then again, maybe not.

He really didn't care.

CHAPTER TWENTY

The outside light didn't reach my bedroom, making it impossible to figure out what time it was without looking at my cell phone. And that was a death sentence to sleep. The moment the screen lit up, my mind would start racing in a hundred ways. I'd either slept through my alarm, or it wasn't even six in the morning yet. I tried to resign myself that I didn't care. Two minutes later I grabbed my phone. 5:20 a.m. Close enough. I showered, dressed, and managed to escape the house before the old lady knew I was up.

The sunrise was vibrant this morning with thin wispy clouds providing a textured canvas for the colors to play with. I stood next to my car and watched for a few moments, enjoying the cool morning air. It wouldn't last, that's for sure. By ten in the morning it'd be close to ninety if today was anything like yesterday.

Cassie and I had agreed to meet at a diner close to her place for breakfast. I almost slammed my forehead into the glass entry door when I saw Pennington and Cervantes sitting at the table. Cervantes noticed me first. He flashed a cocky grin, like he knew something I didn't. My stomach churned. Anything could've happened overnight. Pennington didn't alleviate any concerns when he broke off eye contact a second or two after making it.

I navigated the crowded diner, dodging old women and young waitresses. The air was laden with syrup, coffee, and floral perfume that was twenty years past its expiration date.

"Nice to see you, Tanner," Cervantes said. "Now get the hell outta here."

"The hell you talking about?" I said.

"You heard me," he said. "You need me to escort you?"

"Cerv, chill out." Pennington gestured to the empty seat at the table. "Sit for a second, Tanner."

For a second, huh? I glanced around the room. "I think I'm fine standing. Where's Cassie?"

"Not here," Pennington said. "Look, Cerv here got our boss involved and he doesn't want you coming along anymore."

My old friend rage dropped by for a visit. I kept him waiting on the porch within shouting distance. "Then Cassie's not gonna help you. Simple as that."

"You really that much of an asshole?" Cervantes said.

Knock-knock-knock.

Pennington extended his arm out in front of his partner. "She'll help, Tanner. She might say she doesn't want to, but she will. It's in her blood now. She can't refuse even if she wanted to."

"You bastards can arrest me then, 'cause where she goes, I go as far as this case is concerned. I'm here on her behalf, at her request, acting in a private capacity. Now, does one of you want to tell your chief to piss off, or should I?"

Pennington leaned back, fingertips scratching the stubble on his chin. I could tell he still didn't have a good read on me. Cervantes grinned as his hand traveled to his belt, about where he'd keep his cuffs. Maybe they were going to arrest me. Well, let them. Wouldn't be the first time I spent a night on the wrong side of the bars.

"I'm gonna ask again, where's Cassie?"

Neither man responded. Pennington glanced toward the door. A quick movement, not intended for me to see. I spun around and saw Cassie pulling the door open. She walked up to me shaking her head.

"I'm sorry, Mitch."

"Don't be," I said. "If they want to arrest me, they can. I'll sue the whole city over it."

"Won't be necessary," she said.

"Why's that?"

"I spoke with their boss. You're not going anywhere. Definitely not to jail."

I didn't have to look back to know Cervantes was pissed. What went through his mind at this point was anyone's guess. I figured he was devising a plan to get me into the woods and accidentally shoot me. Could be weeks, maybe even months, before anyone found my corpse if he picked the right spot.

The two men rose. Cervantes drove his shoulder into mine as he passed. Neither of us gave any ground to the other. Just one punch, that's all I wanted from him. That would give me reason to lay him out.

Pennington stopped in front of Cassie and me. "You two have five minutes if you want to come with us to the suspect's apartment."

"Speaking of which," Cassie said when Pennington was at the exit. "Anything turn up on whether he was there or not?"

The detective froze with the door half open. A warm breeze sucked into the restaurant. "We'll grill him on it after we find him."

I became aware that most eyes were on us. Could they piece it together? Had they seen Cassie on the news before? The woman who blew open a case by talking to the dead now stood in their presence. Maybe they wanted to ask her to reach out to a deceased relative, or give them the winning lottery numbers.

"Hungry?" Cassie asked.

"Yeah, I was planning on having a good meal to get me through the day."

"Not gonna happen." She gestured toward the counter. "Let's get some coffee and a Danish to go."

Five minutes later we were immersed in the morning humidity. Pennington tapped on his watch as we passed their sedan. They were parked a block from my rental. We drove in tandem through the historic district, winding around the garden squares. Though humid, the air still had that early fall cool feeling to it. We rolled the windows down and enjoyed the rush. A few musicians were already out. An older Black fellow with a patchy white beard belted the dark story of his life through his sax.

Pennington hiked his arm out the window and pointed at an apartment complex. It was a decent enough place. Not the best of buildings, but a far cry from the ghetto. The detectives continued another block, turned right, and pulled over next to the chipped curb. I stopped behind them and cut the engine.

"It's on the second floor," Pennington said. "You two can go as far as the landing, but you have to wait there."

We moved in time with one another. Every move I made, the other two detectives did as well. They took in everything, including possible escape routes and hiding places. For the first time I felt a little better about their abilities. Still didn't trust that they wouldn't get me or Cassie killed, though.

Cassie and I remained behind after climbing the seven stairs to the landing. The echoes of the detectives' footsteps deadened when they reached the corridor that ran the length of the building.

It must've been Cervantes pounding on the door. Sounded like two bulls colliding.

Fifteen seconds passed with no response. A trash truck rolled past, stopped, began backing up. Its alarm shrieked through the silence.

I slid to the other side of the landing. There wasn't much of a view, just the stairs and a stretch of wall. The persistent wind tunnel carried the scent of Chinese food. A bit early, but what the hell, I might grab some if we made it out of there empty-handed.

Cervantes pounded on the door again. Another fifteen seconds passed. The trash truck hoisted a dumpster overhead. The contents clattered and banged and shattered in the empty metal bed.

The two detectives appeared at the top of the stairs. Pennington shook his head.

"Where do you think he is?" I said.

"Who knows?" Cervantes said, huffing past me and avoiding eye contact.

Pennington stopped on the landing. "It was a long shot. We've already grilled him, and I'm sure he's doing his best to stay away from us."

"Might be hiding inside. Could be worthwhile to put eyes on the building."

Pennington nodded. "We're planning on it. On to the house."

Cassie and I moved in slow motion, letting the detectives advance out of earshot. I was apprehensive about her returning to the house after her incident outside. Was she feeling the same?

"You don't have to do this if you don't want to," I said.

"I do, Mitch. There could be something else in there."

"That's what I'm afraid of."

In that short span of time we'd been at the apartment building, the temperature rose enough that we had to turn on the air conditioning. The cabin smelled like the diner. Coffee and grease. Did little to settle my hunger. The Danish I had only sent my blood sugar soaring up, and it had already crashed.

"So have you received anything new?" I asked.

"About Robbie?" she said.

I gripped the steering wheel tight enough to snap it. "Well, no, that's not what I was asking. But, have you?"

She reached for my free hand. "Nothing yet."

"What about Alice?"

"Nothing there, either. Part of the reason I want to go to the house again. See if I missed something. If there's an item that might churn up some images."

We passed the old woman and her little dog as we approached the house. Her track suit was red today. Were they always out walking? Her sagging eyes popped as she caught sight of Cassie. We'd avoid any kind of questioning since the house stood a half block away. No way the woman would make it there in time.

What kind of questions would she have? No doubt the neighborhood residents knew something had happened. They might not know exactly what, but the cops had been around for the past few weeks, and the women hadn't. Word had gotten out. It always does. How quickly and to what extent it would spread was anyone's guess.

Pennington waved us into the driveway. He peered over the top of the car, eyes scanning.

"Let's head inside," he said, already trotting toward the door.

I cast a glance over my shoulder. Six people stood on four porches, watching us.

Word had most definitely gotten out. And it was spreading.

Cassie entered the house. She wasted no time in the main living area or kitchen. Instead she walked straight to the hall and disappeared into the darkened corridor.

"Tanner." Pennington stood by the back door. I saw his partner's silhouette amid the shadows of leaves through the screen. "Let's head outside again and wait for Cassie to do her thing."

There wasn't much conversation to be had between the three of us. Cervantes and Pennington stood at the other side of the yard while I waited by the door.

We all moved at the same time when Cassie's scream cut through the silence.

CHAPTER TWENTY-ONE

I ripped the screen door open, breaking one of the hinges. Pennington rushed in right behind me and finished the job. The metal frame clanged on the concrete patio. Cervantes cursed as he kicked it out of his way. The deserted kitchen and living room felt heavy. The place was as silent as a tomb. I kept reaching for the pistol I'd left in Philadelphia. Didn't stop me from rushing to the hallway.

Cassie yelled again, though not as loud as before. Something banged against the door. A man said something, and once more Cassie screamed.

I felt a hand on my back, gripping and digging into my shoulder. My momentum changed. I twisted and faceplanted into the rough plaster wall. When I had recovered, Cervantes hustled past. I lunged forward and knocked him to the side. We were fighting for sloppy seconds, though. Pennington had already reached the end of the hallway and was struggling with the door.

"Look out," Cervantes said, pushing his partner back. He drew his knee up and struck the door with his foot. The lock gave way and the hunk of wood swung open. Light knifed through the parted blinds. Cassie was engaged with a man slightly taller than her.

The two detectives started yelling, guns drawn. A chaotic scene meant to confuse the man. The guy released his grip on Cassie and threw his hands in the air. I rushed to Cassie's side and pulled her out of the room while the detectives threw the man to the ground. They kept yelling at the guy.

"What the hell happened?" I asked once we were safe in the living room.

"I felt drawn to the bedroom again," she said. "And when I went in there, he jumped me."

"Do you know who it is?"

"Yes. Seth, Alice's boyfriend."

"Well what the hell was he doing in there? Stealing panties?"

"I don't know. I didn't even know he was here. Think I would've gone in there if I had?"

Cervantes sidestepped through the door, his left arm wrapped through Seth's right. The young guy bucked and kicked. All that got him was a right hook to the stomach. A hollow gasp escaped as he bowed forward. The two detectives carried him down the hallway, knocking his head into the wall a couple of times.

"She all right?" Pennington asked over his shoulder.

"Yeah, fine, man," I said. "We'll be out in a second. Just make sure those neighbors are clear of the yard. Got me?"

I wrapped my arm around Cassie's waist and led her toward the front door. We stopped short and surveyed the surrounding street. The people I had seen on the way in, including the old woman and her dog, congregated across the road in an empty driveway. They held their hands in front of their mouths as they spoke. I supposed it was so we wouldn't hear them. Their stares were fixed on the cops and the handcuffed perp.

"Okay," I said. "Let's be quick about it. Head straight for the car. Don't look at any of them."

I stepped out first and did my best to shield her from the onlookers. Didn't work.

The old woman pointed, and said, "That's her. That's the one that was here yesterday, passed out on the ground. Maybe she knows what's going on." She rushed up to us with her barking dog in tow. "Miss? Miss?"

The rest shuffled like a hoard of zombies closing in after we reached the car. I pulled Cassie's door open and stood there, blocking them from her while she settled inside. Her hands and arms were shaking. The surprise attack had rattled her.

"Pennington," I said.

He looked over at me as though the crowd was my problem, not his. To be fair, Seth wasn't going easy. It took both of them to get the man in the backseat.

"Do something about these people so we can get out of here." I slammed Cassie's door shut and pushed my way to the other side of the vehicle. "You don't want to have to escort two people to a cell after I run these folks over, do you?"

He sent Cervantes over. The lumbering detective with his badge in one hand and pistol in the other was enough to send the mob into retreat mode. For the first time, it felt like the two of us were on the same page. It only took an attack on Cassie to bring him to my level. He shot a quick glance my way and gave me a slight nod. And with that, I ducked into the car and slammed it into reverse. A half-block later, I whipped the car around and sped away, leaving the neighborhood behind. A few turns later and we were on I-16 West. I figured putting a half-hour or so between us and Savannah would be a good thing for Cassie.

She turned toward me and spoke for the first time after we had cleared I-95. "Do you think he knew?"

"Knew what?" I glanced over and saw her staring through the windshield.

"That we were coming."

I adjusted the vent so the air hit me in the face. How was it that every rental car spat out the same stale-smelling air? "I doubt he would've been there if he knew that."

"Maybe he was trying to hide something and hadn't managed to get out in time. Figured a hostage was his best bet."

"I guess that's possible. But, still, that's a big risk considering the house has been combed over thoroughly. We're practically on cleanup duty in there."

"What was he doing there?" She looked away, toward the trees that passed by in a blur. The question had been asked of someone other than me. Had they responded to her?

"Could be like you said, trying to cover something up. Or maybe he was there for the same reason as us."

She remained fixated on the view through the side window. "How do you mean?"

"Looking for something, anything, to help find his girlfriend."

Cassie said nothing.

After a few moments, I said, "Tell me, coming into contact with him, did you feel anything?"

"Besides his fist in my stomach?" She looked over and offered a wry smile. It was good to see she could joke about it already. She'd survived much worse than this, and if that hadn't stopped her, there was no way this would. "No, I didn't *feel* anything. It all happened too damn fast, and I doubt I'll pick up on anything in the house again."

"Why's that?"

"That dumbass changed the energy in there. No telling what it'll be like next time."

"It's doubtful Pennington will let there be a next time. He

won't let you back in after this. Not to mention the integrity of the scene has been compromised. They'll shut it down now."

Cassie drew her left foot up and under her right thigh as she shifted in her seat to face me. "And what does that do for those women? How does that help them?"

I shook my head. "You're arguing with the wrong guy. I'm on your side, remember?"

"Yeah, I know." She angled the air vents away from her body. "This is just so frustrating."

"It usually is."

We kept pushing west for a couple more exits, grabbed a quick bite to eat, and then went straight to the precinct. Cassie led me to a rear entrance. We stood in front of the smoky glass door for a few moments. The door was tucked in and shielded on two sides by brick walls that prevented any airflow, making it feel ten degrees hotter. There was a buzzing sound followed by the lock clicking open.

Stale, chilled air met us in the doorway. Cassie walked to the desk where a portly woman waited with a fake smile on her face.

"Good to see you again," the woman said to Cassie. "They're waiting in interrogation room one. Have your associate sign in and I'll let Detective Pennington know you're on the way."

We walked through the industrial gray halls. Fluorescents illuminated the walkways. I caught a whiff of corn chips. Either someone was snacking nearby or it'd been a while since they last cleaned the carpets. After a few turns we entered the interrogation hall and then the outer area of room one. Standing in a dark chamber behind mirrored glass, we watched as Pennington and Cervantes asked Seth a series of questions. The man sat at a table with a half-empty glass of water in front of him. It appeared as though they had been at it for fifteen minutes or so already and were past the formalities. They grilled him on his relationship with each of the women in the house. He'd known one of them since childhood, and met the other three through her, eventually becoming romantically involved with Alice.

I tuned out the monotony for a couple moments and thought about what had happened earlier. Why was Seth at the house? Had someone tipped him off? One of the neighbors, maybe? From Cassie's account, there was no hesitation. Seth went right at her, attacking with intent to hurt.

I was dragged from my thoughts at a simple phrase Pennington uttered.

"Seth, that's not what you told us the last time we spoke."

CHAPTER TWENTY-TWO

Cassie and I both leaned forward. Our foreheads grazed the glass as though it would allow us to hear better.

"What did he ask him?" I said.

Cassie frowned at me. I presumed it was for failing to pay attention. I didn't bother to tell her I was boggled down with her earlier concerns.

"He asked him about being at his apartment. I guess his answer differed this time."

"What was his answer?"

She shot my reflection a look. "How have you managed to remain a detective for so long if you can't follow this?"

"I was lost in thought. Now what'd he say?"

"Said his power went out early, so he headed to a friend's house. The friend wasn't there, but Seth knows where the spare key was, so he went in and stayed there for the night."

In the interrogation room, Cervantes had positioned himself by the door. He leaned back with his arms crossed over his chest and his mouth clenched shut. He'd save his words for the right moment.

Meanwhile, Pennington continued. "So, before you told us you were home the entire night of the storm. Now you're telling me that you went to a friend's place, but the friend can't vouch for you because he wasn't there? I gotta tell you, this smells of bullshit, Seth."

"I was scared," Seth said.

"Scared of what?"

"That you'd arrest me for breaking and entering or something like that."

Pennington straightened up, pointed at Cervantes, then himself. "We're homicide detectives. You think I care about some petty ass B and E charge?"

Seth stared at the table and said nothing.

"See, the problem I have here is that you lied to me, and now you're trying to cover it up with more lies. And all this after we found you inside your girlfriend's room in a house where three women were murdered and one, your girlfriend, was abducted. What do you think she'd think about you sniffing her pantie drawer while she's missing? Huh? Or maybe you were there for a different reason?"

"To hell with her!" Seth slammed his clenched fists against the table. He gritted against the unexpected pain rifling through his wrists and arms. I'd seen it happen before. "If she'd have just taken me back, this wouldn't have happened to her. To any of them."

Did we have a confession coming?

Pennington shot a look at his partner, then toward us. He walked in a complete circle around Seth, stopping on the other side of the table. He pulled the empty chair out and sat down.

"What happened to her, Seth?"

"I don't know."

"Where were you that night?"

Seth looked up, but said nothing.

"We know you weren't at home because it was rented out for the week. And we both know the friend story is a fabrication."

Seth sat still and said nothing.

"You went over there, didn't you? Headed out in the storm, to see Alice. Why? Were you trying to win her back?"

"There was nothing to win back," he said. "We were still together."

"Not according to what some of her other friends said. They told us you two had broken up over a month earlier, and that you kept showing up at her work, her classes, the house. Always uninvited and unexpected."

The young man's cheeks burned red, but he kept his mouth shut. An attorney would have told him to shut up long ago. The house was awash with evidence. If Seth was innocent, forensics would clear him. It was time for Pennington to turn the screws on the guy. Seth knew something that would help to unravel the mystery further.

"Guess you figured the storm was the perfect chance," Pennington said. "Show up there with nowhere else to go. Soaking wet. She'd take you in. Get you out of those wet clothes. Dry you off. Warm you up. Next thing, you'd be in bed together while the wind howled and rain battered the house."

"It wasn't like that!"

And there we have it, folks. Seth had said something to implicate himself.

"Then what the hell was it like, Seth?" Pennington leaned in closer, ducking his head to make eye contact with Seth.

Seth lowered his head until his brow touched the cold metal table. His shoulders hitched up and down a few times, like he was crying, but there was no sobbing. Then after a few moments, he moaned. A high-pitched sound that bottomed out into a throaty growl. He was experiencing a physical and psychological release. The images of that night took over his every waking and sleeping moment.

"Talking will feel good, Seth," I whispered. "Just do it."

"What?" Cassie glanced at me.

I shook my head and said, "Thinking out loud. I have a feeling he's about to tell us everything."

Pennington remained silent. He leaned back in his chair and crossed his arms. No doubt he'd seen suspects try a multitude of tactics to throw him off. The threat of life in prison leads people to do and say anything to save their skin. Speaking from experience, little surprised you after several years on the job.

Cervantes left his post by the door, whispered something to his partner, then exited the interrogation room. The door fell shut like a brick hitting the floor. Cervantes stepped into the dark chamber and stood next to me.

"What do you think?" he said.

"Me?" I said.

"Yeah, you."

"You want my opinion?"

"I asked, didn't I?"

"I thought maybe it was a rhetorical question and you'd try to throw me out after I answered."

"Christ, Tanner. I'm trying to build bridges here. Bridges. Don't burn them down."

Back in the room Seth had straightened up and sat rigid. A red spot covered his forehead. He stared at the window, almost as though he were looking at me right through it.

"I think he's full of shit," I said. "Or he's a psycho stalker who wouldn't leave his ex alone."

"So you think there's a chance he did it?"

"You're the one with access to the evidence, man. You tell me."

"Really think you'd be standing here if we had something solid on him?"

I folded my arms over my chest. "No, not at all."

Cassie said, "It wasn't him."

"How can you be sure?" Cervantes said.

"I can't."

Silence lingered inside and outside the interrogation room for a minute or so. My aggravation bled over and increased my breathing, fogging up the glass. The hazy mist grew then retreated with each breath. Could they see it on the other side? I'd never looked for that before.

Seth cleared his throat and shifted in his chair. "We were broken up."

Pennington nodded, but said nothing. No reason to. Seth had broken the cardinal rule in a negotiation. He spoke first.

"It had been a couple months, like you said. I'd go over to pay her a visit sometimes. She still let me in, but not when her friends were around. And if one of them answered the door..." He clenched his mouth tight. The muscles on his jaw stood out behind his thin, scraggly beard. "When they were around, Alice wouldn't even see me. She'd tell them to send me away. But I'd hang around the hedges at a neighbor's house, and late at night, when everyone was asleep, she'd open her window for me."

"You sure it was for you?

"You calling my girlfriend a whore?"

"Ex-girlfriend, Seth." Pennington stifled a smile. A little twitch at the corner of his mouth. He'd gotten under his subject's skin, and that was often the moment the truth came out.

Seth's cheeks burned red again, but not out of anger. Body language gave it away. His shoulders slumped. His chin dropped to his chest. His eyes cast downward again. "Look, man, I know she's kind of casual with guys. That was why...that's why she broke up with me. I couldn't take it while we were exclusive. While I was exclusive, I guess. I yelled at her one time too many."

"You ever strike her?"

"No, man. The hell? I ain't like that."

Pennington nodded. "Okay, fair enough. Let's get to after you were broken up. Were there any confrontations the times her friends wouldn't let you in?"

Seth shrugged, said nothing. I knew where Pennington was going with it, and hoped he'd stop short. He'd rattled the man and shaken Seth's confidence. Any more might cause the guy to shut down and clam up.

"All right," Pennington said. "Just tell me the truth."

"About what?"

"Where were you that night?"

Seth glanced up. He was biting his bottom lip while clenching and unclenching his hands into fists. The raw emotions from the night of the storm were flooding in. What had he seen? What had he done? Or, perhaps, what did he wish he had done?

"If I tell you what I saw, you promise nothing will happen to me?"

CHAPTER TWENTY-THREE

The three of us stood with our faces pressed against the glass. The air vents directly above piped frigid air over us. The two-way mirror felt like ice on my skin. The tension in the room immobilized us where we stood. Seth appeared on the verge of confessing, or at the very least, placing himself close enough to the crime scene that he'd be upgraded from person of interest to a full-blown suspect. Cassie had her doubts, and so did I. Seth didn't have the look of a man who could kill three and kidnap another. Then again, they didn't always look like you expected.

Pennington said, "Seth, I can't promise something like that until I hear what you have to say. I mean, if you tell me you went in there and murdered those women, there'll be consequences. I'm sure you understand there has to be. This is the kind of case where the DA will recommend the death penalty. That being said, confessing now will greatly help your chances of avoiding serious punishment."

"I ain't did it, man," Seth said. Tears were falling now. "Christ, it wasn't me."

"Okay, so what's this about then?" Pennington's voice rose in anger. He was getting tired of the run around.

"I went over that night, like you said. My apartment was rented, and I had nowhere else to go. Most times, I'd just find a quiet spot and sleep outside. No one really bothers you if you're in the right area. But the rain started. When I checked my phone and saw the size of the storm that was coming, I mean, shit, I knew I had to get somewhere."

"You hadn't heard anything about the hurricane prior to those first few drops?"

"Nah."

"How?"

"Don't pay attention to the news."

"You don't listen to the radio?"

"Why would I?" Seth lifted one eyebrow and looked at Pennington as though the detective had stepped out of a time capsule. "I got all the music I need on my phone."

The guy epitomized everything that they say is wrong with millennials.

"All right, okay, Seth. I'm feeling it. But why not check into a hotel?"

Seth shrugged and looked a little surprised. Hadn't he considered it?

"Well," Seth said, "I figured just like you thought, being trapped in a hurricane gave me an opportunity to get back in with Alice."

"How long had it been since you'd seen her?"

"Seen? Or touched?"

"Both."

Seth looked toward the ceiling, calculating dates and times. "I'd seen her only a week before, leaving the library. She went over to Leopold's with two of her roommates."

"Did you talk to her?"

He shook his head. "Nah, I know better than that. She was with her friends, so I kept on my way."

"Okay, so when was the last time you were in contact with her.'"

"It's been a few weeks. Fifteen days before she disappeared, I'd say."

"And what happened?"

"The usual, I guess. She let me in. We did, uh, our thing." The left side of his face scrunched up, like he was trying to explain to his grandmother what happened in that room. "I tried to talk to her afterward, and she asked me to leave."

"Nice gig for her, huh? Lets you in when she's got nothing better on tap, then gives you the boot."

Seth narrowed his eyes. "I guess. I'm getting something out of it, though."

"I'm sure you are, Seth." Pennington's lips twitched again. He was working overtime to keep from laughing at this clown.

"Anyway, that's the last time I spoke to her. I mean, I tried calling, but she wouldn't answer. I left a couple messages. None were returned."

I nudged Cervantes with my elbow. "Messages?"

"Nothing exciting," he said. "We checked it out already."

Nodding, Pennington said, "Let's get back to the night of the storm. You knew you had to get inside, and didn't bother with a hotel or shelter. Did you try a friend's house?"

"What I was saying earlier was kinda true." Seth leaned back in his chair, crossed his left leg over his right knee. He was getting comfortable. Letting his guard down. Was Pennington enough of a shark to take advantage? Seth continued. "I did go by a friend's house, and they weren't there. But there wasn't any spare key. I tried a few windows and the terrace door, but they were all locked."

"And you did what after that?"

"Alice's. I went to her place."

"Did you walk? Take the bus? Drive there?"

"I rode a bike."

"Through the storm?"

Seth shrugged and said nothing.

Pennington shook his head, exhaled, and refocused. "What did she say when she saw you?"

"She never saw me."

"Why not?"

Cassie drew in a sharp breath about the same time as Cervantes. This was what we were waiting for. Seth was about to deliver the money shot.

Seth leaned forward and tapped the table with his index finger. "'Cause by the time they got to the house, it was raining so hard they ran from the car to the front door. All five of them."

"Five, you say. Who? Tell me as though I know nothing about the residents of this house."

"Her, her three roommates, and that dude."

"What dude?" Pennington did well to hide his apprehension. It was best to string it out, let Seth recount it as he remembered it. And then ask him again.

"The one that slut brought home." Seth leaned back and folded his arms over his chest. He held his head high, lips pursed.

"Did you get a good look at him?"

Seth shook his head as he lifted his hands in the air. As he let them fall, he wiggled his fingers. "The rain, man. It was like a plastic sheet. I can tell you he was about a head taller than her, but other than that, I don't know if he was old, young, bald, whatever."

"Was he white?"

Seth leaned back and glanced up at that spot on the ceiling where the inner recesses of his memory resided. "Yeah, he was. I could tell that."

"So what happened next?"

Seth picked up his cup and turned it over. "I need some more water."

Pennington looked back and nodded. Cervantes exited the room, leaving the interrogation on hiatus until he returned with a pitcher of ice water. He left it on the table, then rejoined Cassie and me on the other side of the glass.

Pennington filled Seth's cup. We all waited while the guy took his time sipping on it.

"All right," the detective said. "You're re-hydrated. So now tell me what happened after they went inside."

"I went to the door, the front one, and tried to get in. It was locked. I checked the flower pot, but the spare was gone. Guess she removed it after the last time I went over."

"Thought you said she invited you in."

Seth shrugged. "Kinda. I guess I showed myself in, and that was good enough for Alice. It wasn't the first time, either, so don't start thinking I did something wrong."

"The door was locked the night of the hurricane. No key."

"Right, yeah. I went to the back. Same thing. Power was out, so I couldn't see anything through the windows. Checked each one. Either the curtains were drawn, or the darkness was too...dark."

"How long did all this take?" Pennington shot a glance at his watch.

"Fifteen minutes, maybe?"

"You must've been soaked by this point."

"Yeah, I was."

"So what'd you do next?"

"The storm was getting bad. I went down the street and

stopped at every house that had a garage until I found one I could get into."

"What'd you want with a garage? Refuge from the storm?"

Seth slumped in his chair, eyes focused on the table. "Yeah, I mean, for a while."

"How long?"

"An hour. Maybe two."

"Must've been tough in there," Pennington said. "Knowing that your girlfriend was in that dark house with some strange man."

He was baiting the young guy. Judging by Seth's reddening cheeks, it was working.

"They were all wet from the rain," Pennington said. "Get to the house, guy has no clothes. Alice offers him something from her closet. Heck, maybe a pair of shorts you left behind. Can you imagine that? She helps him change into your old clothes."

Seth said nothing. Kept his eyes focused on a scratch on the table. His expression told a different story, though. His eyebrows knitted together while his nostrils flared wide.

"Wonder if she even got dry clothes back on him? But you probably weren't thinking about that, were you?"

Seth balled his fists and hit the table. "Yeah I was thinking about that. I stewed on that the whole time I was in there. What the hell was she thinking? I mean, I was right there, available, and she knew it. She knew I'd be over. She asked me to come over, man. And she still brought some asshole home."

Pennington remained quiet as Seth shifted in his chair.

"And all around me, in that dark, ass-smelling garage, all these tools."

"And what'd you do?"

"I took a big ass knife off the wall and went back out into the storm."

CHAPTER TWENTY-FOUR

The room felt as though the air had been drained from it, like it'd been hit in the gut, until Cervantes broke the silence.

"Shit, this little creep? He did it?"

As much as I couldn't believe it either, it appeared a confession was forthcoming. I had questions, sure. What happened to the other man? But I supposed that would come in the next few minutes.

Cassie placed both hands on the window. I glanced over. Her eyes were shut. Her head swung side to side.

"What is it?" I asked her.

She said nothing. Someone else had her attention.

"The hell is wrong with her?" Cervantes said.

"You've worked with her," I said. "Shit like this just happens."

Inside the interrogation room, the mood had changed. The scared, scrawny man no longer looked so scared. His lips formed a slight smile. He sat up, shoulders back, hand clutching an imaginary knife.

Now Pennington hunched forward, like a leopard ready to

pounce. He only needed Seth to make one statement. The trick was leading him there.

"What was the weather like at that point?" Pennington asked.

"Felt like walking through a hailstorm of bullets, man. Wind was ripping down the street. Water pelting me in every direction. I figured out pretty quick that if I huddled up next to a house, it was a lot easier than walking down the middle of the road."

"And how far away were you?"

"Couple blocks is all."

"Okay. So on your way back to Alice's house, did you see anything?"

"Nah. Too dark. Rain was too thick."

"What were you thinking as you were making your way back to the house?"

Seth smirked. "I'm gonna kill that bitch. Only thought going through my mind." He hummed a few bars of blues, then sang, "I'm gonna kill that bitch tonight."

Pennington placed his hands on the table, palms down. He lowered himself an inch or two, slightly below eye level of the other man. He was going for the close. "Seth, did you? Did you kill Alice?"

A long silence ensued. It sounded like the three of us standing behind the glass were in the middle of panic attacks. Our breathing was rapid, shallow. The glass in front of me fogged up with every exhale. It felt as though my heart was going to explode.

"I got there and the front door was still locked. I checked for the spare again, figuring maybe I was being too hasty last time. Still didn't find it. Was about to try and kick the door in, but I changed my mind at the last second."

"Why? Seems like the quickest way inside."

"Someone might be watching. Might call the cops."

"You didn't think standing out there in the middle of a hurricane with a large knife was enough to raise suspicion?"

Seth shrugged. "Dunno."

"So what'd you do to get inside?"

"Went around back."

Pennington nodded. "You broke in through the rear door."

Seth took a deep breath, puffed out his cheeks as he exhaled. His lips flapped together. Sounded like an eighteen-wheeler blowing out a tire. "I didn't break in," he said after a few moments, shrugging and holding out his hands.

"The back door was unlocked when you returned?"

"No, Detective." Seth brushed his open hand across the table. "It was open."

"Unlocked?"

"I mean wide open, man. I stepped in and the little bit of light there was glinted off the floor. At first I thought the rain had gotten in. I bent down, stuck my fingers in the puddle. Knew right then it wasn't water."

"What'd you do?"

"There's a junk drawer by the sink, next to the door. I found a cheap flashlight in there. Switched it on. Sure enough, kitchen floor was covered in blood. Tracks and trails, leading from the hall to the back door."

"You sure about this?"

"Of course I'm sure. I saw it."

"Was this the first time you saw it? You don't recall a time lapse, anything like that?"

"You think I blacked out and killed all of them?" Seth pushed back from the table and stood.

Pennington mirrored him. Cervantes exited the room and joined his partner.

"Seth said 'all,'" I said, not sure if Cassie had rejoined us yet.

"And?" Cassie said. Whoever had grabbed her attention was gone.

"What was he doing in Alice's room? Trying to find a clue or something? Mourning her? Jerking off?"

After some shouting by Cervantes, the situation in the interrogation room returned to normal. Seth sat back down. So did Pennington. Cervantes remained in the room by the door with his hand where his pistol normally resided.

"I saw all that blood," Seth said. "And I panicked." He chuckled softly. "I freaked out is more like it. Ran out of there, tossed the knife into some hedges about a block away, and just ran until I reached a park, where I took shelter in the bathroom with some homeless guy until the storm let up."

Pennington asked a few more questions, but they led nowhere. Finally, he cuffed Seth.

"What's this?" Seth asked. "Are you arresting me?"

"You won't have to worry about where you're staying for a few nights," Pennington said. "We're keeping you on suspicion."

"Suspicion of what?" Seth thrashed against the man. "I told you, I didn't do nothing. Let me go."

"Get him out of here," Pennington said to his partner.

Cervantes escorted the yelling man out of the room. His shouts faded a few moments later. Pennington joined us behind the glass.

"What do you think?" he asked.

"I dunno, man," I said. "Lots of probable cause from what he told you. Then he admits entering the house with a weapon and intent to kill."

"I know. His DNA is all over that place, too. Practically every room. But he'd been going there for months, so that's easy for the defense to write-off."

"Was it on the women?"

Pennington shook his head. "We weren't that lucky. It's one of the reasons we've been hesitant with him."

"Yeah, I can see that. Maybe the story about the other guy isn't the truth. Maybe they were working together."

Pennington shrugged and then reached out for Cassie's arm. "What about you? You buy what just happened?"

"It makes sense," Cassie said. "On a couple levels. His rage, I can see, I guess. But why kill *all* the women? Alice was the one who fueled his rage. And if you charge him, are we to believe that Alice is dead? And why would he go back to the house?"

"You gotta find that knife, Pennington," I said. "If what he said is true, that he chucked it, it'll provide an answer. Even if only a partial one. Something will be left behind on it if he used it on the women."

"I'm with you, Tanner. I'll get a group together to search once he gives up the location. In the meantime, you two get going. We've got a ton of paperwork, so nothing to do here for a bit. I'll be in touch soon."

We parted with Pennington in the hallway. Cassie led me to the rear parking lot. It was midday, and hot as hell. The sun beat down on the asphalt. Smelled like walking through a tar pit. I had to check and make sure the soles of my shoes weren't melting to the ground.

"Always this hot this time of year?" I said as we got inside the sweltering car.

"No," Cassie said. "Nothing like this."

I put the AC on full blast and rolled down the windows. All it did was push hot air around. At least there was the promise of cooling off soon.

"It's been a rough one," I said. "Want me to take you home?"

Cassie adjusted her vent, looked at me, said, "No, I want you to take me out to eat."

CHAPTER TWENTY-FIVE

Cassie picked a historic place on the outskirts of town, an old Victorian converted into a restaurant. The wide plank flooring wasn't level and after a long day had a funhouse effect as I followed the hostess to our table. There were hundred-year-old portraits on the walls above panels that appeared to be aged copper, pounded into a pattern. We were seated next to a window that overlooked a manicured garden.

The menu was full of low country favorites and overpriced drinks, which we both indulged in. The second one went down easier than the first. My shrimp and grits arrived after I'd had my fourth vodka and soda.

"You gonna take it easy now?" she said.

I waved her off. "I'll be all right. Rehydrating is all."

We were silent for the next several minutes while we ate. Afterward, we both ordered coffee. I filled her in on a few of the details about my life. She listened, and offered little in return about hers. About what I expected.

Waiting for the check to arrive, she said, "I forgot how much I hated this place."

"Why? Seems all right by me. Maybe a bit pricey, but I suppose any place in a touristy area will be so."

"The food's fine." She looked up and smiled, softening her features. At times I failed to recognize how attractive she was. "It's the extracurricular activity that goes on here. It's an old building and has seen a lot. I get lots of visitors here. That can be distracting when all I want to do is enjoy the human company sitting across from me."

And that was something else I failed to recognize, or even think about. What was the world like through her eyes? Even if the shit wasn't real, *she saw it*, which I supposed made it real enough. A life sentence of wandering souls pestering her.

"Does that happen a lot?" I asked.

Sipping from her mug, she offered a slight shrug. "Sitting across from a human I want to talk to? No, not really."

I offered her a smile. "That is intriguing, but I meant the ghost thing."

She sighed into a soft smile in return. "Sometimes it does. Other times, it's like they're off bothering someone else. I can go days without a visitor. Then, boom, they're all over me. Everyone needing something different. I have to prioritize who to help, which, if you knew me before I was nearly killed, was not something I was ever good at."

"A bit disheveled in your former life?"

"You have no idea."

I noticed the patrons at a nearby table glancing over. "You'll have to tell me more about that. But not today. It's time to take you home. Let's get going."

The alcohol enhanced the funhouse effect of the flooring. We exited the cool, dim foyer, out into the heat again. Did it ever let up? Even with the sun setting it felt the same as it had a couple of hours ago.

We drove across town to Cassie's place. I threw the car into park in front of her house and left the engine idling.

"You gonna be okay?" I asked.

"I guess," she said.

Seemed like something was bothering her. The reality of the attack could be settling in, but not having time to process it, she couldn't speak about it. Or perhaps it was the event she experienced during the interrogation.

I placed my hand over the ignition. "Want me to come in for a while?"

"Yeah, that might help."

I cut the engine and followed her across the yard. Birds occupied a nearby tree, whistling with the breeze. I caught a whiff of chicken burning on a grill. Dark clouds filled the western sky. The descending sun cast an orange hue around the grey. The Spanish moss hanging from the trees stood out.

Cassie's house was cool and dark and quiet. The heavy front door swung shut, separating us from the madness of the day. She disappeared into her bedroom as I made my way to the kitchen and put on a fresh pot of coffee. I was still feeling the effects of the drinks, and it was too early in the day to keep that chain going.

About the time the pot was finished brewing, Cassie stepped into the kitchen. Her hair was damp. She walked past me, leaving me in a wash of her fresh scent. She had on a new pair of gym shorts and a plain blue t-shirt with a pocket stretched over her left breast.

"Feel better?" I asked.

"I guess in some ways."

"And in other ways?"

"Worse."

"The ambush?"

"Yeah." She stretched to her tiptoes and reached into the cupboard. Her shorts hiked up a couple inches. She pulled down two mugs and filled them both. Turning to me, she said, "What if he'd been armed, Mitch? I held my own for those thirty seconds between him knocking the wind out of me and you guys showing up, but if he'd had a weapon, there's no telling."

"There never is," I said. "Could have gone any number of ways. And a weapon might not be needed. He could've snapped your neck, stepped on your throat, collapsed your trachea."

"Thanks." Her eyes widened as she handed me my coffee.

"Sorry, I know that's the last thing you need to be thinking about."

Neither of us spoke for a few minutes. Our gazes traveled around the room, meeting every so often, each holding the other's for a second or two before moving on again. I marveled at how ignorant I was to her beauty, especially with her hair wet and combed back, falling to the sides. That smell, too. Like an angel recently descended.

She lifted her mug to her mouth, but stopped about an inch short. Her lips formed a smile.

"What?" she said.

"What what?" I said.

"You're staring."

"I was?"

She rolled her eyes and took a drink. "Anyway, you have that postcard on you? The one from your son?"

I reached into my pocket and traced the edge of the thick card stock. "Sure do."

"I'd like to see it again."

Would she find something different now, considering what

she'd been through today? Did the chaos have an effect on her where it cleansed her palette, so to speak?

I pulled out the postcard and set it on the table. My fingertips lingered on top, at around the middle where Robbie wrote my name. Cassie reached out. Her fingers grazed mine. We glanced at each other, our gazes steady for a moment. I don't know who looked away first.

She slid the postcard toward her, stopping at the edge of the tabletop and laying her hand over it. I looked up again. She'd closed her eyes. Her breathing was rhythmic, slow and steady. In through her nose, out through her mouth. Her French roast-scented breath washed past me.

What did she see? Hear? Feel at that moment? Robbie's laughter? It rang out clear as any day I'd heard it in my ears. Me and him and Ella Kate, playing on the floor. Wrestling. They were winning. Had me pinned down.

"May I?" she asked, her thumb and forefinger pinching the corner.

"Of course." My heart pounded. Had she heard something that left her unsure? Would holding it, reading it, help?

The house ticked with every second that passed over the course of five long minutes. Cassie barely moved. She was so deep in her trance, it looked as though she'd stopped breathing. I didn't dare move out of fear of bringing her back to this world. What if she'd made contact? What if she was unlocking the secret? I questioned myself for asking those questions, but to hell with it. I had no other hope outside of Cassie.

She took a deep, loud breath. Opened her eyes. She forced a smile as she set the postcard down again.

"Well?" I asked.

"Sorry," she said. "There's too much clutter. I can't tell what's going on right now, or where he is."

"Clutter?"

She shrugged. "Don't know how else to explain it. It's like watching television through thick static. You can kind of see what's happening, but it would be really easy to misinterpret it, too."

"I got you. I figured it's a long shot, anyway." I tried to hide the disappointment from my expression. It wasn't her fault, and I didn't want her to feel like it was.

She reached for my hand. My skin tingled at her hot touch. "I'll keep trying, Mitch. Maybe after this murder investigation is sorted, it'll be easier for me."

"I hope so."

We both rose. I reached for the postcard. She reached for my hand again. We stood there for a moment, me looking at the table, her looking who knows where. I wrapped my fingers around hers, pulled her closer. I couldn't place the smell of her skin. It was soft and herbal. Her hair, too. Her lips tasted of the coffee at first.

"We shouldn't do this," I said, pulling back.

"I know," she said, leaning forward.

We kissed again. Our hands traveled along the other's body. She pulled me out of the kitchen and into her room, where we retreated to her bed.

CHAPTER TWENTY-SIX

We lay there for an hour, talking about nothing in particular. I kept thinking that I'd butchered a professional relationship I'd built for a decade. Perhaps Cassie read my mind, because she said a couple times this wouldn't change things. How could it not? Even if we never laid down together again, it would always be there between us. But there was no use in arguing that point at the moment. Because if the opportunity arose again, I'd take it.

"You should probably go soon." She lay on her side, the sheet barely covering her breasts. She traced her finger along my chest.

"Kicking me out already?"

"You know it wouldn't be good for Pennington and Cervantes to show up here in the middle of the night and discover you in my bed."

"They have that kind of open door policy with you?"

She smiled and lifted an eyebrow. "You'll never know."

I laughed at the suggestion. "Guess I should be on my way

then. With the hard-on Cervantes has had for me, I don't want to be in the room like this when he shows up."

She planted her palm firmly on my chest, pinning me to the bed. "There's not that much of a rush."

I surrendered to her again.

Two hours later, I was finally on my way. The sun had long since set, but the humidity remained. The clouds had thickened across the night sky. I walked through dim pools of light cast down by the streetlights while the cicadas trilled like ancient warriors rushing a city. I scanned my surroundings, looking and listening for anything out of place. Footsteps. A ticking muffler. A sudden silence. There was none of that.

Driving through the city with the windows down was a different experience at night. The air had cooled enough that it felt chilly at forty miles an hour. It rushed through the car, encasing me in an invisible tomb, dulling Cassie's scent on my skin.

A parking spot remained in front of the house where I was staying. I hadn't pulled in and cut the engine before the old woman stepped out onto the stoop. I glanced up and saw her hugging on her beau. She playfully shooed the man away, then called for me after I stepped onto the sidewalk.

"Mr. Tanner?"

"Yes, ma'am."

"You've had a long day, haven't you?"

What did she know? And how did she know it?

"How do you mean?"

She trekked down the stairs, smiling, and came up to me. "Been gone a long time today. And what's that smell? A woman's perfume? Either you were shopping and trying out a new lifestyle, or you've got a lady friend here in Savannah."

"I've got a lady friend in lots of cities, ma'am."

She slapped my shoulder. "Mr. Tanner, I'm an old woman. I can't take hearing that kind of talk."

"Oh yeah." I jutted my chin toward the gentleman walking away from us. "I guess you and your fella were just playing bridge then, huh?"

"And with that," she said, "I'll be retiring for the evening. Breakfast is at seven if you are interested."

I stayed on the sidewalk until she'd made her way back inside the house. Voices rose behind. I turned and saw a group of people waiting at the light at the end of the street. Despite the late hour, the intersection had enough traffic that they decided to wait for the signal to walk.

The apartment was cool and smelled of the old woman's dinner. Some kind of pasta dish. I felt a pang of hunger and pulled out a half-eaten burger from the small fridge. After washing it down with a glass of water, I turned in with plans of joining the old lady upstairs for breakfast at seven.

CHAPTER TWENTY-SEVEN

The Spanish moss danced in the breeze like lost souls floating down Hades' river. Cassie reached up and let it glide along her palm. The physical feeling matched the psychological impact her visitors had on her. She looked down and saw that the ground beneath her had disappeared. A black void threatened to suck her in. She clutched at the moss, twisting her hand in an effort to wrap it around her wrist. It wasn't that far to the tree trunk, which was still rooted in the earth.

But the moss gave way and she dropped fifty feet in an instant. A stifled attempt at screaming gave her pause for a moment. Overhead, dozens of crows ascended from the old oak tree, leaving behind barren branches. There had been leaves there a moment ago. Or had that been the silhouettes of the birds?

"Think it through," she muttered to herself. "You've been through this before."

The dream was one she'd had several times. After the first few instances, she came to realize it was a harbinger that always started the same way with the moss and the void. Someone communicated with her this way, though she wasn't sure who it was. It was after this moment that things changed.

Just let go.

She spread her fingers wide and let the moss unravel. It clung to her skin as it did so. Cassie breathed in the blackness as she descended through the void. Thirty seconds passed. The light began to filter in. She was near the end. Almost at the place where the message, if there was one, would be revealed. What was it last time? She struggled to remember. While she recognized the beginning of the dream rather quickly, the endings always faded.

She braced for an impending collision with a roof. Would she gain entry this time? The question was answered a few seconds later. She hit the bed and bounced three feet in the air before settling onto the mattress again. The walls and ceiling were coated thick with blood. It dripped like rain off of leaves. She leaned over and stared at the pool of crimson on the floor. Every drop from the ceiling splashed and sent out a wake. Small waves crashed against each other.

The room seemed familiar. Cassie realized where she was when she saw a flash of Alice's face.

"Speak to me, Alice," she said. "Tell me who did this."

The center of the room started to spin, forming a whirlpool. It widened by a foot every ten seconds. The bed broke free and started to swirl. Cassie leaned over and saw the black void again. She'd never gone through twice before. Where would it lead? Panic set in. What if she went through and never came back? What if she was accosted by spirits she had never encountered before?

An arm reached through the ceiling and extended toward her. It was a man's arm with thick muscles covered in a layer of hair. The scarred knuckles gave her reason to pause. But as the front of the bed tipped forward, she reached out and grasped the hand.

A layer of blood coated her as she was pulled through the ceiling into the night sky. The tree loomed larger than ever, every inch of its branches covered in Spanish moss that twisted in gale-forced winds. A face appeared. A face she knew all too well.

Novak smiled at her.

"Welcome back, Cassie."

CHAPTER TWENTY-EIGHT

He watched the mixture of dried blood and dirt swirl around the sink basin before it slipped into the drain. Streaks that looked like Georgia clay clung to the porcelain. It hadn't been his intention to dig a grave in the middle of the night. If she hadn't pushed him, he wouldn't have killed the other woman. Wouldn't have had his way with her before slitting her throat in front of Alice, holding the woman upright as her blood sprayed across the cell. It coated the wall, floor, and yes, even Alice.

These things happen, he reminded himself. And, perhaps it was a blessing. After all, he only had so much room in his cellar and another visitor would be coming soon. Expansion was not in the cards right now. No, his time at the penitentiary saw to that.

He wasn't keen on returning to his shack outside the city. What if he'd been on the news? Would the neighbors have reported him? Hell, how many had even seen him or could recount what he looked like? It wasn't like he had been there long. Few, if any, knew him. And if he knew who those few were, he'd kill them, too. They wouldn't get the benefit of an extended stay in his cellar, either.

After washing up, he changed into fresh clothes. He thought it would be a good idea to pack a few pairs of jeans and shirts since he'd been wearing the same ones for two weeks and now they were ruined. There just wasn't time to get away as often as he'd like anymore. He stuffed the blood-covered clothing into a trash bag and carried it out with him. A light dash of pink littered the eastern sky as he left the small house. Sunrise was still an hour off. Plenty of time to get away from the streetlights and the watchful eye of the city.

He tossed his bag into the passenger seat of his truck, then climbed in behind the wheel. He kept the lights off as he backed down the dirt driveway, not that it made a difference. The truck rumbled something fierce, and was sure to arouse the suspicion of anyone who was awake. Perhaps it was time to look for a new vehicle.

Ten minutes down the road he stopped for gas and coffee. Figured it was the best time of the day to do so. The clerk would have been on shift since eleven or so at night. By this point, they'd be over it and ready to go home. They wouldn't remember him if their jobs depended on it. It was the beard. Helped him blend into the background.

He spotted a stack of newspapers next to the register. It had been a while since he caught up on current events, and who knew when he'd be in a store again.

He stepped out into the fresh morning air. It was a beautiful time of day. He missed it greatly while locked up. He tucked his chin to his chest and looked away while blue strobes sped past. It was obvious they weren't there for him, but why tempt fate?

He pulled the driver's door open and tossed the newspaper onto the passenger seat. The guts spilled out. He cursed at the mess. After securing the cardboard mug in the cup holder, he reached over and began scooping up the loose insides.

And then he froze at the sight of the photo on page B1. The cabin light dimmed off. He reached up and tried to switch it on, but it didn't work.

"Dammit."

He shifted into reverse and backed into an empty spot in the gas bay. The overhead lights provided some illumination, but not enough, so he rolled down his window and hauled the paper over, shoving it through the opening. His arms and head followed. The wind rustled the paper. He stretched it wide to get a good look. His heart jumped at the sight of the house he had been in a few weeks ago. His stay had been short, but had created a devastating impact. Three dead women, and a fourth still in his custody. The only one in his custody, as a matter of fact. But he could see that changing soon.

Because she was there.

"Oh, my dear sweet woman," he whispered amid a spreading smile.

He scanned through the article until he came upon her name. He had never known it. They had falsified her identity in court for her protection. They wouldn't even let him see pictures of her face. All he had to go by were the images from that moonlit night so long ago.

"Cassie," he said.

"What?" There was a man holding a credit card and wearing a red ball cap and a blue puffer vest on the other side of the pump.

"Nothing." He retreated into the cabin, rolled up the windows and pulled away from the gas station. Driving with the paper in one hand, the wheel in the other, his stare traveled back and forth between the road and the photo.

"My sweet Cassie, what were you doing at that house? I

thought you were gone. They told me you were gone, removed, in witness protection. They were going to kill me because I almost killed you! You bitch. I bet you think I deserved that, don't you?"

He knew it was a lie to blame only her. He had killed many women. Far more than the six he confessed and eventually led detectives to. Perhaps they were wise to lie about her. If he'd known, she would have been the first he visited after escaping instead of picking those random women the night of the storm.

"I have to know where you are, Cassie."

He pulled over at a twenty-four-hour pharmacy where he purchased a throwaway cell phone. He couldn't make the call without one. At one time, he'd have used a pay phone. Good luck finding one now, though.

The line rang seven times before cutting to voicemail. He hung up, called again. It rang seven times more. He tried again. This time an out-of-breath man answered.

"Who is this?" the guy said.

"It's me."

There was a long pause on the other end. "Why are you calling me?"

"Don't worry, my friend. This line is clean. Just bought it and I'll run over it as soon as we hang up."

"What do you want?"

"Page B1."

The guy exhaled heavily into the speaker. "What?"

"The paper, you idiot. The woman on page B1. Her name is in the article. Tell me where she lives."

"Uh, okay, hold on."

He waited, listening to the man fumbling around. The distinct click-clack of a computer keyboard filled the ear piece.

"I'm gonna have to get back to you," the guy said.

"Christ. Well, if you find something, you know how to reach me."

"You got—"

He ended the call, then powered off the phone. After it shut down, he stripped the battery and tossed it into a trashcan. The phone wedged nicely underneath the front tire. He rolled over it in reverse, then forward, repeating the process three times. Backing away for good, he stopped, got out, and inspected the cell.

"Digital pancake."

Light filled the eastern sky as he continued out of town. Cool wind rushed in through the open windows. Wouldn't be long before the unseasonable heat took over. Thank goodness the cellar remained a steady temperature year round, but the old house offered no protection from the hot and cold. It was all he had, though, if he wanted to maintain his anonymity. The other place was no good anymore.

The newspaper rustled on the seat next to him. He looked over and was met with her stare.

"Cassie, Cassie," he said. "Where are you now?"

And at that moment, he had the irresistible urge to return to the crime scene.

CHAPTER TWENTY-NINE

I managed to get up in time for breakfast, and since I didn't have anything planned this morning, I took the old woman up on it. She called me inside before I rapped on the screen door. The whole place smelled like bacon and butter. I followed the aroma until I found the dining room. She had the paper laid out on the table next to a steaming mug of coffee.

She poked her head in the room. "Have a seat, Mr. Tanner. Your eggs will be ready in about three minutes."

I sat and flipped open the paper, scanning the pages, reading the headlines, and looking at the pictures. Little caught my interest. Maybe that'd change when I reached the sports section. It felt odd relying on the paper for information. Almost retro. I had it all at my fingertips with my phone, why waste time flipping pages?

And then I saw it. "Oh, shit."

"What is it?" she said from the kitchen.

"Shit," I said.

"Mr. Tanner," she said, standing in the case opening. "I'll not entertain that kind of language in my home."

"Yeah, uh, sorry, ma'am. I apologize, but I have to go."

I clenched the paper tight and ran through the house. She chased after me, hobbled steps echoing in time with mine.

"Mr. Tanner," she yelled. "My newspaper!"

I was in the car by the time she hit the landing at the top of the concrete steps. The engine drowned out her calls.

I rolled the window down, said, "I'll bring it back in a little bit. I have to go check on something important."

Racing down the city streets, I hoped to get pulled over. I didn't have Pennington's number, and doubted the operator would patch me through to him. Maybe a patrol car could reach out to him for me. Then I could rip him over this.

How the hell did we end up in the paper?

How could they let Cassie's picture be shown, given the circumstances?

A killer on the loose, and they reveal she's helping to investigate. If the psychopath saw that, he might track her down and take her out, too.

I pulled into her driveway, left the car running, and sprinted to her door. Didn't bother knocking. It was unlocked. I ran to her room, shouting her name along the way. The door was open. A soft light illuminated the space. The smell of coffee, strong and thick, greeted me in the entry foyer. I raced into her bedroom. The bed had been made and an outfit laid out on the comforter. I looked around for the shorts and t-shirt she had on the night before. They were nowhere to be found. And neither was she. I checked the bathroom and kitchen, found both empty. Her car was missing from the garage.

"Cassie, where are you?" I checked the counters, fridge, and tables for any scraps of paper containing a note or phone number. Anything that might indicate why she had left without notice. The investigation turned up nothing.

Where could she have gone so early? Maybe Pennington and Cervantes uncovered another suspect, or managed to break Seth, and called her in. She would've called me though, right?

I pulled out my cell. There were no texts or voicemails. The only missed call was from Sam, and I didn't have time to deal with that.

"Think logically," I told myself.

The best answer was that she had been called into the precinct for her protection. That's where I had to go next.

CHAPTER THIRTY

"I'm sorry, dear," the old woman said. "Mr. Tanner took off like a headless chicken this morning. One minute, he's sitting at the table drinking coffee, and the next he's stomping through my house with my newspaper. He didn't take a bite of bacon or wait for his eggs. Who does that?"

"Your newspaper?" Cassie said. "Why the paper?"

"I don't know. I thought all you young'uns used those cellular things for your news these days. Why else is everyone's face buried in them all day long?" She pointed at the square across the street. There were a handful of folks sitting on the benches, all of them staring at their phones.

Cassie smiled. "Let him know I came by. Okay?"

"Will do, dear." The old woman pulled the door shut, but stopped short. "You're the lady friend he's spending so much time with, right?"

Cassie looked back and nodded.

"He's got good taste. You tell him I said that." She winked before retreating back into her house.

Cassie had wanted Mitch to ride over to the crime scene with her. The dream had left her with more questions than answers, and the only place she might find them was at that house, in Alice's room. It hadn't been the first time she'd dreamed of Novak, but it was the first time he'd touched her. The dream was often a harbinger of sorts, though she never knew exactly what for. She could only hope she'd now receive the message she had been waiting for. Only question was, which message was in store for her?

Her focus and energy had been on Mitch last night. He needed her help. Likewise, the case absorbed much of her energy. It had to be related to one of the two. Dragging Mitch to the crime scene was her best option at figuring it out. But since that wasn't in the plans, she had to move forward.

Cassie walked the half-block to her car, passing the small cafe. She glanced inside and saw two large bookcases full of used books for sale. She made a mental note to return there some day. Might find a good read, or a tortured soul who needed her help. It took a little over ten minutes to reach the girls' house. She drove past, sweeping the street for any of the onlookers who had tried to accost her with questions. It would be inviting trouble to park in front of the house, so instead she made two rights and pulled to the curb in front of an empty lot on the next block.

No one noticed as she cut between the two houses that backed up to her destination. The grass was wet with dew, shining in the morning sun. The dampness penetrated her shoes. Her toes grew cold. She climbed the chain link fence. Her hand slipped off the slick railing. She came down awkwardly on her right leg and turned her ankle. She stifled a pained yell, gritting her teeth hard.

"Dammit," she muttered as she rose to her feet, more aggravated at having possibly drawn attention to herself than at the injury. She extended her leg and rolled her foot in a circle. The pain wasn't blinding. It was only a strain. She limped across the yard as fast as her injury would allow her, sidestepping the screen door the detectives had broken from the hinges. At the back door, she glanced over her shoulder to see if she'd been spotted. Windows remained blank. Curtains didn't rustle. She was in the clear. In their haste the day before, no one had locked up.

"Easy, peasy," she muttered as she pulled the door open.

Mindful of the bloodstains, she crossed the floor to the hallway, then continued to the end. The air was still with a hint of fragrance. A visitor? From which realm? She stood outside of Alice's room, staring through the opening, recounting what had happened the day before.

What if he was in there now?

Impossible. Seth had been taken into custody, and Pennington and Cervantes found enough probable cause in his statements that they had detained him. He'd be locked up for at least forty-eight hours.

She inched into the room, one hand on the wall, the other reaching out, ready to defend herself should something materialize in front of her. It was quiet and empty, and about fifteen degrees warmer than outside. Had it been that hot the previous two visits? The events were so intense in her memory that she could not recall what it had physically felt like in the room.

Cassie sat on the stool in front of Alice's vanity. There were a dozen or so pictures tucked into the mirror's frame. Most had Alice in them. Some were of her and her roommates. Her and a few different guys. A family photo from when the girl was fourteen or fifteen. She wore too much makeup to compensate for her youth back then. Her parents were older than Cassie would have expected. If the others in the photo were Alice's siblings, they had at least ten years on her.

Cassie grabbed a brush off the vanity and clenched it with

both hands.

"Talk to me."

CHAPTER THIRTY-ONE

I parked across from the precinct's entrance. Cassie might be able to get in through the back door, but I would not be afforded that luxury. And I'm sure if Cervantes saw me try, he'd have me locked up for trespassing. Once inside, I headed straight for the reception desk and asked for either detective. The cop there barely acknowledged me. Didn't even ask what this was about. He picked up a phone, punched in a code, and told whoever answered that they were needed out front.

"You can take a seat," the guy said.

Hell with that. I paced from his desk to the first bank of chairs, and back again. A minute passed. Then another. What was this bullshit?

"Can you call back there again?" I said.

"He'll be up when he's up," the officer said.

"Sonofabitch," I muttered under my breath.

"What'd you say?" He rose from his chair. "You think I can't hear you?"

"Nah, man, I—"

"Tanner." Cervantes rapped on the counter, startling both of us. "What're you doing here?"

"Where's Cassie?" I said.

He shrugged. "How should I know? Last I saw her was yesterday back in interrogation. You left with her."

"So neither of you called her to come down here this morning?"

"Nah." He turned and started toward the hallway, stopping about halfway and glancing back at me. "That all?"

I hoisted the paper up for him to see. "You taken a look at this yet?"

Cervantes did a one-eighty and rounded the counter. I felt each of his steps under my feet. He grabbed the paper from my hands and studied the photo.

"Shit," he said.

"Yeah, shit is right," I said.

"No, Tanner, you don't understand."

"What don't I understand?"

"This is bad."

"I'm not thick, man. I know it's bad."

"Come with me." He turned and waved two fingers over his shoulder and started off without me. I didn't wait for any further invitation. The desk officer called out something about a visitor's pass, but if Cervantes wasn't concerned with it, neither was I.

Cervantes glanced into each room we passed. Finally, he halted, turned, extended his arm. "In here."

It was an empty office with a desk littered with paperwork and three worn-down chairs. Family photos revealed a middle-aged black woman with three kids and a husband twenty years her elder. Framed accolades said she had reached the rank of lieutenant.

Cervantes stepped in after me, letting the door fall shut.

"All right, you got me alone," I said. "What's up?"

He rubbed his temples with his thumb and middle finger. He kept his eyes clenched and worked his nostrils in and out with deep, raspy breaths. When he glanced up at me, I got the distinct impression that he wished the situation would just go away.

After a few seconds, he spoke up. "The name Novak mean anything to you?"

I felt the blood draining from my head. The world went a bit fuzzy, hazy, like shining a flashlight into fog. It came in from the front and sides. Cassie had told me the chilling story on a couple of occasions, with each retelling going into more detail. The pain and then numbness with each subsequent thrust of the knife into her flesh. How she bled out in the graveyard and could sense the slow soaking of her blood into the soil. She spoke of the feeling when her soul departed her physical being. She compared the sensation of it returning to that of slamming your body into a concrete wall.

"By the look on your face, I'm gonna say it does," Cervantes said.

"He's doing life plus some for killing those women and leaving Cassie for dead, right? Pled out of his death sentence."

"Yeah." Cervantes' face paled. His forehead shone with sweat. "He was."

"What do you mean 'was'?"

"Escaped."

"When?"

"Before the storm."

I fell back into a seat and stared up at the recessed lighting. The bright LED looked out of place in a precinct building. They must be going green.

"You mean to tell me that this guy's been on the loose for some three-plus weeks now and you haven't told Cassie?"

He raised a defensive hand. "Novak doesn't know her real identity. It was blocked at trial. He doesn't know where she lives. They told him she'd been relocated by the FBI. Last thing on his mind is her."

I somehow doubted that. She was probably on his mind dawn till dusk. She put him away. I snatched the paper off the desk and shoved the photo in his face. "You still think that? Huh? Holy shit, man. We gotta find her and get her under protection before this psycho reaches her!"

The color returned to his cheeks. They burned red. Was he angry at me? The situation? The system? Or himself?

"Let's take my car," he said. "We'll go by her house."

"I was already there. She wasn't home. Car wasn't in the garage."

"House was unlocked?"

"Yeah."

"I've never known Cassie to be like that. She's the most uber-cautious person I know."

"I didn't see any signs of foul play. Nothing broken. No tracks left behind."

Cervantes fumbled with his keys. Said nothing.

"Let's go to the crime scene." I stopped at the door and looked back. "Maybe something happened overnight after I left her house."

"What if she went out for coffee?" Cervantes moved past me into the hallway. "I think we need to go to her house first. If Novak is able to get the address, that's the first place he's gonna check."

"You're wrong, man." I fumbled my keys out of my pocket. "Tell you what, you go there. I'll carry my ass to the crime scene."

I bolted past him, shrugging off his attempt at stopping me, and made my way to the front of the building. Cervantes followed close behind, calling for me to stop. I did at the front door.

"What?" I said.

"You step one foot inside that house, and I'll have you arrested."

"Do what you gotta do, then. Hell, follow me over there. I don't care. My gut tells me she's there, and this guy knows it."

CHAPTER THIRTY-TWO

Cassie hadn't realized that the air conditioning had cut on. She felt the cool air forced through the vent as it brushed past her, chilling the thin veneer of sweat on her face. She paused and looked up at the ceiling. It had been so hot inside on each visit. If the AC had been on its cycle, that wouldn't have happened. Come to think of it, had the house even had power?

Her skin pricked at the realization someone might be there. Spirits she could handle. They could only do so much damage. But someone in the flesh? She reached into her pocketbook for the small 9mm.

Cassie sucked in a few deep breaths and steadied her nerves. It could be a glitch, after all. Maybe the unit had shorted after the storm, and now that it had dried out, it was working again. Why would the crime scene guys cut it off intentionally? Wouldn't the uncontrolled temperature damage the remaining evidence?

For all she knew about her part of the investigation, Cassie knew little about the rest. She often felt she had it best considering she didn't have to rely on logic, science, or even deductive reasoning. Voices spoke. She listened and passed on the information. For that, they called her a hero. She rolled her eyes at the title. There were real heroes in the world. She was not one of them.

She took another trip around the room in search of whatever the dream had sent her back for. The trip had turned into a dud. Nothing had happened. Nothing had been left behind, at least not that she hadn't seen in person on the previous trips.

What the hell had Seth been doing there yesterday? He came with nothing. Didn't appear to have tried to take anything. Perhaps she interrupted him. But what would he have been looking for? She had checked under the mattress, in the closet, and gone through all the drawers. There was nothing.

Cassie sat down on the edge of the bed and stared up at the vent. Strands of hair fluttered in the forced breeze. "Come on, Alice, or anybody for that matter, talk to me."

Seconds passed before she heard a creak on the floor. Cassie turned to the open doorway and stumbled as she tried to get up from the bed.

"Hello, Cassie."

CHAPTER THIRTY-THREE

"Tanner!"

I stopped on the concrete walkway and turned back toward Cervantes, holding my hands out. "What, man? We're wasting time here."

He jogged up to me. "Why do you feel so strongly about this?"

"Why don't you?" I said. "I already went by the house. She wasn't there. Yeah, maybe she's returned. But we both tried calling her and neither of us got an answer. We go over there, we're wasting time. Let's get to the house before something happens."

He rocked from foot to foot, fingers twitching, like a linebacker over the A gap ready to blitz the moment the center snaps the ball. The hell was the guy's problem? I could get him not trusting me since I was from a different area. The 'Big City,' as he'd referred to it. But my argument was sound and logical. And Cassie was in danger.

"I can't wait all day, man," I said. "And neither can Cassie."

"Get your car and meet me by the rear entrance," he said. "I'll lead the way."

And he did. Like a pulling guard he cleared a path through the city with his lights swirling and siren blaring. No easy feat, either. Seemed every second intersection we came to required us to slow down or stop all together and wait for a pedestrian or two to get out of the way. The squares made it tricky as well. There was no speeding at eighty miles per hour when you had to turn sharp right every hundred feet.

We finally broke free when it happened. Cervantes didn't hear my blaring horn. And he didn't see the oncoming truck that had failed to hear the sirens or spot the flashing lights.

CHAPTER THIRTY-FOUR

Ice streamed through Cassie's veins. Her heart ramped up to two beats every second. There wasn't enough air in the room. Her extremities began to tingle and her head felt light. Thirty-seven scars on her neck and torso and arms raged with fire. Though she'd been shielded from his view, she would never forget the sound of his voice. She'd heard it every day in the courtroom for two straight weeks. It grated against her soul every day since.

"I thought I'd never see you again, Cassie," Novak said. "It always made me so sad. No, frustrated is a better way to put it. I'd sit in my cell thinking over our special night. Over and over and over." His head bobbed with each utterance of the word. "What more could I have done to you to achieve my goal of killing you? I mean, I stabbed you, what, forty times?"

"You..." She choked on the word. "You know how many times you stabbed me. And you did kill me."

"Yet here you stand." The floorboards creaked as he stepped closer. "Here you crumble." He laughed softly. "I don't believe all that 'died and came back' shit, either. Just lucid consciousness. Know what I mean?"

Cassie fought her frozen muscles and turned to face the man who'd left her for dead. All she had to do was slip her hand into her pocket. The pistol was there. *Use it, girl!*

"What are you doing here?" she said. "They sent you away. Locked you up."

He shrugged, both hands out. One clutched a knife. "I escaped. Imagine that. They blinked for a second too long and I was gone."

"How did...how'd you find me?"

"Please," he said. "It wasn't that hard. They took your picture in front of this house, my special house, and put it in the paper. They begged me to find you, for Pete's sake."

"Your special house?" She retreated backward, stumbled over her feet and fell. His image in her dream had been more than simple imagery. They were telling her who did it. "You did this?"

"I'm sure you saw the crime scene photos if the police went through the trouble of bringing you here. Aren't I the reason they involved you? The similarities? Young women, stabbed and assaulted violently. I suppose that's not quite a single person's MO, but really, in this small town, it's not too much of a stretch. Especially when you consider how long I've been out of jail."

Through his babbling she determined he didn't know about her ability. He thought she was there because of him. What did the paper say? What did the photo show? It had to have been taken yesterday, with the crowd surrounding the house. They saw an arrest at a house where three, maybe four, women had been murdered, and she was caught in the photographic crossfire.

"Now, Cassie—lovely name by the way, and you know, they never told me that. I'm surprised I can even remember your face. It was so dark out there that night, and they never let me see you in court. I get this feeling we've been meeting in another world, in our dreams. Anyway, I've been thinking since I saw your picture this morning, what to do with you?"

She backed up to the window to create some space between them. It would take a few seconds to draw on him with the pistol. He'd come at her with the knife. "Let me go. Please. You've done enough already. I'll lead them in a different direction. I promise."

"Lead them? What?"

The last thing she wanted to do was let him in on her secret, and she'd almost blurted it out.

"I'll tell them it's not the same," she said. "Just go, Novak."

"Hmmm, let me think about that." He turned and walked to the door. Slammed it shut. "How about no."

She reached into her pocket when he turned his back, but the pistol snagged when she tried to pull it out. Novak spotted it and rushed forward with the knife leveled at her throat.

"Remove your hand at once."

She choked down a sob to go with the tears flooding her eyes. This was how it ended? Why? And then it happened. Something gripped at her soul and pulled.

Not now!

She needed her wits about her more than ever before. Novak was not without reason. As insane a person as he was, Cassie knew she could buy some time and get him to take her out of the house.

But it didn't matter. The walls closed in and immobilized her. She was on the floor. Had he hit her? She couldn't tell. Her body was numb. A voice, loud, distinct, female, spoke to her. The same woman she encountered the first time.

"Him. It's him."

Then it was over. He yanked the 9mm free and laughed. "Safety on. Half-loaded magazine. You did yourself a favor letting me see you reach for this. Had you pulled it on me, you'd be dead right now.

She rolled over and shuffled backward on her elbows, scraping her feet against the floor, until her head touched the wall.

"Where are you going?" Novak approached, no longer wielding the blade. In its place was the pistol. He racked the slide and thumbed down the safety. He moved a few more feet forward, aiming the weapon at Cassie's head.

"Don't," she whispered.

"So many choices, Cassie. I could kill you." He paused while his gaze traveled to her chest, then crotch. "Or I could have fun with you, then kill you. Damn these decisions."

Think, Cassie. Throw him off.

"What did you do with Alice?" she blurted out.

Novak cocked his head and smiled. He tapped her forehead with the pistol. "What do you know about Alice?"

"I know this is her room. I know you were in it the night of the homicides and her disappearance. What did you do with her? Is she dead, too?"

"Oh, I wouldn't worry too much about Alice. She's doing just fine. Better than you at the moment, that's for sure." He took a step back, nodded at her. "In fact, I think it's time you found out, Cassie. Get up."

Fear immobilized her, but after a few seconds her limbs responded to his demands. Did she have a choice? She could handle herself, but he was bigger and stronger. The deciding factor was he had armed himself with her weapon. Combine that with a confined space that had only one means of egress leading to a long corridor, and she knew her chances of survival plummeted.

"Now I want you to turn around, cross your legs, and hold your hands behind your back." When she didn't respond, he shouted at her. "Do it!"

Novak twisted a towel and wrapped it around her wrists, binding them together. It wasn't foolproof. Once outside, she could throw her weight to the side or the ground and take him with her.

"Good girl, Cassie. Now let's get out of here. I've got someplace special to take you."

His hand grabbed her hip, pulling her back tight to him.

"What are you doing?"

He said nothing. His fingers worked their way into her pocket. They wriggled against her leg. She tried to jerk away, but that resulted in Novak tightening his grip. He found what he wanted and pulled her car keys out.

They walked through the house, stopping at the end of the hallway, and again by the back door. The towel went slack. Her arms parted and swung freely to her side.

"You run," he said, "Alice dies. If I don't return to where she is, she dies. Got it?"

It was a punch to the gut, and Cassie felt as though the wind had been sucked from her lungs. She tried to breathe, but her muscles were too constricted. Her one chance to get away was on the line. Was he serious? Would he do it? And would he just let her go? She could risk it. Now that she knew who did it, there might be enough there to help lead them to Novak and Alice. But would it happen fast enough?

Cassie knew it wouldn't. So she opened the door and led him through the back yards to where her car waited, slipping in behind the wheel, while Novak kept the pistol aimed at her.

CHAPTER THIRTY-FIVE

I yanked on the crumpled door, but it refused to budge. Cervantes hunched over the steering wheel with the deflated airbag in his lap. Tiny rivers of crimson flowed down it. "Cervantes," I yelled into the splintered glass. "Are you all right?"

He looked up at me. Had a small gash on his forehead and a bloody nose. He didn't wear his seatbelt. The accident could've been a lot worse for him.

The other driver hopped out of his truck and ran over. "Shit, I'm sorry, man. I didn't hear the siren. Is he okay?"

I redirected him back the way he came. "I suggest you go wait over there. Don't think about leaving, got it?"

Cervantes climbed over the passenger's seat and exited the mangled vehicle. With his feet on the ground, he looked like a beaten fighter, staggering until he placed his hand on the hood to steady himself. Even then I thought he might drop at any moment.

"Sure you're all right, man?" I said.

He pinched his nose, tilted his head back. "Yeah, just a busted nose. I'm fine."

"Look, why don't you wait here for the medics while I go check on Cassie. You might have a concussion after that blow to the head."

He circled the back of the vehicle, waved one hand at me while keeping the other planted on the car. "No, we both go."

"You need to get checked out. You're bleeding and limping. I think I can handle this. Give me your cell number and I'll call you."

Cervantes continued past me and walked toward my rental. Why was he refusing to let me go alone? Wasn't like he was any good to me like this.

"Fine, have it your way." I popped the trunk and grabbed a towel for him to hold under his face. "I'll bill you if you get any blood on the seat or carpet."

Ten minutes later we pulled up to the house. I scanned the street. No one lingered outside. No faces peered from behind closed windows. I glanced over at Cervantes. His white shirt was stained red. So was the lower half of his face.

"Man, I hope you don't have hepatitis or anything like that."

"Asshole," he said. "I'm clean. You got a gun in here?"

"I flew in and this is a rental. What do you think?"

"I dunno, Tanner. You know Cassie, so I figured you might have some other connections down here."

"Just her. Don't think I can call you and Pennington confidants quite yet."

"Quite never," he said. "All right, you stay behind me. Got it?"

"Yeah, whatever, man."

We exited the vehicle and cut across the lawn. Cervantes was moving better now. He'd shaken the cobwebs and worked out whatever had aggravated his knee. The breeze was hitting my face, but I was so amped, I couldn't tell if it was warm or cool. A couple birds occupying a nearby tree silenced as we approached.

Cervantes went right for the door. He squeezed and turned the handle, then looked back at me.

"Unlocked," he said.

"Surprised?" I said.

"I thought we locked everything up yesterday."

The door stuck at first. Cervantes lowered his shoulder into it and it popped open with a cracking sound. "AC's on." Cervantes gestured toward the thermostat with his pistol. "Remind me to get prints on that."

The main living area of the house stood empty. The hallway and kitchen looked the same as when we had left.

"Cassie?" Cervantes called out.

There was no reply.

He yelled her name again.

Still no answer.

"Let's go check in back." He held his weapon so the barrel pointed at the floor. He'd grown a little too calm for my tastes. Maybe the blow to his head had done more damage than to just his nose.

We walked back to Alice's room and found the door wide open. I had no idea if it had been closed after they dragged Seth out of the room. Cervantes didn't seem bothered by it.

"Room's empty," he said. "Wait here while I check the others."

Light knifed in through the space between the curtains and the wall. It stretched across the floor and ran up the wall a foot or two. Were the curtains parted like that before? I was so amped up yesterday, I had no recollection of the placement of anything in the room.

Something glinted in the light, catching my attention. I dropped to a knee and fished the item out from under the bed. I recognized it right away.

"Cervantes," I called out. "Get in here."

The stocky man thundered down the hall. "What is it?"

"Look at this."

"What?" He squatted next to me. "A watch?"

"That's Cassie's watch."

"Think she lost it here yesterday during the struggle with Seth?"

"She had it on last night, man. I remember it..." I couldn't tell him the rest. I recalled it so vividly because it was the only thing she had on. My stomach knotted and the air grew heavy.

"You sure, Tanner?"

"Yeah, more than sure. I'm positive. That's Cassie's watch."

"I'm sorry, Tanner, but I've gotta ask you to step outside."

"What?"

"Crime scene integrity."

"Crime scene integrity, my ass."

"Any defense attorney gets wind that you were in this house and found that without me around, they'll get the defendant off in a heartbeat."

The sonofabitch was right. I might not trust him, and the thought lingered that he might be attempting to cover something up, but my presence here could bring down a case. Cervantes followed me down the hall. He stopped at the front door as I stepped outside.

"Hang tight," he said. "Pennington is on his way. I don't want you leaving 'til he gets here."

"Yeah, no problem." Pain knifed through my eyes as they adjusted to the bright sunlight. There were no crowds gathered. Perhaps the scene yesterday was enough to keep them at bay. Or rather, the aftermath.

I heard a yip and noticed the old lady and her dog approaching. She had on a baby blue track suit with a leash and collar on the dog to match.

"You fellas any closer to solving this?" she asked.

"I'm not at liberty to discuss, ma'am," I said.

"Sure you're not." She glanced over at the driveway. "Saw the lady again today. Never seen the cop she was with, though."

I left the porch and met her at the end of the driveway. "She arrive with him?"

The old lady shrugged. "I didn't see her arrive. Looked out the window while drinking my tea and saw the car drive past and park. Was glued to the seat after that. This is better than daytime TV, you know."

If only these people knew what crime scenes really looked like, and the amount of work involved in processing them and tracking down the killer.

"Where at?" I pointed up and down the street. "Where'd the car park?"

"I live over there, sugar." She aimed past the house. "On the other block. Anyhow, she cut through my yard, went in alone, and left with the guy a short time later."

I choked down the anxiety threatening to overtake my body. "How long was the car there?"

"Maybe ten minutes."

"Do you remember the guy she left with? What he looked like?"

"I guess."

"Describe him."

"Kinda ragged looking." She tapped her finger to her lip. "Come to think of it, he really didn't look like the detectives I've seen. Was he undercover?"

"I'm afraid he might've been." I craned my neck to get a visual on an approaching car. "Ma'am, wait right here, okay? I think this detective is gonna want to talk to you."

CHAPTER THIRTY-SIX

"Where are you taking me?" Cassie said as they passed the outskirts of town, driving west. The land ahead was sparsely populated. A place Novak could easily dispose of her. She doubted that mattered much to him. He had tried to kill her in a cemetery. He'd slaughtered those women in a residential neighborhood, then kidnapped Alice, dragging her out of the house battered and bloodied in the middle of the night during a hurricane. Hell, he'd led Cassie out of the same house at gunpoint in broad daylight.

Novak's head dipped and swayed with the movements of the car. His stare seemed distant and unfocused. The pistol remained aimed at Cassie, and she didn't dare try to do anything to test his concentration.

"If you were going to kill me," she said, "why not do it back at the house? What's one more dead body there?"

He said nothing. Had no visible reaction to indicate he'd heard her. She switched her attention from the road and studied his face as though she was seeing it for the first time. In some ways, she was. Novak had only ever been the monstrous presence who'd risen from a grave and attempted to steal her life. In court, they were never face to face. She was shielded while testifying, not allowing him the satisfaction of gazing upon her. She only saw him on a monitor with crappy resolution. He'd been fuzzy, like a character in an old television show.

But now, up close, she realized he wasn't near the villain she'd built up in her mind. His build was sort of slight. His features were soft, almost feminine in the right lighting. Where did the evil live? Certainly not on the exterior.

"I can kill us both, you know." Her fingers gripped the steering wheel tight enough that her knuckles turned white.

"You'd be no better than me," he said, still staring off into a distance that Cassie wondered if anyone else could see. "A murderer. At least I took pleasure from my killings. You? Well, you'd be committing two sins by taking your own life, too."

She relaxed her grip and slunk back in her seat. She didn't want to die. Not even at her own hand. Her glimpses into what came next were enough for Cassie to want to remain on this earth, inhabiting her fleshy cell, as long as possible, despite the constant bombardment for help. And as much as she hated to admit it, some days those requests were what got her out of bed.

"See that sign up there?" Novak stretched a slim finger out and aimed it ahead toward a billboard with a cow painting on it.

"Yeah."

"Slow down. You are going to turn right immediately following that sign."

Cassie glanced into the rearview in hopes that someone was behind them. The road, however, was desolate. Did he know? Had he taken his eyes off that imaginary point in the distance long enough to check the side mirror and see for himself? Or did he not care if they were seen leaving the road? What was his plan? Was he going to have her creep into the woods far enough that he could do whatever he wanted to her, then leave her for dead?

Today was the day he'd finish what he started. Cassie's throat constricted, and her eyes burned in anticipation of salty tears. She fought them back, forcing herself to swallow the fear. Now more than ever it was important she keep her wits about her.

"Slow down, Cassie." He shifted in his seat so that he leaned back against the door, allowing himself better control over his weapon and aim.

She wished they were in a cartoon, in one of those cars that had a button where she could eject him from his seat, flinging him high into the air.

"Just relax," he said. "Nothing is going to happen to you here."

Here.

Why was no one else chiming in? She'd been there for them when they needed help. If there was ever a time for them to repay the favor, it was now. Cassie took her foot off the accelerator and pressed the brake. The sound of the tires on the asphalt rose in ferocity as the friction built. She spotted the two dirt tracks that ran behind the billboard. She looked up and saw that the cow was hanging in front of the billboard, not attached in any way she could see. How'd they do that?

"That's right," Novak said. "Turn there and follow that old road."

Her small car pitched and swayed as the tires found their place in the dirt ruts. How long would it last in these conditions? Enough grass covered the path that it looked abandoned now. But at one time it had been used regularly enough that the tracks had been etched permanently into the earth. Hunters, she figured, drove it during deer season.

She followed the trail, weaving around trees, trampling over new growth. In some spots, the grass grew past the hood, hitting the grill with a soft *thunk* and swishing underneath the vehicle.

The woods thinned out. The tracks split and formed a V.

"Go left." Novak remained seated against the door, facing her, no seatbelt on. If she had a chance, this was it.

Cassie pushed as hard as she could on the accelerator. At first, nothing happened. The wheels roared and ripped into the soft earth. The car shook, but didn't move forward. She glanced over and saw Novak's eyes widen. Much like the vehicle, he was stuck, processing what was happening.

Cassie grabbed the gearshift and yanked it toward her, dropping the transmission into second gear. The engine screamed at her for doing so. She feared it would burst due to her actions. Then she was slammed back into her seat.

Had he hit her?

In her peripheral vision, she saw Novak flung forward. His head smacked the windshield. The glass splintered. The car had lurched forward, stopped abruptly when she hit the brake, and was now bouncing in the rutted ground. She kept her foot pressed on the gas as they blew through the middle of the V in the path into the field. Ahead, she estimated fifty yards before they reached the wood's edge.

She pressed harder on the accelerator. Gripped the wheel. Let out a scream that had been building since the moment life had been restored to her shredded body.

Then the world went black.

CHAPTER THIRTY-SEVEN

The sedan pitched forward as Pennington slammed the brakes. Scorched rubber polluted the air, enveloping me like a cloud. He drove his shoulder into his door, stepped onto the asphalt, slammed the door shut. He ran up to me. "The hell is going on?"

"Slow down, man," I said. "Cervantes is inside, securing the scene. You need to talk to the dog-walker over there. She saw them leaving."

"Who?"

"Cassie and her abductor."

Pennington's face went slack. Beads of sweat formed along his perfect hairline. "This isn't happening."

"Afraid it is, man. Now you need to tighten up and do your damn job. Go talk to that lady over there."

He looked past me, his eyes narrowed, and studied the woman. Fixing his gaze in my direction again, he stepped forward. "I swear, Tanner, if you had anything to do with this..."

I moved to block his path. "Me? You better step the hell back, man. I've known Cassie a long time. She means a hell of a lot more to me than you'll ever understand."

"You were the last one with her," he said. "I know you were at her house late last night. Spent the whole day together, didn't you?"

Had he been watching or having her house patrolled? Keeping tabs? On who? Her? Or me? Perhaps he'd had someone else doing it. Told them he was concerned for Cassie's safety because of what happened earlier in the day, and assigned a unit to her neighborhood, with the focus being her.

I got close enough to his face I could smell his breakfast lingering between us. "What exactly are you accusing me of?"

He said nothing, focusing on my face, my expressions, looking for the tiniest of signs of deceit. Problem is anger can trigger some of the same responses cops are taught to look for. And my blood was boiling at that point.

"Look, Pennington, I left Cassie last night and haven't seen her since. Then I saw the paper this morning. You seen it?"

He nodded tersely.

"Then you understand the implications." I put my hands on my hips and took a step back. "I couldn't reach her by phone. Went to her house, and she wasn't there. Went to the precinct to find you guys, to find out if you'd seen the paper yet. How many guilty men you know walk right into a police station?"

He mulled it over for a second. Almost smiled. "Dirty cops do it every day."

"Pennington," Cervantes said. "Come on. We ain't got time to dick around with this."

He brushed his shoulder against mine as he passed. "We're not done, Tanner."

I turned and followed him, stopping halfway. "One of you needs to talk to that woman. She saw something this morning. I'm outta here now."

"You leave Savannah and I'll make you our number one suspect," Pennington said. "Stay put until you hear from us."

The keys dangled and glinted in the sunlight as I held them high and waved back at the other detective. He could go to hell. I got back in my rental and drove straight to Cassie's house. Maybe they'd use it against me later. I didn't care. Stepping into her house, I caught a whiff of the smell of her hair, raising hope for a few moments. It didn't take long to determine she was not there. I searched the kitchen, her bedroom, even her computer desk for something, anything, that might indicate why she went back to the crime scene, and who she thought might've been there.

It was busy work meant to keep my mind from diving into the reality of what Cassie was going through at that moment. What else could I do? I didn't have the ability to talk to the dead, like her. I had to work with logic. Not the easiest thing when dealing with a psychotic killer. There was little to go by at this point, but all I needed were one or two clues and I'd be off to the races.

The photo in the paper, and the revelation from Cervantes that Novak had escaped from jail more than three weeks earlier, left little doubt in my mind that Novak had followed her to the crime scene house. Or perhaps he sprung a trap, baiting her to come. Hell, he might've been waiting for her there, knowing somehow she would show up on her own. Were they inexplicably linked through a bond created by attempted murder, a bond that gave him such powers?

I stood in the hallway underneath an air vent. The cold air washed over me, chilling the last of the sweat that covered my skin. I listened with my eyes closed. For what? Hell if I knew. Maybe the same spirits that spoke to Cassie would chew on my ear a bit, too. It'd never happened. Christ, I doubted it happened to her. Yet I waited there for a couple minutes anyway.

Beep-beep-beep.

The sound nearly startled me into a cardiac event. I rushed into the kitchen expecting to find a bomb taped under the table with a note written *To the Late Mr. Tanner*. The red light on the coffeemaker blinked with each subsequent squeal until the machine cut off.

I walked over and pulled the pot off the burner. Held it to my nose and inhaled. The brew had gone stale and had a burned smell to it, but it was piping hot. I poured half into the sink before thinking better of it and stopping. I had a thought. The machine had an auto-cutoff. That time had to be programmed into the device. With that information, I could pinpoint the earliest possible time that Cassie left the house.

I spun around to check the brand.

"Shit."

The coffeemaker refused to cooperate. On the top were three buttons, labeled "two," "four," and "six." Select one of those and it would turn off in that many hours.

I knew it couldn't have been two. I was there more than two hours ago. Was it on at that time? I couldn't say yes for sure, but I did smell coffee when I came in. So between five and roughly seven-thirty am. It was a start, and we could cross reference the time I was here earlier, along with the dog-walking woman's estimates from the window of her breakfast nook.

Draped over the back of a chair was one of Cassie's shirts. I grabbed it, held it to my face, inhaled her scent.

I pictured her walking through the house, alone, and encountering someone. I felt her fear. My response wasn't hers, though.

She knew the man, and seeing him caused every muscle in her body to cramp, locking up and rendering her immobile. But in time I knew she'd adapt, and overcome her assailant.

I hoped so, at least.

CHAPTER THIRTY-EIGHT

Glass sliced through Novak's skin like a hot knife through melted butter. Blood flowed warm down his back, pooling near his waistband. He limped around the vehicle, every step sending pain up his right leg from his ankle to his knee. It didn't look broken. Time would tell, he supposed.

He had managed to strike Cassie and free her grasp from the wheel. Had he not, he surely would've been ejected from the car, through the windshield, and splattered among the trees. Instead, he grabbed the steering wheel and yanked it toward him. Cassie's foot must've slid off the gas pedal, too. The car spun and decelerated and hit at an angle that spread out the impact along the driver's side. He didn't escape unscathed, but the wounds he suffered when he collided with the side window weren't life-threatening.

After pulling Cassie free of the wreckage, he slung her over his shoulder. She still hadn't come to. He wasn't sure how far he could carry her. She wasn't heavy, but damn if his lower leg wasn't screaming at him. Luckily, he didn't have to make it to the van, only into the woods far enough that they wouldn't be seen if someone had heard the wreck and found the car. The chances of that were slim, he admitted to himself. Still, he had to remain vigilant. He'd only been free for less than a month, and going back to prison was not in his plans. He'd rather die in a hailstorm of lead than go back there.

Cassie coughed, then moaned. Novak bent forward and let her slide to the ground onto her back. He found a thick tree trunk to lean back against and catch his breath. She wasn't going to get up and run off. She could try to crawl away, but he'd jump on top of her. Her eyes fluttered open, wide at first, then squinted. She looked to the side, up, down. She licked the dirt off her lips, then spat it out. Her gaze came to rest on him.

"Hello, Cassie," he said through heavy breaths. He'd managed to stay in shape in prison, but the wounds from the glass and the pain in his leg combined with carrying her in the humidity had left him winded.

"Where are we?" she asked.

He looked up at the green foliage above and around them, held out his arms. "Oh, you know, nowhere."

She started hyperventilating. It seemed as though the situation had slapped her back to full consciousness.

Novak drew the pistol from his waistband. He'd somehow managed to find it after the car came to rest against that tree.

"Cassie," he said. "Don't worry. I've got you covered."

She lifted herself up on her elbows. He pushed off the tree. A hundred crows swooped down and settled on the branches above. It looked like night for a moment. Their shrill voices drowned out everything else.

Novak motioned for Cassie to rise, then aimed his pistol toward a narrow path. She complied without hesitation. Aside from being rendered unconscious, she appeared to have escaped the accident unscathed.

"Good girl," he said, unsure if she could hear him over the squawking from the trees.

A few minutes later they were walking along a set of ruts in the ground. The left path. The one he'd wanted her to take when she had decided to take matters into her own hands. What was she thinking? Novak gripped the pistol tight in anger. She could have killed him in the most unceremonious of manners. It would have been weeks before someone came across his remains.

At times, Novak could be a normal, thoughtful person. He felt empathy for those in dire situations, was cordial to restaurant wait staff and store clerks, and he pretty much left things as they were in the world. But that was not always the case. Sometimes the anger would rise. One he couldn't control. Violence had become the only way for it to subside.

This was one of those times.

Novak rushed forward, ignoring the pain in his leg. Like a soccer player, he planted on his good leg and used the other to sweep Cassie's feet out from under her. She seemed to freeze mid-air before crashing hard on her side. There was no yell or cry. There couldn't be. He stood over her, staring at her twisted, reddening face, her mouth open, trying to force out a scream for which the required oxygen didn't exist.

He reached down, grabbed a fistful of her t-shirt, and yanked. The fabric tore from her collar to mid-breast, revealing a pink and blue bra. He let go and swung his arm wildly, grasping and coming up with her hair.

She still hadn't taken a breath. Her face had turned dark red. Primal moans escaped from her mouth. He didn't care. He pulled upward until she was on her feet again. He dragged her along the path by her hair.

When she finally pulled in a gulp of air, it sounded like someone emerging from underwater, their lungs about to burst. She sucked it in, coughed, heaved like she was going to vomit.

"You puke and I'll do it again," he said.

She bowed forward, hands on her knees, breathing hard and loud. One yank of her hair and she'd go flying forward.

"We're almost there," he said. "Stay on your feet or this forest will be your grave. No one will ever find you here, Cassie. The creatures will pick your bones clean before the hunters bag the first buck of the season."

She staggered forward, one step much shorter than the other, in obvious pain. He expected later he'd see a large black mark on her right hip. And at that point, the rage drained like water swirling down a drain. He moved in closer, placed a hand on her shoulder, squeezed lightly.

"Forgive me, Cassie. This was not the appropriate place or time."

He withdrew before she could react. It wasn't smart getting that close with his weapon out. He knew it. Cassie was a *survivor*. And she probably prided herself on that. Probably took classes. Self-defense classes. So that she could deal with someone like Novak.

"How's that working out for you, Cassie?" he muttered.

She looked back at him, confused. "What?"

He shook his head and prodded her forward. A short while later, looking ahead, he saw the sun glinting off the chrome side mirror. Cassie stopped. She must've seen it, too.

"Keep going," he said.

"Who's there?" she said.

"No one," he said. "That's my van."

Novak watched her face draw tight. Fear? Anxiety? Her eyes darted left and right, looking for a way out, no doubt. She wouldn't find it. Wouldn't get more than ten feet before he shot her. Judging by the slackness that overtook her features, she knew it, too.

"What's inside it?" Cassie asked.

"Let's go find out."

She didn't seem all that keen on doing so until Novak threatened her. Again. It was a game he'd grow weary of if they didn't get out of the woods soon.

When they reached the van, Novak pulled back on the handle and slid the side door open. He had Cassie wait with her arms around a nearby tree, cheek against the bark, ass toward him. He pulled a length of rope from a cargo bay.

As he approached, Novak instructed Cassie to reach her arms behind her back. She failed to comply, forcing him to drive his knee into her lower back and wrench her arms around. He secured them at the wrists with the rope. She grunted as he tightened the knot, digging the rope into her flesh.

"Yeah," he said. "Let me know how it feels, Cassie."

"Fuck you," she said.

"Not yet." He ran his hand over the curve of her hip.

She craned her head around and spat. The trajectory was all wrong, though. Didn't come close to hitting him. Novak laughed as he returned to the van. He waited for a second and watched her. Would she run? Was she that brave? Oddly, he wanted her to try to escape. He desired the chance to hunt her down. Again.

But she didn't move. Strange. Perhaps she was waiting for a better time or place. If only she knew this was her best and last chance to attain freedom. From this point forward, Cassie belonged to him.

Novak opened the glove box and retrieved a black bag. He carried it over to where Cassie stood with her forehead pressed against the tree bark. Inside the carry case, a metal syringe and bottle of fluid banged together with a soft thud with every step he took.

He stopped a few feet away from her. No point in getting any closer yet. It would only give her an opportunity to wreck his plans and make things more difficult for him.

Novak unzipped the case slowly, hoping to spark some fear in the woman. It was obviously a zipper, but to what? His pants? Something else? A smile played on his face as he leaned to the side and searched hers for signs of a reaction. Sadly, there was none. He unscrewed the lid from the bottle. The needle encountered a slight resistance and then slipped through the membrane. Clear liquid rushed into the chamber as he drew back the plunger.

"This will pinch a little, Cassie," he said, yanking her shorts down, exposing pale skin. "But there's no harm being done."

Before she could react, he penetrated the flesh of her right buttocks with the needle and injected the fluid into her. Her glute flexed and tightened, but it was too late. The drug has found its way into her system. Cassie swayed to the side, stumbled, started to collapse. Novak lunged forward and broke her fall for her.

"Don't go passing out on me just yet." He stroked her hair while easing her to a seated position. "We've got to get you inside the van."

Her eyes glazed over. Her stare was distant. Her pupils grew until there was nothing but black and white and tiny strings of red. She mumbled something incoherent.

Novak wrapped one arm around her, lifted her off the ground into a standing position. He draped her other arm over his shoulders. She felt like a noodle, all wobbly. Not the first time he'd had to assist one of his victims in such a way. He could carry her, but why waste the energy when she could sort of walk? She managed a step here and there, but her feet mostly dragged along the ground.

They reached the van. Novak untied the rope around her

wrists, then laid her on her back. At her torso, thighs, and ankles there were two steel eyelets on either side of her body. He grabbed two more lengths of rope and strapped her thighs and ankles to the floor. With the third rope, he retied her wrists in front of her.

Then he climbed into the front seat and navigated out of the woods.

CHAPTER THIRTY-NINE

I went through every drawer, cabinet, and closet in Cassie's place in search of any scrap of evidence I could use to locate her. My gut told me it was a waste of time. The trail started at the triple-homicide crime scene with her watch. She'd intentionally left it there knowing three detectives would be by at some point.

But it only told us she had been there.

Where was she now?

I paced down the dark hallway, checking my cell every few seconds, hoping a text or call would come in from Pennington or Cervantes. I'd already looked past Pennington's behavior earlier today. He was in the same place I was. Scared shitless for Cassie. That would affect any man's emotions. Sure as hell did mine. On any other day, I'd have knocked him flat out.

At least they couldn't suspend me in Savannah.

In one of the kitchen drawers there was a keychain with five or so keys attached to it. I grabbed it and tested each in the front door. One matched. I removed it from the chain and tucked it in my wallet so I could lock up on my way out. No sense in letting anyone inside the house to cover up their tracks.

Back outside, the humidity enveloped me. It was more stifling today than it had been. That was saying something. The day had started off sunny, but now the skies thickened with dark gray. Thunder rumbled in the distance. Maybe the rain could wash the last eight hours or so away.

I imagined by this point the forensics team was combing through the crime scene again for clues as to Cassie's disappearance. It was their job, of course. And things had to be done by the book. But little doubt was left in my mind who perpetrated the crime.

I knew little about the man aside from the few details Cassie had told me over the years. I put the chances of anyone inside the Chatham-Savannah Police Department telling me any more about Novak at less than slim. If I didn't come up with something helpful on my own, they'd blacklist me from participating in the investigation. That'd be a bad idea.

The first raindrops thudded on the ground, prompting me to get back to the rental. A sheet of rain raced toward me. I managed to slide into the car as the brunt of the storm hit. After wiping my hands off on my jeans, I pulled out my cell and placed a call.

"'Bout damn time you called me back," Sam said.

"Look, bro, I know you're ready to light into me, but we got a hell of a situation down here."

Sam's tone changed. "What's going on?"

"Any chance you can get away for a couple days?"

"None."

"You sure?"

"I really doubt it." He paused for a beat. "You're making me a bit uneasy. What's this about? You still in Savannah?"

"Yeah, man, I'm here. Hang on." I took a moment to compose

myself. There weren't many people I could unload my feelings on, but Sam was one. "Cassie's been abducted."

"Shit. You're kidding right? This ain't for real."

"Yeah, it's for real. And that's not the worst part."

Sam said nothing. His heavy breathing filled the line.

"Novak got her," I said.

"You sure?"

"No doubt in my mind. Turns out the sonofabitch escaped from prison three weeks ago. These assholes down here didn't bother to warn her because someone had told Novak that Cassie was in the witness relocation program. He'd never find her. And remember, he never knew her identity. Never saw her outside of the time he attacked her, and that was in the dark of night."

"So they figured she was safe," Sam said. "Maybe letting her know would somehow draw his attention toward her, or at the least, cause her undue anxiety."

"With that girl, you never can tell."

"What's that?" he said.

"What?" I said.

"You said 'that girl.' You don't speak like that usually."

"Shut up, man." I dropped the shifter into gear and eased away from Cassie's house. "Anyway, look, I need you to do me a favor."

"What's up?"

"Get me anything and everything you can on Novak. I need you to dig for me, Sam. Find out who he talked to most at the prison if you can. What he preferred for lunch. His favorite porn. Anything and everything."

"I'll see what I can do."

"One more thing."

"Yeah?"

"Get whatever you got going on wrapped up and see if you can get a couple days off."

"It won't happen, Mitch. We're seriously strapped with you out and a couple guys on special assignment. But, hey, if I can string two days off in a row, I'm there, bro."

We wrapped up the call. I drove around the city for a half-hour before returning to the apartment to grab a shower and change of clothes. I wasn't sure where I'd go next, but I had to stay active. Proactive. An idle mind was the tool of the devil. Sam would turn something up soon. Hopefully it was something I could take and run with.

I parked the car about a block away from the apartment. The rain had let up. A tenor sax saturated the air with jazz that sounded like smoke and velvet. The guy playing in the square looked too young to know the tune. Hell, his sax was older than him. He'd lived that song, though. The goosebumps on my arm were a testament to that.

Twenty-plus years as a cop had taught me how to compartmentalize. It was a necessary evil. If I hadn't learned the skill, I'd have been out after five years. But it was only possible to stifle your feelings so much. Everything you shut out returned eventually. Usually with the force of an eighteen-wheeler slamming into a house made of matches.

And as I opened the door to my home away from home, leaving the steamy city behind for the frigid air inside, Cassie's predicament slammed right into me. Was it her reaching out to me?

"I'm here, Cassie," I whispered.

I hadn't managed to get the door shut when a car squealed to a stop on the street behind me.

"Tanner," Cervantes yelled. "We need to talk to you."

CHAPTER FORTY

"Why in God's name are you so heavy?"

Novak dropped Cassie to the ground. Her torso hit with a thud. It always seemed when someone was unconscious, they weighed thirty pounds heavier. He stood over her, watching the empty expression on her face. It was unlikely she felt the collision with the ground. With the drug he'd injected into her, she had three or four more hours in dreamland before she felt anything.

She looked peaceful, lying there on her back, twisted at the waist, right leg draped over her left.

Novak looked around the deserted overgrown field. The grass swayed in the stiff breeze left behind by the storm. Not a soul in sight. No one to stop him from doing anything he wanted. He could strip her bare and have her on the spot where she lay.

Don't be a fool. You never know what lurks behind the veil.

His gaze drifted away from her exposed flesh and traveled toward the tree line. What if a wayward hunter or a couple of day trekkers lingered just out of sight?

More killings.

Fundamentally, not a problem. Practically? Another story. It would involve effort. And risk. One could get away from him, and the last thing he needed was for authorities to close in on his special place. Even all of the probing he went through during the trial and afterward in jail, they had never uncovered this spot.

The place where he brought the special ones.

Novak knelt next to Cassie, shielding himself from view in the waist high grasses. "You are the most special one, Cassie," he whispered. "Maybe not at first. I was blinded that night, I suppose. Didn't have the sight to realize the magnificence of you."

He hovered over her, waiting for a response that would not come. At least, not yet. Novak dragged his fingertips lightly along her arm. Her skin pricked in response. Not all senses were dulled or deadened.

"Now, I don't want you thinking that you're gonna make it out of this, Cassie. No one does. You've just got a little more time. And perhaps the most minute of chances to sway me."

Rising, he scouted the field and wood's edge and determined it was safe to move on. Cassie felt like a hundred-and-thirty-pound sack of sand. He scooped her up, hoisted her over his shoulder and moved on.

"Only a couple hundred feet to your new home."

CHAPTER FORTY-ONE

"The hell is going on?"

Pennington and Cervantes approached, pistols drawn and aimed at me. I didn't know whether to retreat to the back of the apartment or throw my hands up in surrender.

"Step out here, Tanner," Pennington said.

"Why don't you point that thing somewhere else?" I said.

"Come out here, let us make sure you're unarmed."

I was in position to slam the door and make a break for the back of the house. They'd have to travel to the end of the block to get to the back alley. And then, they'd have to choose which end to run to. No car was fitting through that narrow lane. Then what?

If they wanted me, they'd find me. And that was the reality.

"Come on, Tanner," Pennington said. "Let's not make this any more difficult than it needs to be."

"Just tell me what this is about," I said.

"Can't do it right here," he said.

"Why the guns drawn?"

Neither man spoke.

By this point, a few people had gathered across the street. Before long it'd grow, someone would start filming with their damn phone, and I'd be on the news. And if that reached Philly, I'd never get my badge back. Chief Warren would choke on the hard-on he'd get knowing he could get rid of me once and for all.

"All right," I said. "I'm coming out." I crossed the threshold. Pennington put his pistol away and retrieved his cuffs. My legs and back stiffened. The door shut behind me.

"Turn around," Pennington said.

"The hell?" I said.

"Do it," Cervantes said, his body rigid, his aim steady.

"Christ, I'll go peacefully." A lie that wouldn't work.

The cuffs dangled from Pennington's fingers. "We just want to get in the car and ask you some questions."

"About what?" I was out of options and didn't think I could delay them any further. They weren't going to reveal anything standing on the sidewalk, which was expected. Tell me I'm arrested and I'm gonna put up a hell of a fight. "Come on, Pennington. Level with me. What's going on?"

Pennington backed up to the sedan, reached backward with his left hand and opened the rear passenger door. He never took his eyes off me. Didn't he trust his partner to cover his ass?

"All right, Tanner." Pennington tucked the handcuffs away. "Let's do this your way. Okay? Climb in and we can talk."

I bounced on the balls of my feet, looking left and right, ready to sprint. Their sedan blocked the path straight ahead. The closed door behind me made a dash through the apartment impossible. And the two detectives blocked a sidewalk escape. The crowd across the street expanded, spilling into the road as they jostled for position to see the out-of-towner taken down by their local guys.

Pennington remained in position holding the door open for me. He swept his hand in front of the opening. "Sooner we do this, the sooner you can get on your way back home."

I stopped a foot away. Raised my voice. "Home? Philly? Just what in the hell is going on here?"

Pennington glanced over his shoulder at the crowd across the street. A few more of them had their cell phones out, recording the action. His lips drew thin as he turned his head back to me. "Get in the car, Detective Tanner."

I wanted to call Sam, leave the phone on so he could hear everything that happened. But Pennington shut me down when I reached for my cell in my pocket.

"Hands where I can see them." He reached for his piece but stopped short of pulling it back out. The point was made. I was going one way or another. It was my choice whether there'd be handcuffs involved.

"I'm a reasonable man," I said. "I'll go along for the ride. But if you think you're getting me on a plane back to Philadelphia before we find Cassie, you're out of your goddamned mind."

Perhaps he'd learned from his previous outburst, because Pennington didn't say anything. He stepped back as I moved forward. He pulled his hand off the door as I stuck my leg in the car. Once I was fully inside, he kicked the door shut. I reached for the handle without thinking, pulled it back. The door didn't move. I felt like a caged tiger. Unless I planned on ripping out the barrier separating us and climbing over the front seat, they had me where they wanted me. The vinyl was cold to the touch from the frigid air that blasted from the vents. I slid to the middle of the backseat where the air streamed into my face.

Pennington took his place in the driver's seat. At least the guy saved me the humiliation of flipping on his strobes and sirens. I might skirt the law at times, but I'm far from a common criminal.

Cervantes climbed in after talking with the folks who'd been watching. The detectives shared a quick glance, then Pennington dropped the car into gear and sped away.

I waved at my crowd of supporters. If the window had been down I might've yelled something to get them riled up. Instead I decided to save that for my fellow detectives.

"One of you clowns gonna read me my rights, or what?"

Pennington looked up into the rearview. "Did you do something that would require us to do so?"

I shrugged and offered no reply.

"You know this looks bad, right?" Cervantes said. His tone had grown menacing, more so than usual. "Cassie's gone missing, and since then, you've been inside her house and spent time at the murder scene." He half-turned in his seat to make eye contact with me. The look on his face matched his voice. "Someone might think you were trying to cover your tracks."

"And someone with even half a brain might realize I was trying to be proactive rather than sitting on my ass. You know, do something, anything, to help us locate Cassie." I threw up my arms and fell back against the seat. "You guys are wasting your damn time. Mine, too. Let me out here so at least one of us can do something other than sitting on our thumbs."

We were heading west out of the historic district, presumably on our way to Cassie's house. It'd be a pointless exercise. I'd already combed the house. They needed to send a forensics team over there instead of us tromping through and destroying any remaining evidence, if there was any to begin with. Could they find something proving Novak had been there? Sure, I guess. Point was, neither he nor Cassie were there now.

"What'd you guys find out at the girls' house?" I craned my head to watch each of them in the rearview.

Pennington kept his eyes on the road. Cervantes stared down

at his phone. I asked again and they continued ignoring me. Guess they didn't want to talk to me, at least not now in the car. Whatever they had to say was going to wait until we reached Cassie's house, and hopefully it didn't include the words "you have the right to remain silent."

We pulled to a stop. A group of six girls walked in front of the car. One had on a SCAD t-shirt. Did they know the recently deceased? I resisted the urge to tell them to be careful when picking up strangers. Doubt they would've listened, anyway. Those girls hadn't a care in the world, despite what had happened recently. After they passed, I took note of the intersection. Montgomery and West Hall Street. We were west of Forsyth Park. That didn't seem right. Then to make matters worse, Pennington turned right on Gwinnett, taking us in the wrong direction.

"Where're we going?" I asked.

Neither man replied. Shocker. Less than a minute later we were hugging the on-ramp for I-16 West. Pennington pinned down the accelerator, only taking his foot off to slam on the brakes as he wedged into a small space between a black Chrysler minivan and an eighteen-wheeler carrying a load of empty cages. Loose chicken feathers floated off the bed and onto the windshield. Some remained caught in the slipstream, spinning and circling in the air.

Pennington gunned the engine again and whipped the wheel to the left. For five minutes he wove in and out of traffic until it had thinned enough he could do ninety in the left lane.

"Are you assholes gonna tell me what's going on?" I said. "Where're we going?"

Cervantes looked over his shoulder. His brows were knit together, a crease forming between them and running the length of his forehead.

Pennington glanced up in the rearview. He didn't share the

same concerned look of his partner. It almost looked as though the bastard was smiling at me. "You sure you don't already know, Detective?"

CHAPTER FORTY-TWO

The voices told her to leave. They instructed her to get up and get out. They said she was not safe. Problem was, Cassie couldn't see anything. She had no idea where she was. The musty smell stifled her lungs. She blinked in the darkness, shedding fragments of uncertainty, revealing memories that she started piecing together.

The time she spent with Mitch lingered like champagne on the tip of her tongue. Warmth filled her, but only for a moment. The memory passed and then she was back at the girls' house. The bodies strewn about, discarded as though they were refuse. The weight of what had happened to them pressed firmly on her chest, strangling her heart and lungs.

She kept her eyes clenched shut to avoid the spirits. There was no escaping them, though. They remained close, whispering to her, pleading with her to leave. That was not an option at the moment. She tuned them out as best she could. A banging from somewhere within the room grabbed her attention. She opened her eyes again, surprised to see an overhead light had switched on to a low setting. The thin filament burned light orange, clear in the round tube. Slowly a warm halo of light began to spread around her.

Cassie attempted to push off the bed, but discovered her wrists and ankles were bound. She lifted her head and saw the restraints were tied to four short posts that rose from the frame like skeletal fingers about to close in on her. She laid in the palm. The thumb hovered behind, ready to smother her face.

A shadow moved in the corner of the room. She turned toward it, but it was gone. Something smacked against the wall from the other side. The sound was muted and hollow. Her breath caught in her throat. Tingling raced down her arms. Her abdominal muscles began clenching, cramping.

"Slow down," she whispered to herself. She breathed in through her nose, held it for five seconds, then expelled hot air out through her mouth. She caught a whiff of her metallic breath and squinted against it. There was hardly enough saliva available to swallow the taste away.

Light flooded the room in a growing cone as the door cracked open, groaning on rusted hinges. A howl of wind blew in and swept over her sweat-soaked body. She looked down and saw only a sheer nightgown, which offered little protection and revealed everything. Where had it come from? Where were her clothes? She stifled the disgust overtaking her that someone had stripped her down and put her in the lingerie.

He appeared in the entryway, bright light silhouetting him. The dim room cast shadows over his face. Fine. Cassie didn't want to look at his features anyway. She struggled against her restraints but gave up as he shook his head. There was no way out.

Not yet.

The activity in the room died down as he stepped foot inside. The spirits ran from him. Even in death they feared his touch.

Cassie couldn't blame them. She had spent countless nights agonizing over what had happened to her at his hand, reliving every horrible detail in slow motion. She could still feel the rain washing over her, stealing her life.

Why was he standing there? He hadn't advanced more than two feet into the room. She swore he was smiling, even if she couldn't see his lips peeled back, revealing the whites of his teeth. It was a game. Who could go the longest without speaking? Cassie clenched her eyelids shut. For the first time since she'd awoken, she pleaded for the voices to return. Anything to pull her focus away from the deranged asshole staring at her from the doorway.

The ticking of a clock echoed around the room. Tick-tock. Click-clack. It wasn't a timepiece making the noise. He was doing it. A plan to add to the madness of the moment? Perhaps so. And it was working.

"What do you want?" she screamed.

He chuckled softly. She couldn't help but think it sounded like a child laughing at a joke he didn't get only because his parents found it amusing. But she knew that was not the case. He'd won, and he knew it. She gave him the in, and now he could say whatever he wanted. "You look beautiful in that dress."

"Piss off," she said. "This isn't any dress I'd ever wear for you."

As he glided through the entryway, the overhead light burst into a strong glow. No longer was the filament visible. Cassie blinked against the brightness until the pain in her eyes subsided. The bed dipped and bounced a couple of times. She lifted her head on the thin pillow. He'd joined her on the mattress. He sat with his left leg pulled under his right, facing the door, which remained open. She strained to see what lay beyond but couldn't make anything out other than part of a table.

Several seconds passed. Now what? Was he going to stay there until she said something else? What would his next move be if she said the wrong thing?

She opted for something a little more subtle.

"Where am I?"

His right hand drifted backward, fingertips skating along the top of the blue fitted sheet. Inch by inch they drew nearer to her. He was on a collision course with her bare flesh near the spot the nightgown met her thigh. Cassie arched her back and lifted her buttocks off the mattress, sliding over as far as she could. It was only a few inches, but at least it would take that much longer for his repulsive touch to reach her.

He turned his head far enough to see her out of the corner of his eye. He'd shaved since they'd arrived. The corner of his mouth twitched. "You'll come to appreciate what I can offer you, my dear."

"Only if that means you'll finish the job you started in that graveyard," she said through her clenched teeth.

He pulled his leg out from under the other, then turned and leaned over her, one arm on either side of her torso, leaving them face to face. "What makes you think I'll do that?"

Cassie matched his intense stare with one of her own. She didn't have to pretend. All fear had left her body. All that remained was rage.

"Why else bring me here?" she said, knowing she couldn't believe any response he could muster. "You can kill and dispose of me here and no one would ever know, right? I mean, if they knew, they'd already have broken down the doors to rescue me."

"I do not have any plans to kill you, my dear Cassie." He lowered his gaze to her breasts. Her nipples showed through the sheer material. His eyes settled in on them. "That is precisely why I brought you here."

She looked down her body. "For my breasts?"

He smiled, his gaze returning to meet hers. "To not kill you." His mouth hung open as though the words still needed time to escape his brain. He leaned in closer. Their lips were inches apart. "I tell you, though, that is entirely up to you. Cooperate with me and you live."

"Kind of hard to do otherwise when I'm tied up like this." She pulled hard with both arms toward him, fingers clutched like talons. They barely made it past her elbows, but she felt the bedposts give a little, like maybe they weren't as secure as they should've been to hold an adult.

His stare diverted to the corner of the bed. He'd noticed the posts moving, too. How long until he took care of it? The calm look on his face dissipated in the blink of an eye. She hardly noticed him lift up and draw his right hand back across his chest.

She sure as hell felt it when he backhanded her across the face.

Cassie's head snapped back into the thin pillow. The initial flash of pain dulled and then spread across her face. She felt a warm trickle from her nose. It settled into her upper lip and slid around the corner of her mouth and down her cheek.

He hopped off the bed and made it to the door in three steps, stopping there and looking back at her. "That, my dear, is precisely how you will wind up dead."

With a flick of his wrist he shut off the overhead light. The soft glow from outside the room offered a glimpse of the table in the outer room, but it didn't last long enough to make sense of anything else. He slammed the door shut, and Cassie once again descended into the darkness.

CHAPTER FORTY-THREE

"You backwoods assholes better not have any sick ideas running through your heads." I slammed my fist into the seat to the left. We'd been driving for more than half an hour and they hadn't said hardly a word to me or each other. Whatever the plan was, Cervantes and Pennington had worked it out prior to picking me up in front of the apartment.

The distance between exits grew. Trees lined either side of the highway and stretched out ahead as far as I could see. Were they going to treat me like an unwanted dog and drop me off on the side of the road? I lowered my chin to my chest and settled my gaze on my knees. It was all I could do to keep my anger at bay. Not like it would serve me any purpose from the back seat.

Pennington swerved to the right at the last second and exited the highway. The tires yipped against the move. Which exit were we getting off at? He hadn't given any indication he was about to leave the highway, so I hadn't taken notice of where we were. Our gazes met in the mirror for a moment, then his diverted back to the road.

I sat up and looked for a street sign at the end of the off-ramp. The metal pole stood six feet in the air. The sign was missing. Maybe some drunks with a shotgun or a bat had taken care of it. Or it could've been a popular name, the kind that'd tempt someone to steal it. Stoner Avenue, or some such nonsense.

He turned right, headed north for a couple of miles, then made a left. Best I could tell we were running parallel with the interstate now, but that'd be hard to track long-term. As long as I had some kind of idea where it was, I could make it back to the highway after they stranded me.

That plan went out the door as the road started winding and twisting through the woods. It was close to noon, and the sun sat high above. I couldn't tell whether we were on the right or left of it. I'd have to sit for a while to get my bearings straight.

Nothing like wasting hours when every second counts.

We emerged from the woods and stopped at an intersection. Finally one with a name I could attach to it. Pennington turned left, pinning the accelerator down. The car lurched so hard it slammed me back in my seat.

It wasn't long after that I saw the strobe lights on the horizon.

Pennington and Cervantes shared a look. My stomach turned, then sank, nearly sending its contents back up my throat. This did not bode well.

"What happened to her?" I choked on my words.

Cervantes turned in his seat. His stared at me through narrowed eyes for several seconds, not saying a word. Whatever it was, it wasn't good. And I was suspect number one. The last to see her alive. I'd been in her home and knew where she was going.

"You wanna go over what you were doing this morning again?" Cervantes said.

"For Christ's sake." I knew what he was doing, trying to get me to slip up, and I understood why. But I was getting tired of the act the detectives were putting on for me. "I don't have a damn clue where we even are. Look, if you truly believe I'm a suspect, then take my ass to jail. Otherwise, quit with this damn territorial nonsense and tell me, what the hell happened to her?"

"You don't know nothing about a van?" he asked. "Didn't encounter one, or have anyone at either house mention seeing one?"

"I didn't see one, and nobody mentioned seeing one."

Cervantes kept staring and said nothing else.

Pennington rolled down his window as he approached the parked patrol car. A uniformed state trooper stood off to the side, waiting for us to reach him.

"Picked up a trail," the trooper said.

"How far back?" Pennington asked.

"Quarter-mile."

Pennington turned to Cervantes. "Better if we walk it."

Cervantes didn't take his eyes off me. "Don't think about running, Tanner."

"Why not? Your thick ass can't keep up with me."

Pennington maneuvered past the trooper's car and cut the engine. I scanned the area, spotted a light blue early-2000s Tercel parked on the other side of the road a few hundred yards away. Its trunk was popped open. The detectives exited the car and spoke with the trooper, leaving me stuck in the back. With the AC off it didn't take long for it to heat up. A thin sheen of sweat dampened my forehead. When they finally opened the back door, the young officer had stepped away.

"Thanks." I stepped out and spit on the ground between them. "Gonna finally fill me in?"

Pennington took a deep breath as he looked past me into the woods. He hiked his thumb over his shoulder. "Stranded motorist called it in."

I looked at the Tercel again. This time I spotted a woman sitting on a five-gallon bucket off to the side. She had her phone pressed to the side of her head.

"Saw a vehicle pull off right about here and head into the woods over there." He aimed his finger in the direction of two faded tire tracks. Long grass covered the dirt ruts in the ground. "She didn't think much of it. Figured someone lived back there, I guess. But then she heard it."

My stomach did another somersault. There were only so many sounds that would give a bystander reason to call the cops. "Heard what?"

Pennington slammed his hands together. The clap echoed throughout our surroundings. The woman across the road looked up at us, shook her head. "She thought maybe it was a gunshot."

I peered into the woods as though I could see the details through the maze of trees and leaves. "Was it?"

Pennington shook his head. "Come on, let's go see for ourselves."

"Let's leave him here," Cervantes said. "We don't need someone else trouncing all over our crime scene."

Before I could say anything, Pennington silenced his partner. "Cerv, we don't have a lot of time here. We're gonna bring him along. He might spot something we don't."

If I knew anything at that moment, it was that Cassie's body wasn't waiting for us in the woods. And with the way Pennington stood up for me there, I almost began to feel accepted by my southern counterpart. But the look both gave me wiped that feeling away. Neither man wanted me there, but I'd become so entrenched in everything that had happened they had no choice. I also had a better relationship with Cassie than either of them. If she left some kind of message behind, it would be for me, something I'd pick up on before them.

"Let's move."

Pennington took the lead. Cervantes gestured for me to go ahead of him. I fell in line between the two detectives as we trekked into the woods, following the trail left by the vehicle. We studied our surroundings as we walked. Nothing looked out of place, not that it would be easy to tell.

I saw what had happened before we reached the clearing that opened up like a football field in the middle of the forest. Across the span of overgrown grass and weeds was Cassie's car, wrecked into a pine tree. I started to wonder if I had been wrong about there being no body here.

"Anyone left behind?" I asked.

Pennington shook his head as he pulled out a pair of latex gloves and tossed them to me. "Scene integrity. Got that, Tanner?"

I blew off his remark and stepped into the clearing. At this point I didn't want to disturb any evidence, so I walked about ten feet to the right of the tracks left by Cassie's car. I was the first to reach the wreck. The car appeared to have hit the tree at a speed faster than you'd expect a small sedan to be traveling through high grasses. It didn't make sense. There were two other trails they could have followed instead of trouncing through unseen obstacles. Something had happened between Cassie and Novak in the moments before the crash. I eased the passenger door open and stuck my head inside to see if I could figure out what that was. Blood spattered the dash and passenger seat.

"Wait for us, Tanner," Cervantes called out. The grass whooshed as they hurried toward the car.

Pennington appeared on the other side of the vehicle. The dented driver's side door wasn't shut all the way. He eased it open and leaned in. He nodded as his gaze met mine. "See anything?"

I ignored him as I searched for something, anything, that Cassie had left behind to let us know she had been there. That she was still all right. My gut told me the accident was anything but that. She had fought back. They hit this tree because of her. There was no way she'd let Novak take her twice.

"Detective?" Pennington said.

I knelt down next to the car. My knee sank into the soft ground. The breeze that wafted past smelled of radiator fluid. Angling my head to the side, I checked under the seat.

And I found what I had been looking for. I looked up at Pennington. "She's been here."

"What, you got her gift now?" Cervantes said.

"Don't be an asshole," I said.

"How do you know?" Pennington said.

I leaned back and scanned the ground for a stick, locating one with a forked end. I used it to retrieve the bracelet from under the seat. It glinted in a ray of sunlight.

"You sure that's hers?" Pennington asked. "And even if it is, it could've been under that seat for months."

"It was on her wrist last night," I said.

"Sure about that?" Cervantes said.

"She told me the story of how she got it. So, yeah, I'm pretty damn sure, man."

"Kinda strange how you found the watch at the girls' house, and now this bracelet? You sure you're not planting evidence?"

"Shut up, Cerv." Pennington looked back at his partner as he headed into the woods. "Give him an evidence bag."

I didn't want to hand the bracelet over, but it might have DNA on it. Novak was my prime suspect, but I couldn't allow tunnel vision to set in. That's when the biggest mistakes were made. The discovery gave me what I needed. Proof that Cassie was alive after the accident.

"Tanner," Pennington yelled from within the woods. "Come check this out."

CHAPTER FORTY-FOUR

I knelt over the deep impression in the leaf-covered ground. Sunlight trickled through the overhead canopy. The still air did little to keep the effects of the humid day at bay. Sweat trickled down my neck and settled into my collar.

The vehicle had sat long enough to work the tires into the ground. But as I scanned ahead, I noticed that the trails leading away from the scene only left the grass bent. Novak had left the vehicle, presumably a van, knowing he would need it to transport Cassie's body. Hopefully her live body.

I rose and took a long sweeping look around the area for any evidence of foul play. There had been blood in Cassie's car, but that was easily explained by the accident. The trail stopped in the car though. Whoever had been injured must have managed to cover or wrap the wound. There was none to be found around the perimeter where the vehicle had been parked or near these tire marks.

Cervantes entered the area with a scowl on his face.

I stopped him from plodding through. "Let's be careful where we walk. Try to land in my footsteps. Your crime scene guys still need to process this. There could be plenty we're not seeing."

Cervantes shrugged, pushed his sunglasses over his brow, and headed straight toward me, ignoring everything I had said. Why was he risking compromising the crime scene just to be a hardass toward me?

I intercepted him before he trampled over the tire tracks. "You got a problem with me, that's one thing. You can settle that anytime you want to step in the ring. Hell, I don't even need a ring for you. Any street corner will do."

He looked away, clenching his jaw.

I continued. "But goddamn, man, this is someone we all know. Cassie's helped out all our asses at one time or another. Maybe you pricks aren't capable of it, but she's become my friend. The hell is wrong with you potentially ruining evidence that might help us find her?"

Cervantes struck me in the chest with both hands open-palmed so fast that I didn't have time to get a hand up in defense. Guess he decided to take me up on my anytime-anywhere challenge. The blow knocked me back a step. I set my feet and readied a haymaker meant to land on his head. But before I could launch my attack, another set of hands grabbed me from behind.

This was it. It was going down.

Cervantes disappeared from view as I was spun around by Pennington. The man kept me at arm's length. Good idea, too. I was hellbent on throwing that damn punch.

"Enough of this shit!" Pennington looked past me at his partner. "Cerv, dammit, I've had enough. If you can't get on board with what we're doing, then I've got no choice but to recommend you be removed from this case."

I felt like it might be time for me to referee. Another challenge had been issued to Cervantes. I turned sideways, breaking free from Pennington's grasp, both arms up, palms facing either man.

"I don't know why you're sticking up for this asshole," Cervantes said. "He shows up, Cassie goes missing. You don't think there's some link there, man? Come on, give me a break."

Pennington pushed me aside and stepped up to his partner. "I see a guy standing there who is more willing to do what it takes to get her back safely than the guy who is supposed to be my partner."

Cervantes said nothing. A wrinkle between his eyes deepened as his cheeks got redder.

"Go check the car again," Pennington said. "Cool off while Tanner and I talk."

Cervantes didn't move. Pennington took a few steps back, turned, and motioned for me to follow him. I kept my eyes on Cervantes. He matched my steps one for one until he reached the edge of the clearing where he turned around.

"What was all that about?" I said after catching up to Pennington.

The detective looked back to where his partner had been standing. "I wish I could tell you. Something about you, I guess. Really sets him off. He's normally not like this. I mean, he can play it up with a suspect like an award-winning actor. You should see him when he gets going. I swear the guy could get a confession out of his own mother."

"But you don't see that happening here."

Pennington shook his head. "It's a battle of instincts right now. Apparently his are telling him there's something about you that should cause him to worry."

"He's probably right. But it ain't over what happened to Cassie."

Pennington smiled for a moment like he knew more about me

than he let on. "You're no angel. And neither are either of us. But I can tell you're in this with us, Mitch. Not against us. Just keep doing what you're doing, and I'll work on Cerv. He'll come around eventually."

I pointed past him. "Where do you think those tire tracks lead?"

"First officer on scene said they followed them out to the road. It's not far, not even a quarter-mile."

"Let's go then." I looked back and saw Cervantes poking his head in the car again. It was fine with me if he stayed put.

Pennington started off into the woods, keeping the tire tracks to his left. Nature had overtaken the old fire road, and that worked in our favor. Made it easy to follow Novak's path out in the few places where the trail split off. I stopped at each fork for a moment, stood there, scanning the surroundings. I was looking for something, anything that might shed some light on where they'd gone. I knew there'd be nothing there. Novak wasn't the smartest criminal, but even he knew not to leave an address lying around where the cops could find it.

We reached the road after a five-minute trek. It was a narrow blacktop that looked new. Heat rose off it. So did the smell of tar after a morning of baking in the sun.

"This is where the clues end." Pennington stood with his hands on his hips, facing away from me. The road stretched out a couple hundred yards before curving left and disappearing behind the trees on the other side.

"What's down that way?"

He shook his head. "Not super familiar with this area. The computer in the car will give us a better idea." With that, he pulled out his cell phone and called his partner.

We waited another seven minutes or so for Cervantes to arrive. Every second that passed led to more uncertainty. The distance between us and Cassie grew, whether they were screaming down 95, or he'd planted her somewhere. I closed my eyes, felt the light breeze against my dampened face, and tried to feel for her presence. I had no idea how she did what she did, all that talking to the dead and whatnot. I'd asked. She'd explained. It made no sense to me. But I felt if I just let her know I was here, had seen what had happened to her car, maybe she could tell me she was ok.

But all I got in return was silence.

CHAPTER FORTY-FIVE

The greenhouse was the only place on the property where Novak felt like himself. One might think that place would be inside, with the women. But those same women left him feeling out of control. Especially Cassie. She was unlike all the others, and perhaps that's why she survived. Take Alice, for instance. Weak. Weaker than most who came back with Novak. How had he missed it the night of the storm? She could never survive the attack that Cassie did. Novak wondered if Alice would simply give up and succumb to her fear.

He snipped a dying vine from a tomato plant and cut it into short pieces, then tossed the remains onto a bare patch of dirt while recounting that first night with Alice. The realization sunk in that it would have been best if he had killed her, as he had her three friends. His interest in the case would have diminished until the urge returned, which after four homicides would have stretched long enough that Cassie's involvement would have been in the past. He'd never have even known she existed in the same geographic space as him. But allowing Alice to live—despite his future intentions toward the woman—had created the storm he now lived in.

He let her live and that meant someone would be actively searching for her. Novak didn't fear them finding him. The police had always had trouble with that. And on the rare occasion they did find him, catching and then keeping him confined was never an easy task. In time, Novak always got his way.

"Alice, Alice, Alice," he muttered, walking down the aisle with a green hose. He pulled the trigger on the spray nozzle and sent a wide cone of water over a section of vegetables. The dampened soil exacerbated the smell of compost. Novak pulled his shirt collar over his nose and fanned the air away from his face. It was the only part he couldn't stand. Maybe it was time to fix the ventilation in this place?

His thoughts turned to Cassie. Why was it so difficult to keep his composure around her? She was the anti-Alice. Tough, dominant, and she'd just as soon kill him, or perhaps herself, than give in to him. That made him want her even more. In the end, she'd have no choice.

Novak finished his work in the greenhouse. After rinsing all his tools and putting them back in their storage space, he lifted the hatch and descended the rusted metal ladder bolted to the brick wall with a small flashlight clenched between his teeth. As was customary, he dropped to the ground with a few rungs left. Getting Cassie down the ladder had been no easy task. He didn't care if most of his visitors enjoyed a spill to the ground. Cassie had been no different in that regard.

The tunnel was ten feet underground, sealed in by bricks. It was there when he first came across the property almost two decades ago. Over the years several of the bricks had fallen out of place. Novak had been diligent in replacing them, but his time away in prison had led to more and more damage. Water dripped in many sections now, pooling in several spots. This was expected, considering they weren't that far above sea level. He couldn't believe it when he found the property. It had been a steal. He bought it off an old man who had no idea what he was sitting on. The old coot had inherited it from his grandfather, who had grown up on the property. Apparently, the old guy hadn't known about the tunnel between the guesthouse and the greenhouse.

Novak did nothing for upkeep to the property. From outside, the house looked abandoned. Grass stood waist-high. Weeds littered every acre of the lot. The cycle of the seasons took care of killing it all off and exploding it into growth again. The house, guesthouse, barn, and other structures on the property were in such disrepair he doubted teenagers looking for a place to make out would even bother going inside. Old wood siding adorned with chips of paint hung from rusted nails.

In a word, the place was perfect. No one would ever come looking for Novak there. And so long as they couldn't find him, they couldn't find his guests. Dead and alive, they could stay with him there for eternity. So long as he remained in place and stopped looking for new friends. Every time he added another to his collection, he put it all at risk.

He panned the flashlight across the floor twenty feet ahead. There had been a puddle of water there earlier that he would have to keep tabs on. God forbid the tunnel collapse. There'd be no way of repairing it, and the thought of crossing a hundred yards in the wide-open fields between the house and greenhouse was not a welcome one. The puddle had drained through the cracks in the floor. He ran his hand along the ceiling. Aside from the lingering condensation, the bricks felt solidly in place.

Another ladder identical to the first waited for him at the other end of the tunnel. He climbed up, hooked his left arm through a rung and unlatched the trap door with his free hand. There was no point in locking it. The end points were hidden from view.

The trap door swung up and over and collided on the ground with a loud thud that shook dust loose from the floor and ceiling. Novak held his breath as he pulled himself out of the tunnel to avoid breathing in the mold spores. He made his way to the kitchen, which was positioned in the center of the house with a window overlooking a field of cattails. There were two entrances to the room, both equipped with solid-core doors. This was the only room on the main or upper levels that he ever allowed light to be used. With the blinds and shades drawn, no one could see the light from the outside.

He lifted the ice chest lid and pulled out a couple of frozen water bottles. On the table was a bushel of bananas. He grabbed two. And from the small fridge he retrieved a turkey, ham and cheese sub, already cut in two equal pieces.

Feeding time was his favorite time. It was the only time he was certain his friends were appreciative of him.

Novak made his way to the cellar door. He flipped the switch on the wall and a single light over the stairs cut on, casting a dull yellow wash over the worn wood. A few of the stairs had bloods stains. He felt the side of his forehead, where he'd been cut earlier during the accident. Some of that blood on the floor was his. Some had come from Cassie. He ought to make her clean it up. She'd relish that job, though. A woman like her, she'd use it as a chance to get away.

As he descended into the cellar, it crossed his mind that he could put a choke collar on her. He still had one from Brutus, his Rottweiler they'd unceremoniously put to sleep when he'd been sent off to prison.

"Put to sleep," he muttered. He'd like to put those bastards to sleep, starting with the piss-ant judge and his horrible excuse for a public defender. Not to mention all the damn detectives who had been involved.

He flipped two switches at the bottom of the stairs. As the stairwell light dissipated, another came on and lit up the room at the bottom. The low ceilings and concrete walls and floor absorbed light. It was cool and dry. There were no windows. A square iron light fixture hung from the ceiling over a long rectangular dining table. There were eight chairs around the table. He'd never managed to fill all of them. At most, he'd had a special dinner with four women and a friend.

Novak set a bottle of water, one half of the ham and turkey sub, and a banana on the table. He carried the rest over to Cassie's room. He reached for the handle, paused, then rapped his knuckles against the door. Why not try to get things back on the right track? Perhaps if he showed a little kindness, she'd return the favor. His smile faded with every passing second the bitch didn't bother to respond. He'd even been nice enough to untie her earlier!

He cleared his throat, and knocked again.

And again, there was no response.

Novak grabbed the knob and flung the door open. Cassie lay on her back in the middle of the bed. Her hands were folded over her stomach. Her legs were crossed at her ankles. She opened her eyes, but did not look at him, instead choosing to stare up at the ceiling.

"I brought you lunch," he said, leaning against the doorjamb.

She blinked.

"Care to say anything?" he asked.

If she did, she opted not to.

He bit back his anger. That would only lead to him making a rash decision, and those kinds of decisions were often permanent. He didn't want to take any action against Cassie that would result in her foregoing the pleasure of his company. He set the food on the bed and left the room without another word.

He thought about leaving the door open a little, just so she could hear everything that was about to happen. But he thought better of it as he exited. It was too soon for such gestures. She'd take advantage of it. Besides, she'd hear it anyway.

He picked up the next meal and walked to Alice's room. Alice was not one to take advantage of his kindness. That was why her door was left cracked open an inch. And it hadn't moved since he left. He extended his foot and nudged the door open wider.

"Hello, Alice."

The woman huddled in the corner, naked, her knees drawn to her chest. Dark bags under her eyes made it look as though she hadn't slept since she had arrived. Novak reached into his pocket and pulled out a small vial of crushed valium. He'd sprinkle it onto her sandwich.

She got up and went to the bed after he set her food down. Apparently satisfying her hunger was more important than hiding her body from him. She gnawed on the sub and took a healthy gulp of water.

"That's a girl," he said. "Eat it all. You're gonna need your strength in a couple of minutes."

CHAPTER FORTY-SIX

Cervantes sped down the road toward us and slammed the brakes a few seconds too late. The car screeched past, leaving a wave of burnt rubber in its wake. I scrunched my nose against the odor as I climbed into the backseat of the sedan. The vehicle had been on long enough that it had sufficiently cooled down. I pulled my sweat-soaked collar away from my neck while leaning back against the seat.

The two detectives held a hushed conversation that I didn't bother to lean in closer to hear. By this point I realized if they wanted my input, they'd tell me what I should say. Cervantes nodded at Pennington, then shifted into drive and pulled away from the skid marks.

"The witness says she never saw a van or a truck drive by," Pennington said.

"Where's this road come out?" I asked.

Cervantes glanced up in the rearview. "Pretty close to where she was stranded. She would've noticed if Cassie was taken back that way, especially with how wound up the lady was after hearing the accident."

"Or she might've missed it for that very reason," I said. "Or forgot, what with all the other thoughts going through her mind at that time. We sure she wasn't cowering in her back seat, afraid she heard a gunshot and someone was coming for her next?"

Cervantes shook his head and turned his gaze back toward the road. His death grip on the steering wheel told me he didn't care for my assessment.

"I'm not trying to be contrary for the sake of it," I said. "But we gotta consider these things."

Pennington intervened yet again. "Hey, now, we get where you're coming from. But if Novak took her that way—," he aimed his finger over my shoulder, "—then they could be anywhere right now."

"They already are anywhere right now," I said.

"We know what's back there, Tanner." Pennington faced forward in his seat. "We're gonna see what's up ahead. Hell, maybe they ran off the road."

"I don't doubt that possibility." I pictured Cassie in my mind, never giving up. "That girl's a fighter."

"She is," Pennington said. "Any of us went through what she did, forget about it. We're not coming through it like her. She'll hang in there long enough for us to get to her. Bank on that."

The sky grew overcast in a matter of minutes while we raced down the winding country road. The woods gave way to pasture-land. Dozens of cows lined up along a splintered wooden fence as if a passing car was a big event.

Pennington had his phone held up. He was manipulating a map on the screen. "Couple of miles, we're gonna come across a gas station."

"I'll stop there," Cervantes said. "Maybe someone saw something."

"How likely is it Novak would stop five minutes after leaving the woods?" I said.

"How likely is it the guy would abduct the woman who was responsible for putting him away? The guy's crazy, so maybe we need to think a little crazy ourselves." Pennington rolled down his window and let the wind rush overtake the conversation.

A couple of minutes later the gas station crept into view. A rusted roof over the pump island stood out in the deserted parking lot. If not for a neon open sign next to the front door, I would've thought the place had long since been deserted.

Cervantes pulled up next to a pump and cut the engine. We sat there for a moment. The heat quickly penetrated the cabin through Pennington's open window. The cicadas ended their momentary silence and sang their shrill song from behind rows of palmettos.

Behind the front window a man looked out at us as we exited the car and approached the store. Anyone with half a brain could tell we were cops. So the question was did this guy have something to fear from us? If so, it wouldn't be as easy to get any information out of him. He'd be too afraid of uncovering his own tracks.

The door jingled as Pennington pulled it open. He remained in place and held it for me and Cervantes. It seemed they wanted to keep me between them. And I had no doubt they wanted me to keep my mouth shut while inside the store. I'd oblige, for a minute or two. If I didn't like the way the questioning was heading, I'd make my mark.

The guy behind the counter pegged us for cops right away. His lips drew tight and his eyes danced around the store. Drugs? Guns? He was giving away something, but not what we were there for.

"How ya doing, buddy?" Pennington strode up to the counter, hands in his pockets. Seemed a stupid move to me. No telling what the clerk had hidden behind the counter. The guy could pull out a .357 and that'd be all she wrote for Pennington.

The clerk nodded and glanced over Pennington's shoulder at me and Cervantes.

"Can I get a pack of Camels and some matches?" Pennington said.

The clerk turned to the wall of cigarettes and reached for the Camels. Pennington leaned across and took a look around.

"What are you doing?" The clerk drew his hands tight to his chest as though the pack of smokes would protect him.

"You got surveillance in here?" Pennington said.

"Wha—why?" If the guy could've retreated into the wall, he would've at that point.

Pennington spread his arms, placed his hands wide on the counter, making himself look larger and more intimidating. "You see a van come through here in the past two or three hours?"

The clerk's tight face relaxed for a beat as he realized we weren't there to shake him down. "You-you guys are-are cops?" He must've been a thespian in a past life with the way he pulled that line off.

Cervantes and I moved in closer. The label on the clerk's shirt said his name was Craig. I decided to break rank and say something.

"You know we are, Craig. Now at the moment, we aren't here to look into what you've been doing during your downtime."

Craig's eyes darted to his laptop and his hand slowly moved toward it.

"Just leave that where it is," Pennington said.

"Craig, just answer the questions as they are asked and we'll be out of your hair in a few minutes," I said.

Cervantes leaned in and bumped my shoulder. A subtle gesture telling me I better shut the hell up. Now.

"Back to the van," Pennington said. "You seen one?"

We weren't one hundred percent sure it was a van. The forensics team would need to gather all the evidence from the tire imprints, match the tread to specific tires, measure the distances between the impressions, and so on. From that, they could make a determination on types of vehicles and in some cases, provide specific models. But eyeballing and spitballing, I'd call it a van.

"Couple hours ago," Craig said. "An old Dodge or Ford, primer gray, a panel van."

"A family? Man and a woman? Hunting dogs? Migrant workers? A load of illegals?"

Craig furrowed his brow and stared out the window at the vacant gas pumps. "It was a guy. He pumped some gas then came in for some coffee, water, few other things. He kept, um, glancing out at the van."

"That seem strange to you?"

Craig shrugged at the suggestion and smiled. "I mean, what's strange, right? Maybe he loves his van." His gaze darted toward his laptop screen. The guy folded his arms over his chest as his face grew serious. "What was strange was the cut on his head. He kept dabbing at it with an oil-stained rag."

"Which pump were they at?"

"They?" The clerk looked confused.

"Him."

"Three."

Pennington looked back at Cervantes and nodded. Cervantes tugged on my sleeve and we exited the store.

"What are we doing out here?" I said.

"Trash digging." The man headed right for the trash barrel next to the pump. "Maybe we'll get lucky."

"You know that ain't gonna happen today."

"A man can hope, can't he?"

Cervantes rifled through the trash without even donning a pair of gloves. It was enough to make someone with a lesser stomach sick on the spot.

"You look like a natural at that," I said.

"Eat me." After a couple of minutes, he stopped, looked up at me and shook his head.

"Not a damn thing," I said.

He nodded, wiped his hands on his pants.

The door flung open and Pennington ran over to us.

"What's up?" Cervantes said. "You got something?"

Pennington smiled as he hid something behind his back.

CHAPTER FORTY-SEVEN

Craig the clerk stared out the window at the three of us huddled by the trash can. For some reason I couldn't take my eyes off the guy. Maybe it was the way his mouth hung open. I broke off my stare. Standing in front of me, Pennington looked like a kid who'd found his daddy's porn collection. His ear-to-ear grin made me think he had Novak's location printed out.

"What is it?" Cervantes said.

"We've got surveillance footage." Pennington produced a VHS tape.

"Really?" I said. "VHS?"

Pennington shrugged. "Not everyone's up to speed on the latest technology here in the backwards south, Yankee."

Yankee? Where the hell had that come from?

"Tapes still work. The footage is still admissible by law." He held it up in front of my face. "And this is pulling from four different feeds." Pennington pointed at the corner of the building. "There, the main store area, the office, and out back. We might not only get Novak's face on camera, but the van, license plate—"

"And maybe proof Cassie is still alive," I said, blinking him back in focus. "You guys got a VCR at the office?"

Cervantes nodded as he pulled his keys from his pocket. "Sure do."

Pennington called in to have a forensics unit sent to the gas station. It was doubtful anything had been left behind, but if they turned up even one small piece of evidence, it'd be worth it.

We hung around until one of the uniformed officers from the crash site showed up. While waiting, Pennington taped up the gas pump where the van had been, but left the store open. The clerk had told him at least a dozen other patrons had been inside since he had seen the van. It was as contaminated a scene as you could find.

The drive back to Savannah took half as long as the ride out of town. Maybe that was because I knew where we were going and the tension we felt toward each other had shifted to a mix of anxiety and hope over what the security footage contained. It helped that Cervantes pushed the needle past one hundred miles per hour and left it there the entire time we were on the highway. It was driving I could respect.

We entered the station from the back, the same way I'd gone in with Cassie on a couple of occasions. The familiar smell of stale coffee and Lysol hit me and I felt a slight pang of yearning to be back home.

They already had a VCR hooked up to a large display in one of the meeting rooms. There were four conference tables pushed together to form a large rectangle, and probably twenty chairs stretching around the table. I grabbed one and wheeled it closer to the screen. Cervantes sat to my right. Pennington cut the lights and shut the door, then took a seat on my left. He slipped the tape into the VCR and cut on the screen with a remote.

The large air vents in the drop ceiling piped frigid air into the room at around twenty miles per hour. It didn't take long before the effects of being in the heat and humidity all morning wore off.

Cervantes leaned closer to me. "It's every damn meeting room."

"What?" I said.

He jutted his chin toward the ceiling. "The air vents. Freezing in the summer, and hot as hell in the winter."

"Good thing it's fall." I studied Cervantes for a few moments wondering if the current extreme personality shift would last long.

"You ain't lying," Pennington said. His demeanor shifted as he pointed to the screen. "Here we go."

The image on the screen was split into four boxes. The top left showed the empty office. Next to it was an angle that covered most of the inside of the store, shot from the front doors. Bottom left was of the pumps and parking lot. And bottom right was out back.

A brindle pit bull sauntered through the field behind the gas station, stopping every few steps to cock his head and listen. Then he moved offscreen and didn't return.

Pennington hit the fast-forward button and the scene raced by. A couple cars pulled up, got gas, and drove off. The drivers never set foot in the store. Craig the clerk paced behind his counter and played at his laptop. A couple times he came out from hiding and stood in front of the doors, looking the road up and down. At one point, he grabbed a stool and carried it to the back corner. He climbed atop the stool, pushed away a ceiling panel, and stuck his arm into the darkness.

"I knew that son of a bitch was crooked," I said.

"Petty shit," Pennington said. "Nothing to be concerned about. If we notice anything unusual around the time the van shows up, we can use Craig's dealings to get him to talk."

Several minutes passed as we watched the sped-up version of

that morning's events. Then a primer gray Ford panel van appeared.

Pennington slammed his thumb into the remote so quickly he ended up stopping the tape. He cursed, restarted playback and apologized.

The van pulled alongside the same pump we had used. A man wearing a hat stepped out. He tossed something into the trash.

"Dammit," Cervantes said.

"You had the right idea," I said.

"Don't forget it."

I waved him off and returned one hundred percent of my focus to the screen. Sunlight reflected off the van's windshield, making it difficult to monitor any activity within. I doubted there'd be much, though. No way Novak would leave her alone out there if she was conscious.

After pumping a few gallons of gas, the man walked into the store. He moved slowly and casually, without purpose. Didn't look like a man who held a kidnapped woman in the back of his vehicle.

We all shifted our gaze to the box on the top right of the screen. Craig the clerk glanced up from his laptop and nodded at the man as he entered, then veered toward the counter. All we had was a shot of his back so far. After saying something to Craig, the guy went to the back of the store, where the refrigerated coolers were. He reached inside one and pulled a tall can of something out. The film was getting grainy.

"Bet they just record over the same tape," I said.

Pennington nodded. "Not like much happens out there. System is in place in case they need to recoup some insurance money, or catch someone shooting buckshot at the window late at night."

The guy walked down the back row, head down. All we wanted was the confirmation that it was Novak and the son of a bitch was making us wait for it. Finally, he turned toward the camera.

Pennington paused the tape. The image of the guy was one big blur. Pennington clicked through frame by frame, forwards and back, until we had the clearest shot. And it was still shit.

"You know that's him," I said.

Cervantes rose and paced to the back of the room. He threw his hand out. "You think that's admissible? Come on, that could be any number of guys."

"He's right," Pennington said. "This tape isn't going to do much to help us when we're up against 'beyond a reasonable doubt.'"

The feed resumed at normal speed. There wasn't another shot of Novak's face. We followed him out of the store, watching his back all the way to the van. He climbed inside. The sun had risen a little higher. The glare wasn't as strong as it had been. He could be seen climbing between the front seats into the back.

"What was it he purchased?" I said.

Pennington rewound the tape. "Looks like some energy drink and a bag of chips."

"Some lunch, huh."

We watched him exit the store again.

"A few landmarks there," I said. "Forensics guys can figure out his height, approximate size, then match that up with what we know about Novak."

Neither detective responded. We watched the rest of the tape in silence. He spent two minutes in the back of the van before leaving the scene. He pulled forward and made a sweeping U-turn.

Pennington jammed the pause button down. "Either of you make out that plate?"

The three of us huddled as close to the screen as we could in an attempt to make out the tiny set of letters and numbers on the back of the van. It was pointless.

"Too damn grainy," Cervantes said. "We'll never figure that out."

"Don't say never," I said.

"Hey, if you got it, tell the rest of us," Cervantes said.

"No, I don't. But I know someone who can get it."

"Who?" Pennington stopped the playback and ejected the tape.

I sat on the edge of the conference table, cracking my knuckles on the hard surface one at a time. "A guy back in Philly. One of the best in the country at this kind of thing. We can overnight it to him."

Holding the tape up, Pennington shook his head. "No chance this gets out of our sight."

"Then what the hell do you want to do with it? Wipe your ass?"

Pennington chuckled. "You're taking it to him personally, Tanner."

CHAPTER FORTY-EIGHT

Cassie lifted her face from her sweat-drenched pillow. She rubbed her cold cheek and wiped her nose in an attempt to clear the smell. All it did was allow the musty odor of the room to pervade her senses again.

The overhead light cast a dim wash of yellow across the room. It was always the same. How long had she been sleeping? She'd lost all sense of time. It could be two in the morning and she had no clue.

Sometimes she awoke to find her wrists and ankles bound and tied to the bed posts. There were never any memories to go along with it. Had he been drugging her food and water? She wouldn't put it past him.

Right now she was free to move about the room. She rose and tugged the damp nightie away from her chest. She would demand a change of clothing next time she saw Novak.

She crept to the corners. What secrets did the room hold? Cassie closed her eyes, inviting any spirits to speak with her. There had to be a tortured soul or two hanging around. Someone

Novak had killed, or a weak spirit who somehow became trapped there. After a few minutes of no contact, Cassie opened her eyes and looked around. It seemed brighter now. No one had been in, though. Perhaps Novak had a way of controlling the lighting from outside.

She tiptoed to the door, stopping short a few inches. A cool draft coated her toes. She placed her hand on the frame and eased her head to it. Her ear was an inch or so from the crack. It was dead silent aside from the sound of her raspy breathing.

That was another concern. She'd never had problems with allergies or asthma, but since being confined to the room, it had become more difficult to take a deep breath.

Was it the room? Or something he'd given her? Or something altogether different? Psychological reasons, maybe.

She knew he'd drugged her at least once. The ride in the van had been a blur. She had awoken at times. Once at a gas station. It hadn't seemed like they had been moving for long, then he stopped. She managed to lift her head, but that was it. Her legs, arms, torso all felt as though they had been cast in iron.

From there she faded in and out until she finally succumbed to the darkness. Maybe she'd been afraid of dying and that's why she fought the effects of the tranquilizer for so long. In the end, it had been too much for her.

Cassie shook the thoughts from her mind and stepped away from the door. The cool breeze on her feet diminished with every step back. She walked around the other side of the bed. There was only an eighteen-inch-wide gap between it and the wall. She wedged herself between, then lowered herself to the floor.

Did she really want to know what was under there? It was too dark to see anything beyond vague outlines. She swept her left arm in an arc and pulled out the first item she found. A pale towel. She held it up to the light in search of dirt or blood. Aside from dust, it appeared clean. Cassie pulled her nightie off and patted herself down. Then she wrapped the thin piece of clothing in the towel and wrenched it tight.

She didn't like the thought of walking around the room naked. Chances were Novak had some way of monitoring her. Was he watching right now? Getting off at the sight of her bare body?

Cassie unwound the towel to retrieve her clothes but stopped. What better test to find out if he was monitoring the room? Could she stand the consequences of her action? Another visit from the demented creep?

A chance to lure him in while he was in his weakest state.

She eased herself onto the sweat-dampened sheets. Her skin pricked in response to the cold. It took a few minutes to adjust. As long as she didn't move, it was fine.

The ceiling offered no clues. There were no cutouts, no blinking red lights, nothing hidden in plain sight. Where would Novak watch her from?

The overhead light brightened considerably. The sudden change caused a jolt of pain to rifle through her head. It felt as though she had a hangover and moved too quickly. A moment later, the light dimmed again, even lower than it had been before.

She squinted her eyes while staring at the fixture through the bright remnants of light clouding her vision. That's how he was watching her. He had a camera inside the light. She tucked her right foot under her left knee and laced her fingers together behind her head. How long could he take it before he came into the room?

What the hell am I doing?

It was one thing to be forced to wear next to nothing. But it was quite another to provoke a psychopath. She grabbed the nightie and donned it and then wrapped the towel around her waist like a skirt.

No sooner had she curled up in bed than did the light shut off.

She turned her attention to the door where light seeped into the room through the edges. Shadows would give her advance warning of his presence. The dark offered her cover. She could pounce the moment he walked in. Her gaze shifted to the blackened ceiling. What if he had night vision in there? He'd see her setting up the ambush.

The door swung open and violently collided with the wall. Novak's frame filled half the opening. He breathed heavily. Had he run to the room?

He crossed the room and hovered over her on the bed. She couldn't make out his features to tell what kind of mood he was in. He moved quickly, yanking the towel from her waist, then plunged something into her thigh. The needle penetrated her flesh. The stinging gave way to burning as he injected the mixture into her bloodstream. The fire spread up through her hips, stomach, and chest.

Novak took a few steps back. He scrunched the towel into a ball and tossed it at her. It landed on her chest. Her vision started to double. There were two doorways. Two Novaks.

Then there were four of him.

It made no sense. There were still only two doorways.

She saw two of the bodies turn. The other two stood just outside of the room.

Two separate men.

The images began fading as the edges of her vision darkened.

No, this can't be happening.

"Hello, Detective," Novak said. "Have you met the lovely Cassie before?"

CHAPTER FORTY-NINE

I stepped out of the arrivals terminal into a warm and hazy evening. The sun hung low in the western sky, throwing all manner of reds and oranges about. I pulled in a deep breath of smog-ridden air and held it in for a few extra seconds like I'd sucked it in through a joint.

It was good to be home.

A long line of sedans and trucks and SUVs lined the curb. Airport police kept a watchful eye over them, ushering out any who had lingered too long. They were more concerned over those going in than those leaving. But these days, you never knew where a shooter might come from.

I spotted Sam's car idling at the back of the line and waved two fingers in his direction. He flashed his high beams in response. The passenger door swung open. I climbed in and angled the ice-cold air vents at my face.

"Traveling light, I see," Sam said.

I shrugged the backpack off my shoulder. "Not staying long."

"Wanna run by your momma's house and see the little one?"

I thought about how good it would be to see Ella. Hug her and never let go. And that was the problem. "I'd never want to leave if I did."

Sam gripped the gearshift and nodded. "I hear that. They even know you're in town?"

"No point in getting her hopes up."

"So straight to Sartini's place then?"

My stomach cramped and I realized I hadn't eaten since morning. "How about we get a bite to eat first?"

We found a pizza joint not far from Sartini's. It was quick and easy, and I'd probably pay for it in an hour or two with a touch of indigestion. Fair enough tradeoff, I supposed. While we waited for our pie, Sam caught me up on his caseload.

"Sounds like they've been keeping you busy."

He pounded down the rest of his beer and set it down loud enough for the waitress to notice. She asked if he wanted another and then disappeared behind the bar.

"Busy is an understatement. It's like Huff has something to prove now that you've been suspended."

"What's he got to prove?" I tore a chunk off a garlic knot.

"It all happened on his watch."

"I've been causing problems long before he came along."

Sam laughed. "That you have, man."

I swallowed the mass of garlic-laced dough and leaned back into the booth. "So, the old lady convinced the trainer to off her old man? He had plans to kill her and make it look like an accident, but the guy had no idea she was connected to the mob."

Smiling, Sam nodded. "Can you believe that? Worst part is, DA won't touch the case now." Sam's expression turned grim. "You haven't mentioned Cassie once, Mitch."

I had filled him in on the latest details while waiting at the gate in Savannah for my flight.

"Trying not to think about it too much," I said.

"How can you not?"

I thought of Robbie for a moment. "I happen to have a lot of practice in this area lately."

"I'm sorry, man. I—"

"It's all right." I couldn't fault him for not thinking about everything I'd been through with my son. Not seeing him for over a year. No solid lead on where he was. I could let the situation eat me alive, or I could bide my time until the right opportunity arose. I had a feeling it was drawing close so long as I got Cassie home safely.

The conversation died out. Just in time, too. The waitress dropped our pizza off a few seconds later.

After we finished eating, Sam took care of the bill while I headed out to the car. The taillights flickered a couple times as the doors unlocked. A couple of teenagers who were parked in the next spot stared me down as I approached. The engine was off. Smoke wafted from the cracked windows. The unmistakable smell of marijuana filled the air from twenty feet out. I wished I had my badge on me. Incite a little fear and panic into their high.

I leaned back against the tail end of the car and waited for Sam. The pot-mobile cranked to life. The guy grated his gears shifting into first. Sam threw the restaurant door open, stepped outside, and stopped. His eyebrows knit tight as his nostrils flared in and out. He nodded, smiled, crossed the lot over to me.

"Tell me you're not smoking dope again, Mitch."

"Come on, man. How long I been a cop now? It's been at least half that long since I last did."

Sam let out a loud laugh. "Why didn't you bust those kids?"

"They'd probably get me run through for excessive force. Figured it best to let them go on their way."

"There's still time to mess with them." He pointed at the truck stopped at the parking lot exit with their left blinker on. The light there was famous for taking three minutes to change, and then you only had ten seconds to make it out of the lot.

"Maybe just turn on the strobes when we pull up behind them?"

Sam lowered himself into the car. "Deal, man."

As he backed out, my phone vibrated on the dash. "You sure you didn't tell Momma I'm home?"

He shook his head and said nothing.

I unlocked the screen and opened the message app.

"Son of a bitch."

"What is it?" Sam said.

I read the text message back to him. "If you want Cassie to have a chance, stay in Philadelphia, Detective."

CHAPTER FIFTY

Sam stomped on the brakes. A truck trying to exit the parking lot laid on his horn. "Where the hell did that come from?"

"912 area code. That's Savannah." I tapped the phone number to place a call to it. The operator's voice piped through the speaker. It wasn't legit. Someone had spoofed the number specifically for the purpose of threatening me. Rather, threatening Cassie through me.

Sam had eased the car back into the parking spot. The driver of the truck decided to pull up behind us to block our exit and kept honking. "You think it's one of those asshole detectives down there?"

I glanced over my shoulder, making sure no one had stepped out of the other vehicle. "Shouldn't we deal with that?"

Sam held up his hand. "In a minute. Why would one of them send that to you?"

"They'd have to be involved in some way. I don't get that. I mean, they seem like decent cops. Sure, they're giving me a ration of shit, but it's no different from how we'd treat them if they were on our turf."

"This Novak guy, think he got Cassie to talk?"

The thought sent shivers down my spine, quickly interrupted by the sound of two doors opening then slamming shut. "Shit. Now we gotta deal with that."

I guess the car hid our frames well enough, because there's no way in hell the two short guys standing at the rear of the vehicle would ever knowingly pick a fight with Sam and me. We towered over them. One opened his mouth to say something.

"Shut your damn mouth," Sam said. "I'm half-tempted to not even tell you I'm a cop and just whoop your asses instead." He pulled his badge from under his shirt. It was attached to a necklace. "See this? That gives me the right to royally screw up your night if the both of you aren't back in that shitty truck and out of this parking lot in five seconds."

Sam started counting in a deep, menacing voice. The guys were back in the truck before he hit three.

"The hell is wrong with people?" he said.

I had no answer for him.

We didn't linger in the parking lot. It was best to not keep Sartini waiting. We could work on the text message on the way.

"Back to what I was saying," Sam said, once again behind the wheel. "It's possible he had been stalking you or the detectives. Maybe he had an idea who they were, but you were a mystery. So he broke her down and made her talk."

"We were in the paper." I recalled the photo that had been snapped of us outside the crime scene.

"Worthless media." He accelerated to twenty over the speed limit. "Always getting in the way of our jobs."

"No kidding. It was like setting up a billboard telling a psycho one of his victims was alive and well and here's where she's been hanging out."

Sam shifted in his seat and pulled his cell out of his pocket. He punched in a number then waited a few seconds. "Hey, Mac. How you doing? Yeah, yeah, it's Sam. Hey look, I need a favor." He looked over at me and covered the mouthpiece with his thumb. "What's that number, Mitch?"

I read off the number the text had been sent from. Sam repeated it into his phone.

"Sure thing, Mac. As soon as you can. If it's tomorrow, then it's tomorrow. I'll be around."

"Who was that?" I asked after he ended the call.

"You aren't the only one with contacts, man."

"Yeah, I get that. Now who was it?"

"Old friend of mine. Works for the NSA."

"Wait a minute. What old friends do you have that I don't know?"

"We weren't always together. I know more people than you think I do."

"You think he can do something with a fake phone number?"

Sam shrugged. "Hell if I know. But if anyone can, it's Mac."

Five minutes later we pulled up to a small house on the outskirts of the city. I tried not to think of Cassie, but that was impossible. If I wasn't talking about something else, she was on my mind. What was she doing at that moment? Was Novak always there with her, or did she have respite from him? Eventually, my mind always drifted to the place I didn't want it to go. Images of Novak finishing what he started years ago played on the big screen in my brain.

The porch light flickered on. The front door swung open and a balding man with a pot belly and skinny legs covered partly by jean shorts stepped out. Sartini had retired five years earlier at the age of sixty. They'd forced him out. If it had been up to him, he would've stayed on the job forever. He had no wife or kids, no relatives, and only a few friends. Truth be told, I was surprised he hadn't succumbed to a heart attack or some other fatal ailment by this point. He had nothing to keep him going.

I waved as I started up the walkway to the house. "How's it going, Sartini?"

He shrugged and shook his hands in front of his distended stomach. "Can't complain too much."

We followed him inside. There were stacks of boxes lining both walls of the already too narrow hallway. The boxes scraped the ceiling in some spots and were covered in dust. I glanced into the first room we passed. Had to be a dozen black trash bags in the middle. Newspapers were piled along the back wall.

"You feeling all right, Sartini?" I asked.

"Sure, why not?" he said.

"Just making sure." I prepared myself for the next room. Who knew what waited for us there. Would we be sitting on trash while watching the tape?

Sartini slid a pocket door back into the wall and flipped a light switch. I was definitely surprised by what I saw. The light-colored carpet was pristine. The walls were white and bare. A long L-shaped desk took over two walls at one end. The surface was empty. A couch wrapped in plastic was positioned at the other end of the room.

"It's my sanctuary," he said. "Could care less about the rest of the house. This is where I spend my time."

"Fair enough. We're not judging," Sam said. "I see you still got the gear."

Next to the desk was Sartini's setup, an advanced tape player that digitized the feed and connected to his desktop computer.

"I've upgraded a few things since I last saw you guys."

Sartini had lent his experience to us a few times since leaving the department. He was better than anyone they had tried to replace him with. The last case he helped on was about a rich woman killed by her pool boy and the maid. Sartini's work on the security footage nailed the case shut.

"Probably not much need for this these days, huh?" Sam said.

"More than you might think," Sartini said. "I get a call every week or two. I'm the lead expert for some of the local robbery detectives. The old school cops, too. A lot of FBI work lately."

"Anything we might've heard about?" Sam asked.

"Probably." Sartini eased into his Herman Miller chair. At a thousand bucks on a cop's pension, he must get quite a bit of use out of it to justify the price tag. "So, what do you have for me?"

I handed the tape over to him. "Pretty bad feed of a gas station and convenience store. We got a potential suspect and a license plate. Both are grainy. License plate is worse than the face."

"Different feeds?" He wheeled over to the tape player. He stopped short of inserting it. "You got a copy of this?"

"That's the only one," I said.

He thought for a moment. "I can duplicate it real quick."

I shrugged. "Can't you just make a digital copy?"

"Might not stand up if I do. All depends on where it's going to be tried."

There would be no trial. I had no intentions of letting Novak live after we caught up to him.

"I think it'll be all right," I said. "That feed's in such bad shape, it won't hold up. The work you're going to do is what'll make the case."

"I get paid either way," he said.

"Paid?" Sam laughed. "I got a case of Pabst with your name all over it."

"That'll work. Just make sure you have a few with me." Sartini slid the tape into the machine, pressed a couple buttons, then wheeled back over to his command station. He opened up three different programs, one of which looked like something an audio producer might use to mix tracks. A few moments later the feed took over one of his twenty-seven-inch monitors.

"Shit, Mitch," Sam said. "This is bad."

"Don't I know it," I said.

"Got a time stamp?" Sartini asked. After I told him the exact moment the van arrived, he forwarded to it. "What's the first thing I'm looking for?"

I pointed at the store feed. "When he's in there, right before he leaves."

He sped the tape up and froze it at a spot where Novak's face was completely visible. "All right, give me a moment."

And a moment was all it took for the magic to begin. Keystroke by keystroke, the image became more enhanced. Once Novak's mug was fully realized, Sartini pushed back from the desk.

"What is it?" I said.

Sartini looked up at me, the last bit of color draining from his pale face. "I know that son of a bitch."

CHAPTER FIFTY-ONE

The figure hovering over Cassie and blocking out the dim light was one she had seen numerous times. The black shadow was a harbinger of sorts. The message was always the same. Someone was about to die. Of course, the shadow wouldn't tell her who. It could be anyone she had been in contact with. Someone she'd passed on the street. A tourist from Moscow sitting in one of the squares while Cassie walked by could have left a minor psychic imprint on her and now Cassie was being warned of their demise.

But maybe this time the harbinger was there to inform her that her own passing would be happening soon. Considering the events that had transpired earlier, she knew her chances of being freed were less than zero.

"Hello, Detective."

Novak's words played over and over as though they were stuck on repeat. The figure in the doorway had seemed familiar. Though that was likely the drugs thinking for her. She couldn't discern a single feature other than the height. And even that memory couldn't be trusted. Space and time had been distorted in a major way since Novak had come back into her life.

Cassie moved to get up but found her arms and legs were bound to the bedposts. What had those bastards done while she was knocked out?

She took a deep breath, closed her eyes, and scanned her body for pain or signs that she had been violated. Her legs and arms burned, perhaps from thrashing against the restraints. Did she lose consciousness when things went black? Or did the drug only affect her memory? It was reasonable to assume Novak injected her with something which turned her into the walking dead, able to perform acts without any idea she was doing them.

Two people now knew her location. Judging by Novak's greeting to the other man, she assumed he was a cop. Both men had plenty of motive to keep Cassie confined, or push for her outright demise. Novak surely had no intention of going back to jail. And prison was probably a place the detective had no desire to ever reside.

Chills sliced through her body. She knew every detective from Savannah to Charleston, South Carolina. She'd worked with them all. And several others around the country. Chances were this was someone she knew. How close was she to the man?

Her thoughts centered on the last two men she had been in contact with. Pennington and Cervantes had worked with her more than anyone in the area. They'd been with her from the beginning as the detectives who'd put Novak away. No way one of them could be mixed up in this.

She focused her attention on the fleeting memories in the moments before the drugs took her out. Novak's final words repeated again. The detective stood in the doorway. She stared at the now closed door, imagining the guy there.

The figure hovering over her faded a little, allowing some of the light to shine through.

"Why don't you be useful for once?" Cassie chastised the spirit. "Help me figure out who was down here."

The shadow disappeared.

"Must be a man," she muttered. "Always disappearing when I need them most."

Her thoughts turned to Mitch. He was out there, somewhere, doing what he could to find her. He was as relentless as a pit bull and wouldn't give up on her. Even if it were only her remains that could be recovered, Mitch would be the one to do it.

"Can you hear me?" she said softly. "Mitch, I'm trying to let you know where I am."

Chances are it wouldn't work. The dead were so much easier to work with. The living had too much going on around them to tune into the frequencies the majority of the universe communicated on. But she had to keep trying. Perhaps she could reach him in a moment of downtime, when his thoughts weren't tied up with what was happening to her, to his daughter, and wondering where his son and estranged wife were.

A fire burned and welled up inside of Cassie. She had unfinished business. She had to help Mitch find Robbie. The process had already begun. It was a matter of finding the right helper at this point. The call had gone out. The helper would respond. Eventually, at least.

"I have to survive," she whispered.

Cassie silenced the chatter in her mind and went to work freeing herself. The bedposts weren't the strongest thing in the room. Not by a mile. She tugged with her left arm, then her right. The left corner was loosest. She drew herself as close as she could, fighting against the rope burning into her right wrist as she stretched it as far as it would go. Rhythmically, she pulled her left wrist down to her stomach, then out as far as it would go. She repeated it over and over, loosening the bed post further.

Ten minutes later, it broke free.

CHAPTER FIFTY-TWO

Sam and I stared open-mouthed at Sartini. What was he talking about, he knew the guy? The man pointed at the frozen image of Novak's face.

"You guys don't recognize him?" Sartini said.

I leaned in closer, sliding my hand along the cool desktop. "Who do you think that is?"

Sam straightened up and folded his arms over his chest. The look on his face told me he was searching his mind for something long forgotten.

Sartini puffed out a long breath, flapping his lips. "Guess this goes back more than fifteen years now."

Novak was older than he looked. The guy had a boyishness about him. Still, fifteen years would put him at about twenty-five or so. And some five years or so before his attack on Cassie.

"What's his name?" Sam asked.

Sartini leaned back in his thousand-dollar chair, tipping his head over the backrest. He stared up at the plaster-swirled ceiling. "O'Connor, I think."

"O'Connor?" I said. "What was—"

"No, that's not it." Sartini did a one-eighty and hopped up from his chair. There was no old-man moan or pushing off of the arms to get there. He just hopped up like he was twenty years younger. "O'Connell. Mark O'Connell. You guys were a couple of rookies back then, I guess."

"I was still in the Army," Sam said. "Mitch had around five years in at that point."

Sartini offered a contemplative nod, though it didn't seem he cared about the information. "O'Connell was under investigation for a string of incidents surrounding teenage girls. Lots of coincidences, like he'd be linked to an area, and someone would go missing at the same time he was there. We could never get anything to stick, though."

"How long was he being watched?" I asked.

"Eighteen months?" Sartini made for the door. "Wait here."

"You ever hear anything about this?" Sam said after Sartini left the room.

I shook my head. "I've heard a lot over the years. Back in those days, I focused on my job mostly. I didn't think about all that was going on outside of that. If I wasn't directly involved, there was little chance I paid attention. It was the only way to stay sane."

"I hear you," Sam said. "I'd go crazy if I tried to follow every evil deed that happened around here."

Sartini re-entered the room carrying a white and blue banker's box. He set the heavy-duty cardboard box on the desk and lifted the lid. There were a dozen or so red folders inside. He rifled through them and pulled out a stack.

Sam shot me a grim look. They were murder investigations. Sartini must have kept copies over the years of the various cases he had worked or helped out on.

"Each one of these," he said, "we had O'Connell pegged as a suspect."

"And with all of those nothing ever stuck?" Sam leaned over the stack, blocking the overhead light.

"We were cinching the noose. Almost had it tight enough he'd hang. And then Stacy Darlington happened."

A memory rammed through my mind like a falling boulder. "Now that I remember."

"It was a big deal." Sartini held out the file.

Sam cocked his head. He had never heard of this.

"Yeah it was," I said. "Her father was running for governor at the time, right? Ended up becoming a senator."

Sartini snapped and pointed at me. "Correct. The spotlight was huge on this one."

"So, what happened?" Sam was fidgeting with a pencil, spinning it one second, drumming it on the desk the next.

"She vanished." Sartini looked apologetic. "She was inside a clothing store. The last image recorded of her showed her taking a pile of clothes toward the dressing room. And a second later, we get the guy. Him." He aimed a stubby finger at the image of Novak on the monitor. "O'Connell."

"She was never found," I said.

"And he was never caught. They both disappeared that day. And not too long afterward, there was a fire in the storehouse where O'Connell's file was. All the physical evidence disappeared right there. Not as widely known is his prints were lost from the database, too." He limped over to the bar and pulled down a handle of Maker's and three glasses. "Ain't got no ice, so you'll have to shoot it straight."

That was it. No asking. And at that moment I was fine with it. Processing the reality of how this had all played out was messing with my mind. Cassie had not once, but twice now, been accosted by Novak because people couldn't do their damn jobs. They had this guy. Knew he was guilty. And he slipped away.

I watched Sartini pour the drinks. It was hard for me not to put the blame on him, but doing so would get us nowhere.

He limped back over, doled out the drinks and sat back down in his chair.

"Your injury," I said. "You got it on this case, didn't you?"

Sartini stared into his glass and nodded. After a hefty swig of whisky, he looked up at us.

"Here's the deal," I said. "This guy you know as O'Connell, we know him as Novak. He assaulted a young woman in a Savannah graveyard ten years ago. Made the mistake of leaving her for dead when she wasn't. Because of her, they were able to bring him in and he confessed to six more murders."

"How?" Sartini asked. "This guy was impossible to take down."

"He gave up the details to save his life. They were threatening the death penalty. It was a matter of time, though. The crime scenes indicated he'd started to get sloppy."

"Like most serial killers do," Sartini said.

"Right."

Sartini set his drink down and interlaced his fingers behind his head. He was focused on the image of Novak. "And the son of a bitch is free again. Where?"

"Savannah, Georgia." I leaned back and looked Sartini in the eye. "Things didn't go right all those years ago and more people died. A few weeks back, things didn't go right, and Novak escaped prison. Now he's holding someone prisoner who is very dear to me. I need you to do your best work yet and get me the license plate of that van."

Sartini emptied the contents of his glass into his mouth, bit down, then blew ninety-proof air out. This was what we'd come for. He'd cleaned up the shot of Novak. Now it was time for the big reveal. The pay off. The license plate.

Frame by frame the video played. I tried to tell him that it was still a few minutes away. Sartini didn't care. He said haste might've contributed to missing a vital clue years ago. He wouldn't make the same mistake twice. I was relieved to see he was taking this so hard. We all make mistakes in this line of work. Over so many years, it's bound to happen. Any chance at redemption was welcomed.

"She's in the van, isn't she," he said.

"Yup," I said.

"When did you get the tape?"

"About two hours after they'd been there."

He shook his head. "Can't imagine how you felt, being so close behind. This was in Savannah?"

"About thirty miles away. You familiar with the area?"

"We used to vacation down there. Was years ago, though. Those memories probably aren't much help now."

"He had the van parked in the woods nearby. Used her car to get there. We assume he drugged or beat her, threw her in the van, then left. He'd made the mistake of not gassing up ahead of time, so he stopped at the first place they came across."

Sartini looked up at the wall. "Don't think he might've known the clerk?"

"Anything's possible, I guess. But you saw the tape. Wasn't much interaction between them."

"Wouldn't be if the guy knew what was going on."

"That's an interesting angle," Sam said. "We should follow up on it."

"One of the detectives down there said he knew the clerk was into some things and mentioned he might go rattle his cage to see if he'd make a mistake."

"That's a good move." Sartini set his attention back on the tape. We had reached the point where the van had begun moving.

"And we're off," Sam said.

The license plate came into view. Sartini let the tape run one frame at a time until it was out of sight. Then he ran through it backward and forward again. He was looking for the best shot, the one he deemed most likely to produce a crisp view on cleanup.

He selected his frame, dragged the mouse around to create a square around the van, then removed it from the program. He pasted the picture into another program, blew it up, and began enhancing the pixels. Every so often he'd return the image to its regular size.

"Wait," Sam said. "Leave it there for a moment."

Sartini looked up at him. "What?"

Sam leaned in. A wave of bourbon blew past me. He pointed at the single window on the back door of the van. "You see that?"

Now I leaned in. The three of us were ear to ear staring at a faint outline in a tinted window.

"That's Cassie." Sam glanced over at me, a relieved smile on his face. "She's still alive."

"Well, she was earlier," I said.

"Think about it, Mitch. If the plan was to kill her, he'd have done it in the woods and thrown the body in the van to get rid of it elsewhere. He wouldn't run the risk of her lashing out or breaking free unless he wanted her to arrive alive."

I didn't share his enthusiasm, but it was a fair point.

"The license plate is still shit," Sartini said.

While the van had come into clear focus, the sequence of numbers and letters on the plate were blurry and pixelated.

"Can you get it any clearer?" I asked.

Sartini waved me off. He put the photo through the process again. We all held our breath as he started the final rendering and then shrunk the screen.

The air left the room. Out of seven characters, only the first and fifth were remotely discernible.

CHAPTER FIFTY-THREE

We moved the car to the end of Sartini's street. Sam got out and I sat in silence. A light breeze blew in through the open windows, filling the car with the scents of early fall. Soon enough the ground would be littered with dead leaves and the smell of smoke would linger throughout the day. But for now, it was still warm out.

What was it like where Cassie was? Was she near the city or the coast? Or had they pressed west? Maybe Novak had travelled into South Carolina. Was it possible he'd come back here?

I doubted the last option right away. He hadn't been in this area in fifteen years. Things had changed. Any support network he had back then had most likely been put through the ringer by the detectives working the case. If Novak showed up, he'd hang, and he knew it.

The murders had occurred in Savannah. Several of his previous murders had taken place in and around Savannah. He'd abducted Cassie in Savannah. Call it intuition, gut instinct, or simply looking at and digesting the obvious facts, but I knew he was somewhere near Savannah.

Sartini said he'd continue to work on the license plate. He could try other still frames, and even send it off to the one guy who was better than him. Mostly because the other guy had the best equipment, and it wasn't worth Sartini upgrading, because according to him, he had one foot, both nuts, and an ass cheek in the grave already. I didn't want to know what all that meant, so I simply gave him my blessing to do anything and everything in his power to decipher that license plate. It was all we had.

Sam's cell phone screen streaked past the open window as he shoved it in his pocket. I'd caught bits and pieces of his conversation with his NSA contact, but had been too far into my own head to pay much attention. He dropped into the driver's seat. The car dipped noticeably to his side.

"Anything?" I asked.

"Still working on it. They're one hundred percent certain the call originated from the Savannah area. Now they're trying to trace it to the device it originated from. Since it's a spoof number, it could've been done on a computer or another cell phone."

"It's a start," I said. "That's better than what we had before."

"Don't let the license plate thing get you down. We're gonna figure this out and get her back."

"We?"

He nodded. "I'm coming down to help you."

"Pennington and Cervantes are gonna love that."

"Screw them. Cassie's my friend, too. Yeah, I know she weirds me out sometimes, but the lady has grown on me. Any extra help should be welcome as far as I'm concerned."

I stared out the window at a couple jogging toward us. The guy spotted us and placed himself between the car and his wife. He stared us down as they trotted past.

"We better get out of here," Sam said. "That guy's a threat to call the cops."

He navigated back to the highway. I went back and forth on whether it would be a good idea for Sam to come down. I know I'd asked him earlier, but I hadn't thought it through then. The situation evolved by the minute. Would he help or hamper? I considered several of the cases we had worked, and one thing stood out. I probably wouldn't have solved seventy-five percent of them if he hadn't been my partner.

"All right, maybe it is a good idea to have you down there with me."

"I knew you'd see it my way." Sam hugged the centerline tight on a sharp curve.

"But we need to be on separate flights. Someone's gonna be watching out for me. I don't want you mixed up in it if they try to take me down."

"All the more reason for us to get on the flight together."

I raised my hand, but Sam shut me down quick.

"Mitch, listen. They know you. What makes you think they know about me?"

"Shouldn't take too much Googling to figure out we work together. All the spotter needs is a picture of you and you're done, too."

"Then they'll see me anyway." He turned into a Hardee's parking lot. It was the only fast food I could stand. "Mitch, we're taking the same flight. You'll do everything fifty feet ahead of me. Once they spot you, they'll stop looking elsewhere."

I conceded the point to him. We weren't talking about a trained Special Forces guy on lookout. Whoever would be waiting would be antsy. "That'll work, I suppose. Unless they're just watching the manifests."

Sam shrugged. "I got ways around that."

"Mr. NSA?"

"Miss." He winked. The water was becoming less murky.

"So how long's this been going on?" I asked.

Sam raised an eyebrow and changed his tone. "Hey, why don't we stop by your mom's place and surprise Ella?"

"Changing the subject?"

"It's only about ten minutes away." He picked up his phone and swiped away the lock screen. "I'll give her a call so she's got the coffee ready when we get there."

"All right, all right," I said. "I'll stop talking about Miss NSA if you put that phone down. You know how much trouble I'll be in if they find out I've been in town all day?"

"Who'll give it to you worse?"

"Ella, no doubt." At one time I would've said Momma, but the little girl had grown into her own recently and had a forked tongue, just like her grandmother.

"Wanna crash at my place?"

Sam's house was closer than mine. But something was tugging at me. Pulling me back to Savannah.

"Let's get to the airport and redeye our way down."

Sam sighed while rubbing his temples. "Tomorrow's gonna be a long day."

"I don't doubt that."

Neither of us knew how right we were.

CHAPTER FIFTY-FOUR

My rental car sat in the middle of the parking lot. I could see it underneath the bright lights from inside the airport. And so could anyone else. Had Pennington and Cervantes put eyes on it, watching since I left? I had no doubt they knew I was back. I half-wished one of them would pull up so I could give them the good, the bad, and the interesting news I'd learned back home.

But that would take time I didn't necessarily have.

Sam's flight landed about an hour ahead of mine. In the end, we decided it was best he go first so he could act as lookout for me. I texted him the moment the wheels hit the ground for an update. Since then he'd messaged back every three minutes. Same text every time.

No activity.

Maybe Pennington and Cervantes didn't know I was back. Hell, what if they had made progress with the investigation and had Novak in custody? The thought tugged at the strings of my emotions, and I nearly dialed Pennington's number. That would lead to questions from them. I wasn't ready for that. Plus, it was still early.

I spotted Sam standing outside the terminal, trying to blend in with the arriving tourists and business people catching their early flights. Sam fit in with neither group. The hard look on his face told anyone who eyed him that they'd be better off picking a fight with a crocodile. At least then their punishment would be quick.

I stepped outside into the thick air and walked right past Sam. He took off about the same time, heading straight across the road. A few minutes later I picked him up on the other side of the lot at the exit, beyond the reach of most security cameras.

"Good flight?" he asked.

I stirred what was left of my coffee with the sludge at the bottom of the cup and finished it off. "Nothing special. Managed to sleep for a bit."

"Not me, man," he said. "Whole time I was thinking about Cassie. Almost felt like she was talking to me. Know what I mean?"

I most certainly did. "That's happened to me a few times, too. It's like she's reaching out and playing inside my mind. I wonder, is it really happening, or is it just stress catching up to me?"

"Felt pretty damn real to me."

I eyed him as I merged onto the highway. "What'd you see?"

"See?" He tipped his head back against the headrest. "Don't know if it was as much seeing as feeling restricted both physically and mentally. My limbs tied down. My mind overwhelmed. I've told you about how those bastards waterboarded me when I was captured in Afghanistan. I felt like that again. And then, I was free."

Did it mean she'd found freedom in passing to the next life? Were we too late? Did we ever have a chance?

"I can see those wheels turning, Mitch." Sam placed his hand on the dash. "Don't read too much into it. I was somewhere between sleep and meditation when it happened. Probably just my imagination."

"I've had it happ—"

"Stop right there. Look, don't you think if she was dead, she'd find a way to lead us to her body? I mean, if all this shit that's happened with her is real and we aren't just mass-hallucinating every time she tips us off on a case."

I might have settled for that at the moment. "Maybe she did and you can't remember. Hey, we'll get you one of those regression things. Get some hypnotist to pull the memory out of you."

"I'm afraid of what else they might dig up."

"Can't be any worse than all the other shit I know about you."

Sam laughed and turned toward the window, leading to the death of the conversation. For the next several minutes we were quiet with our thoughts as I drove to the crash site. I'd only been there and back. The ride out was a blur, but coming home I'd managed to memorize the route.

There was no sign from the road that anything had happened in the woods. They didn't want anyone stopping and performing their own investigation. I drove a few hundred yards past the billboard and pulled over. We sat there for a few minutes with the windows rolled down, watching to see how much traffic drove by. There was none. By the time we exited, Sam had a slick layer of sweat on his forehead.

"This isn't going to bode well for me." He unbuttoned his pullover and spread the collar as wide as it'd go.

"It gets plenty hot and humid back home," I said.

"Not like this. Not this time of the year."

I glanced up at thick gray clouds gathering overhead. "We might want to hurry this up."

He pointed at the billboard. "The hell is holding that cow up?"

"More of a mystery than half the cases we worked."

We followed the trail through the woods until we reached the clearing.

"That's where the accident happened." I pointed at a section along the wood's edge where a small tree was bent over, and the grass had been crushed after having a car sit on it for a couple of days.

"It was Cassie's car?" Sam said.

"Yeah, and I know she was in it."

"How's that?"

"Found a bracelet inside."

"She could have left it in there anytime."

"She had it on the night before." I stopped and waited for him to turn back toward me. "And I mean late the night before."

Sam wagged his index finger in front of me. "You and Cassie?"

I shrugged. "Something like that. Don't want to make too much of it. The detectives don't know the details."

He nodded silently before turning back to the accident scene. I hung back while he walked the perimeter. It was best to let him form his own opinions and see things through impartial eyes. Maybe he'd spot something none of us had. Sam spent ten minutes walking from spot to spot, kneeling, spreading the grass and looking at the dirt. In the end he found nothing substantial.

"What happened after the crash?" he asked.

I led him into the woods. Yellow crime scene tape wrapped around several trees fenced the area in. "Maybe they're still working it?"

Sam stood at the edge with his hands on his hips, staring out over the dried plaster-covered tire tracks. It appeared the forensics team had found footprints as well. He threw one leg then the other over the tape and walked through the scene, stopping a few times but quickly moving on. He exited on the opposite side and walked out of view.

A few minutes later, Sam called out. "Hey, Mitch. Come check this out."

I didn't make it five steps before I heard a crack and the lights went out.

CHAPTER FIFTY-FIVE

He'd been told to stay quiet and remain out of sight. But it was just too damn hard to do. For Christ's sake, he had needs.

For chrissakes! For chrissakes! For chrissakes!

Keeping the women there, alive, hurt so badly. It felt like he'd been kicked in the balls and his nuts hadn't dropped back out of his stomach. Novak never liked to keep them around for longer than it took for him to satisfy his desires. Sometimes that only took a day. Other times it lasted for weeks. Now he had two locked up. Used to think that was one too many. But he had begun to realize the benefits. Maybe his partner wasn't so wrong. In some ways, at least. Sure, Alice was easy to deal with. But he needed the magic of pharmaceuticals in order to subdue Cassie. And that just wasn't as much fun. He never enjoyed fucking the dead ones, and it felt too much like that with her.

Only warmer.

The bus ran on a twenty-minute schedule and would continue to do so for another couple of hours. He'd watched this spot before.

It was sketchy, for sure. The inhabitants of this side of town weren't always kind to him, though he'd rarely dabbled in Hispanic or African American women. Not since he'd relocated. They really had no reason to treat him like a jerk here.

"Don't screw around with any more women until we're out of this mess."

His partner was so condescending toward him. Novak had explained his needs, and that was the asshole's response. Novak realized he had little choice in the matter, though. The other guy could put a bullet in Novak's skull, and then the man would be a hero. The world wouldn't know his dirty secrets. And if Novak tried to make a pre-emptive strike against him, well, let's just say that would be suicide.

That might be nice, too.

His thoughts bounced from Alice to Cassie to the thought of taking his life, or perhaps that of his partner. The squealing brakes of the bus pulling up—*a new opportunity to make a friend!*—distracted him from his wandering brain.

The first few women who got off simply would not do. Too old. Too tall. Novak spat across the walkway into the hedges. A man exited, followed by his two sons.

"Keep moving," Novak whispered. "Keep moving."

And then he saw her. My, she was fine. Not too tall, and probably not all that strong. Perfect. He didn't want to deal with another fighter. Someone he could subdue rather easily would be better for what he had in mind.

The woman looked back and waved and smiled at the bus driver. They were on a first name basis. How cute. She was light-skinned with long, straight hair that was black at the roots and red interspersed throughout. Was it a weave? He chuckled to himself. He knew little about such matters. He didn't care, anyway. Her shorts rode into her ass crack and her shirt was cut so that it just covered her breasts. She'd practically invited him over to her place.

Novak shoved his hands into his pockets, tucked his chin to his chest, and began following her. Flecks of stone trapped in the sidewalk cement shone in the sunlight. He traced a path from one to the other. His fist wrapped around the spring-loaded batons he carried. One in each pocket. If anyone got near him, they'd find their skull bashed in faster than they could say *hey what are you doing with those batons.*

With every store and bar the woman approached, Novak felt a tremble of excitement. It would be here, there, the next one. One of them? He wanted an opportunity to talk to her. Try to win her over. It was so much fun that way, you know, when they believed him. Trusted him. Invited him in to play.

But she kept walking, shaking her round ass, the shorts digging in further. She pulled out her cell phone and stared down at it. She better put it away before stepping onto the street, lest a driver might take care of her before Novak could.

A group of guys sitting on a stoop spoke rudely to her. Novak squeezed the baton grips. *Talk to me, cocksuckers.* He averted his eyes after she passed. Before they took notice of him. There were five of them and one of him. The batons only gave him the edge on the first one or two. After that, they could overtake him and then it would be his skull in danger.

The guys said something to him as well, but it went in as noise and was drowned out by the chaos within. He heard their laughter. Chumps. They were good for nothing except sitting on those steps harassing women and trying to intimidate white guys like Novak.

The woman looked back. Her eyes locked on Novak's. His chest tightened in on his heart. The moment was fleeting and gone before he knew it. She'd paid him no attention. She'd regret that. Oh, how she would regret that.

Shit.

What was she doing?

She stopped to talk to another woman. This one was nowhere near good enough for Novak. She wouldn't even do for target practice. Was she testing him? Seeing if he was following her? A quick glance around was enough to realize that he was the least threatening thing on the block. If you went by looks, at least.

He couldn't stop, too. That'd be so obvious. She'd know he was following her. Then the game would have to begin anew. He'd have to find another as perfect as her. And that was no easy feat on this side of town. He spat into a trashcan and kept moving, slowing ever so slightly as he passed by. She smelled of roses and cinnamon. How would she taste?

Ah, there it was. Cover. He ducked into the vinyl shop and greeted the old guy with the gray afro behind the counter with a hello. The guy lifted his chin an inch before going back to his MacBook.

Crazy ass cracker. That's what he's thinking. I'd love to show him how crazy I can be with this baton right here.

"Help you find anything in particular?"

The address of that sweet Black ass outside your store?

"Sir?"

That's right. You better call me sir, bitch.

"No, thank you, I'm just browsing for a present for my mom." Novak lifted his eyes, smiled at the guy, then went back to rifling through a stack of worn album covers while keeping the street in his view.

"All right. Just give me a shout you need anything in particular."

Novak's mind eased a bit. Something about the guy's baritone voice. The maniacal thoughts dissipated and he let go of his baton. For the first time since entering the neighborhood, he removed both hands from his pockets.

A record caught his eye. The Supremes. One of his mother's favorites. The only one he recalled, as a matter of fact. She'd left him early in life. Dad told him she'd run off. But he found out the son of a bitch had killed her after she had found out he'd spent their rent money on a couple of prostitutes. Not that mom had the best reputation, of course. That's why dad was never charged. Cops were happy to get rid of her and must've figured he'd take off sooner or later, too. But when a few more bodies of women similar to her turned up, they couldn't look the other way anymore.

The beauty outside walked past the store, glancing through the window, nodding at the old guy's afro. Her gaze never landed on Novak. Good or bad? He couldn't decide. He wanted her to want him. She would. She definitely would whether she wanted to or not.

He pulled out his wallet, dropped a twenty on the counter and left with Mom's favorite album. He thought so, at least. She was dead, so what did it matter?

Half a block separated him from his latest love. Too much distance. He picked up the pace and got within a hundred feet. Most of the row houses here had a street level apartment. The one she stopped in front of was no different. She disappeared behind the front stoop. By the time he reached where she had been, she was no longer underneath the stairs that led to the house above her little nook in the city. Novak ducked under and out of sight. He backed into the shadows and waited there for a moment.

The front door was solid. The windows were shored up with thick drapes and iron bars. He looked back through the thin slits between the stairs. No one was watching. Hell, there wasn't anyone around.

Are you smart enough to welcome me in?

He reached for the handle. Unlocked! It turned out she had spotted him and knew he was coming and she wanted him inside.

A cool blast of air rushed out. The place had that old musty smell a lot of ground level apartments in Savannah had. He'd adjust. It opened into a large room the width of the place. It was minimally furnished with two chairs and a television on one side, and a small dining table with two chairs on the other. Two chairs... a roommate? The floor was concrete finished smooth. A door protruded into the hallway past the main room. Light seeped out. There was the sound of running water and R&B music. Oh, how perfect. She was getting ready for him.

Novak reached into his pocket and pulled a baton out. With the flick of his wrist, he whipped it open and used it to push the door the rest of the way. The light came from over the shower. Her silhouette danced on the curtain. His mouth watered now.

He pulled the door shut, turning the handle so it wouldn't click, then leaned back against the wall.

His frustrations were about to be relieved.

CHAPTER FIFTY-SIX

I dropped to both knees and managed to get my left hand out to break my fall. A warm trickle ran down the back of my neck. Darkness narrowed my vision to the size of pins. I fought against passing out and collapsing to my chest. No good would come from me blacking out completely. It felt as though there were a stack of forty-five-pound weights on my back, pressing me closer and closer to the forest floor.

"Mitch!"

Sam's voice sounded like it was in an echo chamber. I knew my eyes were wide open, but I couldn't see a damn thing anywhere I looked. There were footsteps all around me. Instinct said to protect my head. But I couldn't find it.

"Dammit, I need a gun!"

The light pierced my skull like a long boring needle. It was too bright to see more than a foot in front of me.

"You all right, man?"

Pressure on my shoulder. A hand gripping me, pulling me up. I couldn't assist.

"He's gonna get away. Stay here and don't move."

Not a problem, Sam. Not a problem.

THE GROUND WAS soft in spots, which made it difficult for Sam Foster and his size fourteens to plow his way through the woods the way he wanted to. The asshole who had knocked Mitch over the head wasn't that bright, as demonstrated by the bright yellow shirt and matching shoes he wore. Had he just come from playing racquetball or something?

The guy had long since ditched his weapon. Sam spotted it, thought about taking it with him to do unto the guy as he had done unto Mitch. Worse, probably. Despite a little blood, Mitch looked okay. He had to shake off the blow. Rub some dirt on it. He'd likely refuse going to the hospital, but if he couldn't stand, he was no help to Sam and the effort to find Cassie.

Sam was gaining ground now. He reached out and grabbed hold of every tree he passed, propelling himself forward. The other guy seemed to be slowing down at the same time. The bright clothes must have been a fashion statement. An unwise one, at that.

Obstacles sprung up at every turn. Sam had no trouble avoiding them. Who knew his trail running hobby would pay off? People always asked why he bothered running at his size. Wasn't it counterproductive? Shouldn't he be in the gym, getting even bigger? Strength had served him well for many years. But now that he was getting older, he needed the extra endurance running provided him. Lord knows he did everything he could to hide his yoga habit.

The guy was almost within reach. His yellow shirt stood out like a single post-it on a black fridge. Sam lunged forward and slammed his hands down on the guy's shoulder. The man twisted in an attempt to shrug Sam off, but Sam grabbed hold and let his bodyweight drag the guy down.

"Get off me." The smaller guy kicked up a storm, managing to connect on a few blows to Sam's stomach and groin.

One he could prepare for. The other he had to clench his jaw and fight through.

You know, rub some dirt on it.

"Who the hell are you?" Sam maneuvered himself until he had the guy's legs locked up. Years of Brazilian Ju-Jitsu training paid off. As the guy squirmed, Sam gained control until he finally had him subdued.

The man mumbled a few words, but they were hardly discernible through Sam's thick forearm.

"You're lucky I don't snap your scrawny neck right here," Sam said. "You hear that, asshole?"

"Mmyhmm."

"That's what I thought." Sam eased up on the guy. Just enough to give him some wiggle room. "You move, squirm, fight against me and it'll be lights out. I won't need a damn club to do it, either."

The guy remained frozen as Sam worked his way to his feet. He lifted the guy off the ground and marched him forward while holding his arms high and tight behind his back. One move and Sam'd dislocate them at the elbow and then yank them out of his shoulder socket.

"That-a-boy. Nice and easy."

THE BLINDING PAIN subsided in a matter of seconds. It had been so intense that I fell again after Sam took off. I made it back to my knees, then wedging my fingers in bark grooves on a tree, got to my feet. It took a few seconds for the world to stop jerking around. The back of my head felt as though it had split in two. I felt around, expecting a large gash. Didn't feel that bad, though. I wiped the blood off on my pants leg and looked for any sign of Sam.

I hadn't seen which way he'd gone. With the way he blew out of there, he had to have a line on whoever attacked me. There was no screaming or shouting going on, so he either hadn't caught him yet, or he'd killed him. I'd put my money on the latter. People were surprised at how athletic Sam had remained over the years. Guys that tall with a thick muscular build tend to stiffen up as the years go by. I couldn't bring myself to tell them it was his yoga practice that kept him so nimble. Cops could be a brutal bunch.

It was unnaturally quiet in the woods. Perhaps the disturbance had sent the birds and squirrels fleeing. After all that had happened in the spot, who knew when they'd return?

I shook the cobwebs from my head and felt steady enough to move away from my support tree. The first few shaky steps made me think I'd made a mistake I might not recover from. But once I got the hang of it, it wasn't so bad. Look at me, Ma. I'm walking!

Sam's voice shook the silence. He was preaching, which meant he had someone in custody. My gut tightened at the thought of apprehending Novak right here, right now. Bastard had come back to the scene of the crime. Couldn't help himself. Didn't count on running into us, though. He got the best of me, no doubt. That only pissed Sam off even more. The poor son of a bitch didn't stand a chance.

"Hey, yo," I called out.

"Mitch?" Sam yelled back.

"Yeah, man. I'm here. On my feet again."

"All right. Just stay put till we get there." His voice trailed off as he gave his prisoner a few instructions.

I resisted the urge to sit down on the ground, knowing I might not get back up. I was out a few minutes ago. Odds were I had a concussion. Sam would insist I go to the doctor. Fat chance that was happening as long as I wasn't throwing up and passing out every few minutes. Besides, I'd been knocked out worse before. One day it would all catch up to me. This was not that day.

Sam emerged from the woods dragging a guy almost half his size dressed like half a banana. I couldn't believe this was the dude who almost brained me.

"What the hell are you doing out here?" I said.

The guy looked at the ground and spat a wad of bloody saliva between us.

"You know him?" Sam said. "It's not Novak, I know that."

"We couldn't be so lucky." I walked up to the guy, made him look me in the eye. "What the hell are you doing out here? You involved in this somehow? Speak up, boy."

He said nothing.

"Who is it, Mitch?" Sam asked.

"Seth. That hurricane night massacre, this poor excuse for a man is the boyfriend of the only survivor. He's withheld some info every time we've run into him, and here he is, popping up again."

CHAPTER FIFTY-SEVEN

"Who the hell is this?" Cervantes blocked the doorway with his thick frame, arms folded over his chest. He eyed Sam, looking like he wanted to spit on my partner's shoes.

"Sam Foster." Sam stuck out his hand. He didn't accompany the gesture with his trademark smile. Cervantes didn't accept the handshake. Still, Sam kept his hand out for a good fifteen seconds, making the moment that much more awkward. The two men engaged in a stare-off I was certain would end up in an MMA-style brawl. Would Sam's height-advantage give him the upper hand, or would Cervantes' stocky build prevail? I'd put my money on Sam.

"Mitch, glad to see you made it." Pennington tossed a casual glance at Sam as he walked toward us. "We think we got something we can use."

They'd sent a black and white and an ambulance to the woods. The officers took Seth back to the station. The ambulance drove me to the hospital to get checked out. There was no way out of it. Even if the paramedics had relented, Sam insisted I get checked out. I'd be of no use heavily concussed. Six stitches later they released me and we made our way over to the station.

Pennington and Cervantes went straight to work on Seth. They'd already pounded the guy on previous occasions, and knew his weaknesses. And now he'd assaulted an officer, albeit an out-of-state one, which gave them a huge bargaining chip.

"Come on, let's get a secure room." Pennington motioned us to follow. He glanced at Sam again. "Who's your friend?"

"My partner from back home. Sam Foster."

Pennington offered a quick nod-smile gesture in Sam's direction. "If you're half as good as Mitch, I think you'll be an asset here."

Cervantes muttered something under his breath as he shot his partner a look that said he questioned what the hell Pennington was thinking letting Sam join the conflicting team we'd created.

"Not now, Cerv," Pennington said. "You can address your concerns with me when we're alone. There's just too damn much to do right now."

We entered a small conference room that looked like the type of place they brought a family to give them bad news in the hospital. Maybe they did the same here. The light blue walls were accented with calming paintings done in pastels. A vase on the round table was filled with fake lilies. I wondered if it was a quiet room, or something. A place the cops here could go when things got to be too much for them.

Everyone took a seat and Pennington proceeded to tell us what had gone down with Seth.

"He was hiding near the house. Claims he was watching it, making sure no one came along and vandalized the place. Says that he was sure we missed something inside. Cerv pushed him on this, but Seth wouldn't give us a clue what it might be. Just a feeling."

They hadn't the time to leave the station, so the clue inside was probably nothing. Something had to have happened while Seth waited.

Pennington continued. "Seth noticed a van pull up sometime late afternoon. A man got out, went around the back of the house. Seth changed his vantage point, saw the man go inside. Seth gets into the back of the van and hides under one of those heavy moving blankets."

"Get the hell out of here," I said. "Seth did this?"

"Tougher than we thought," Cervantes said.

"Or stupider," I said. "So, what happened?"

"The man gets back in the van and drives off. Stops a few times. Opens the back after one stop and tossed some heavy bags inside. One landed on Seth, he had to keep from yelling out."

"What was in the bags?"

"I'm getting there," Pennington said. "After a while, the ride gets rough, like they're off road."

"Took him to the woods." Sam leaned over his forearms.

Pennington smiled and nodded. "You're quick."

"Well that explains why the asshole was out there today," I said. "But why'd he attack me?"

"He thought you had been following him and were going to arrest him," Cervantes said.

"I don't like the guy's meddling," I said. "He's always on the outer fringes of where the action is. Like he knows what's going to happen before anyone else."

"We've said the same thing," Pennington said. "But him being in the back of the van isn't all we got from him. Check this out."

Cervantes pulled five photos from his bag and placed them on the table, facing Sam and me. They were shots of a couple bags of dirt, some fertilizer, lye, and calcium nitrate.

My stomach tightened and I felt my head go light. "You think she's dead? All this was to bury her and get the body to decompose as quickly as possible?"

"We can't know that until we have the van," Cervantes said.

"We think there's an alternative here." Pennington seemed excited over the news. I sensed he cared about Cassie almost as much as I did. If he feared she was dead, his manner would be different.

"What's that?" Sam asked.

Pennington pointed to the fertilizer. "See that brand? It's a local store. I have a small plot next to my house. Grow my own vegetables. Quarter-acre farming... Something the wife and I like to do together. Anyway, that's the store where I shop."

"Local place," Sam said. "Probably know all the employees pretty well, huh?"

Pennington nodded. "Same ten people have worked there for all the years I've been going. I called over right before you guys got here and spoke with one of them. Then I emailed scans of the photos of what was found in the back of Novak's van, along with a picture of Novak."

"Success?" I asked.

"A few of them recognized him."

My pulse quickened in anticipation. "What'd they say?"

"We got them on a conference call," Pennington said. "Might've been better to go do it in person, but we felt waiting for you to get here and then heading over would waste an hour we might not be able to afford."

I'd had all the drama I could take for the day. I wanted him to get to the point, but he insisted on dragging this out. "So, what'd you find out?"

"No one person could give us all the details, but it seems Novak has a need to talk about himself. Maybe he's trying to get the women to loosen up around him so he can decide if they are worthy enough to be one of his victims."

"Why do you say that?" Sam asked.

"They knew the most details," Cervantes said. "The men at the store couldn't tell us much."

"That's right," Pennington said. "He'd revealed more to the women about himself and what he was doing with everything he bought."

Cervantes pulled a notebook and mechanical pencil from his bag. I spotted the Mont Blanc white star emblem on the cap from across the table. Four hundred bucks was some pretty serious coin for a cop to drop on a pencil.

"Here's what it all boils down to," Cervantes said. "Novak has a greenhouse or multiple greenhouses on a plot of land that he maintains somewhere between here and Charleston. Records search shows no indication that he's the owner of the property."

"You mean he's working it for someone?" Sam said.

"Might be squatting," Pennington said. "Or it might in fact be his land. But the public records search shows nothing in his name."

"What about Mark O'Connell?" I said.

Pennington shrugged. "I'm not familiar with that name."

"We learned that Novak has a history up in our area," Sam said. "The guy we used to clean up the gas station footage, he recognized Novak as O'Connell from a case he worked years ago."

Pennington straightened. "And he's sure it's Novak?"

"He pulled out the old file," Sam said. "We saw the photos from over a decade ago. Same guy. No doubt about it."

Pennington repeated Novak's alias as he rose and headed for the door. "I'll be back in a while. Cerv, fill them in on the plan."

Cervantes closed his notebook and leaned back in his chair, taking an exaggerated deep breath as he soaked in the new information. This could be it. The one piece of information they'd been waiting for. He exhaled toward the ceiling as his head tipped back.

"What's up, Cervantes?" I said. "What are you planning from here on out?"

"It's a long shot, at best," he said. "There's so much land to cover. A hundred miles in a straight line. Then you gotta figure forty miles east to west."

My ears and cheeks started to burn. "If we gotta get out there with bloodhounds to find her, then that's what we do. We owe that to Cassie."

Cervantes stared at the ceiling for a few moments before lowering his gaze to me. He held it there for several seconds. "Yeah, Mitch, we do."

"Great, glad you agree with me." I attempted to hold back the sarcasm from my tone. "So, what the hell are we gonna do about it?"

CHAPTER FIFTY-EIGHT

He'd left the woman unconscious on her bed. It was the damn picture of her with her twins. Twins! As in two babies born almost the same time. He never would have guessed it. And now the police would hear about what he'd done because he left this one alive.

Who cared if they knew? The area would now be off-limits. Hadn't it always been, though?

It was a stupid decision to cross into that section of town. Novak didn't belong there. If the desires boiled over again, Novak would take a drive up to Charleston, or head west to Augusta, and look for a tourist traveling alone. No one would miss her for a few days, at least. He might even decide to bring her home if she were nice enough. That's what he'd wanted with the fine ass he'd just left. After all, he'd left her alive.

That's not what he wanted to do though.

He could always get help bringing her to the greenhouse before someone found and untied her. No one would figure out how she'd gone missing. And Novak had the perfect cover. A cop who would lie for him. And everyone would believe that cop when he told them that he dropped the woman off in front of her apartment. What reason would they have to think a law enforcement official would lie to them?

The relationship with the officer had been forged some years ago, before Novak went away for what he had done to Cassie. The guy was a sadistic son of a bitch. Outside of a few incidents, which were swept under the rug, the cop could no longer satisfy his desires through legal means. Abducting and later killing a woman was out of the question, too. That's where Novak's services were valuable. He found that he enjoyed bringing them home, using them for his own needs, and holding them there while his partner and protector got himself off through some sort of sick role playing. Novak was rarely allowed to be around when his partner came over, though he'd relented on that since Novak came back.

And when the cop had no use for the women anymore, Novak disposed of them.

It was the cop who had arranged the escape from that hellhole prison. Novak still had no idea how the man had done it. He hadn't needed to know, either. All that mattered was he got out and had been returned to his land. He'd purchased it several years ago, under his old name. Mark O'Connell had died long ago. If the property had been worth something to anyone else, it would have been claimed years before Novak found it. But no one gave a shit about the land, Mark O'Connell, or Novak.

He was still surprised the cop had given up Cassie the way he did, not that his partner was happy about it. But he realized Cassie would discover or lead them to the evidence they needed to find Novak. And then the cop would be screwed. So, he sold her out.

For whatever reason, she'd been left solely to Novak to do with what he pleased. The woman fought back. Hard. So, he used the miracle of modern pharmacology to assist him with his needs.

Novak pulled the truck to the side of the road and cut the ignition. The wind whistled through the nearby trees. The temperature had dropped ten degrees in the past hour. Felt good sitting there with the windows down.

He pulled a cigarette from the glove box and lit it. Wasn't something he did often. In fact, he used to despise the habit. But you pick up some strange ones behind bars, and smoking had been his. He could go through two packs in a day if his brain was busy. After breaching the walls, he cut down to a few here and there. So much more to do on the outside.

He closed his eyes and leaned his head back on the seat. Images of his new plaything ran through his mind. My, how sweet she looked stepping out of that shower, dripping wet. All he had to do was hold a finger to his lips and she understood. Didn't even try to scream. One crack of the baton to her back stopped her from running. She led him to her bed, prepared for anything he had to offer.

And then he saw that God forsaken photo.

Novak leaned forward, took one last drag on his cigarette and flicked it through the open window. No one had driven by during his pit stop. It was safe to enter the trail. Novak turned the key in the ignition, threw it in reverse, and drove back about fifty feet to a forest service road entrance. The ruts were deep but hidden by overgrowth. They'd been used heavily at one time, but no one other than Novak and the cop travelled on them now.

The journey through the woods lasted seven minutes and ended at the rundown property he called home. The path he took through the field was well-defined after his month of tramping down the grass. It hadn't been hard to find it after he had returned.

The cop must have used the place frequently. Brought his whores out, perhaps? Did he use another partner during that time? At least the asshole kept the crops watered and fertilized.

Novak parked the truck under a rusted carport near the greenhouses. He grabbed his twelve-pack of Budweiser and headed out on foot to the east greenhouse. He spent twenty minutes working while nursing a lukewarm beer. He walked back to the end, paused in the doorway, closed his eyes, and listened. The wind whispered through the tall grass. An airplane droned past high overhead. He was alone on his land, at least above ground.

He hurried to the west greenhouse. His decision to leave the padlock off the door had left him uneasy. Anyone could enter. Anyone could snoop. Anyone could find the hidden exit.

Feeling along the exterior of the building, he knew his concerns were unwarranted. He always attached a thin string to the door and the structure, and found it in place. It wasn't as though the place were Fort Knox. Anyone could break in. And anyone who would go through the trouble to do so would also be more inclined to snoop around. And with their senses on high alert, they'd likely find what he wanted to hide.

Novak walked softly on the concrete pad, not that his footsteps would disturb anyone below. He didn't want to give his position away should someone lie in wait inside. Who? Didn't matter. A number of people would kill him on sight. *That might not be a bad thing, you monster.* He hushed the voice in his head. Damn thing showed up and offered its stupid opinions when it had no idea what really made Novak tick. Take earlier for instance. Gracious. He really needed the release that fine woman would have given him.

Again, he worked for twenty minutes, downing three more Budweisers during that time. The alcohol had started working its effects on him. Normally he wouldn't feel a thing after four drinks. But after the events of the morning, his brain was still abuzz with euphoria. The alcohol accentuated it.

He dug his fingers into the cool, moist dirt and left them there for seconds at a time, burrowing further and further down with each plunge. An earthworm surfaced and slid along his wrist. He had to wash her off of him. Couldn't let his friends below know that he'd almost been with that woman. He didn't want them to think he'd been unfaithful. Then they might want to leave.

Novak gathered his empties and crunched them down to hockey pucks. He placed them in the cardboard container and carried it into the tunnel. Dim lighting from his cell phone provided enough illumination for him to move through without counting his steps. He did it anyway. Habit. He enjoyed the cool air as he traversed the corridor. At the other end, Novak proceeded with caution. Anything could have happened while he was out. The cop could have invited friends over. Though unlikely, Novak had prepared himself for what he would do in that situation. Mass death was the only answer. And he was willing to turn his pistol on himself before allowing them to take him back to jail. Truth was, the cop would kill Novak before allowing him to be arrested. He knew too many secrets.

He paused at the end of the tunnel, next to the hidden entrance. One had to know exactly where to reach to open the door. He listened for a few moments before proceeding inside. Above ground again, he grabbed three cans from the box and tossed the rest in the fridge. Two were for him. One would be for a friend. Which friend depended on Cassie's mood.

Novak walked through the house, checking each room. Once, he'd found a homeless man who said he always stayed there when passing through. The guy got squirrelly when Novak asked if he'd ever told anyone about the place. He offered the man a bourbon, then bashed his head in with a baseball bat. Cleaning that up was a bitch. The cop had made him use bleach. Novak still gagged from the smell alone.

Satisfied that the house was empty, he descended to the basement and cracked a beer. He placed one on the table, and brought the other to Cassie's room. She didn't move when he opened the door. Her eyes fluttered when he cut on the overhead light. She turned her face away. She was still tied up, had been for a while now. If she accepted his offer of a drink, he'd free her.

"Cassie," he said. "I've got something for you."

She did not respond to him.

"Just say yes and I'll untie you. It's nothing nefarious, my dear. Quite the opposite." He chuckled. "It's a can of Bud. Would you like to have a drink with me?"

She kept looking away from him without speaking. Guess her mind was made up.

He backed out of the room, squashing the anger biting at him. She had been sleeping. And was probably pissed at him for keeping her restrained for so long. She'd get over it soon enough.

And there was still Alice.

He rapped on her door and opened it before Alice could answer. The woman sat on her bed and drew her knees to her chest at the sight of him. He lifted his can to his lips and took a sip. His other arm was behind his back. Her gaze shifted to it.

"I've got something for you," he said.

Her lips trembled.

"No, no, sweet Alice," he said. "Nothing like that. It's just a beer. See?"

As he brought his arm around, she flinched as though he were wielding a pistol or an axe.

"Care for a sip?" he said.

She nodded and held out her hand, which he graciously took in his own. Her breasts were exposed. He helped her up from bed and led her out of her room. She sat down at the table without further prodding. So accommodating, that Alice. The powder he'd slipped into both cans hit her first. Somewhere between the table and Cassie's room, he blacked out, too.

CHAPTER FIFTY-NINE

The helicopter hovered a thousand feet over the border between Georgia and South Carolina. The ground below looked like a painting of life a hundred-plus years ago. Quaint and free of the tragedies of modern day. They had their own problems back then, too. That was never lost on me. The scale was smaller to the average person, though. I could've lived with that.

Pennington insisted we start closer to Charleston and work our way back. Didn't make much sense to me. Everything centered around Savannah. Novak had to be close by.

Cervantes and Pennington left before six to drive up to Charleston where they would meet a liaison there who would fly them. Sam and I were assigned to the local department's bird.

We weren't supposed to stop, but Sam spotted two greenhouses on a large tract of land surrounded by woods.

"Probably not what we're looking for." Sam's voice sounded tinny in the earphones. "But worth checking out."

I leaned forward and touched the pilot's shoulder. "Can you get us down there?"

Thirty seconds later he clicked the radio hanging on his shoulder. "I called the location in. Waiting on verification of the property."

Sam leaned his forehead against his window, peering out over the lot below.

I didn't have the same view as him. "See anything?"

"A whole lotta nothing, man."

The helicopter dipped and rose and swayed a few feet. The whomp-whomp of the rotors pervaded the senses if you let it. It was warm in there and smelled like stale chips.

We lurched forward.

"Moving on," the pilot said.

"What's the deal?" I asked.

"Pennington said it's a known private residence with a registered business selling floral arrangements at flea markets and roadside stands. He'd actually been out there in the days before he was in homicide. Couple of kids came across it, thought someone was growing marijuana there. Turns out it was lilies."

"Doesn't sound like Novak," Sam said.

Indeed it didn't. The guy had an interesting psych evaluation. I guess all the crazies did. But nowhere had it been mentioned he was into selling flowers, let alone growing them. Then again, we weren't entirely sure what he was doing in his greenhouse.

As we raced north, I couldn't help but feel we were wasting a whole lot of time. There was too much ground to cover. How were four men in two helicopters searching an expanse of land larger than New Hampshire expected to find a couple of greenhouses holding a couple of women and who knew how many corpses?

They needed to arrange search teams. Bring in more helicopters. We had a lead, possibly a solid one, and the detectives were doing too little in my opinion. Maybe it wasn't their fault. Small-town politics, I supposed.

I stared out the window at the passing scenery. We came across a few more greenhouses, but quickly dismissed them from being top prospects. They were too obvious and visible. The place we were looking for would be away from civilization. Novak wouldn't feel safe hiding out in a neighborhood, let alone with a few captives.

As quickly as I thought it, I had to dismiss it. There had been many stories over the years of kidnapping victims found several years after they had gone missing. They'd been living on busy streets, in apartment buildings, row homes, surrounded by people. Deep cover wasn't required for concealment. You had to be smart. Careful.

Was Novak either of those anymore? He had to be watching his back every step he took. One wrong move, he was either going back to prison, or taking a dirt nap. Did he even care? I doubted he did. A man concerned with his life would not have abducted Cassie in the middle of the day. He broke free from his confinement with the realization that everything could slip away at any time. That made for an even more dangerous psychopath.

The pilot changed his heading to the northwest. Bright sunlight made viewing anything out of my window impossible. It also radiated heat. I pulled my headphones off and wiped my damp ears.

Sam gave me a curious nod. I shrugged and pointed him back toward his window. Couldn't have him missing that major clue we were bound to find up here.

I turned my thoughts to Cassie and tried to reach out to her. Just to let her know I was still looking and I wouldn't stop until she was safe again. I had no way of knowing if it worked. She even joked herself she was more comfortable speaking with the dead than the living. And that was after we'd spent a couple of hours in bed together.

Sam started pointing out his window, tapping it with his thick fingertip. I put my headphones back on to see what was going on.

"That looks like a promising spot," he said.

I unbuckled my seatbelt and leaned over to get a look. The pilot angled the helicopter. An unkempt circular lot surrounded by pine forest held what we were looking for. Two ragged-looking greenhouses stood in the middle about fifty feet apart. Looked like a small garage with a rusted roof was near one of them. About a quarter-mile away I spotted another clearing with an old beat-up house. Best guess says it had been abandoned decades ago.

"You might be right." I leaned forward next to the pilot. "Can you get us down there?"

"I tried radioing to Pennington," he said. "Got no answer. Let's circle for a few and I'll try him again."

"We need to move away," I said. "Gonna spook whoever's down there if we hang out too long. Find a spot to land and shut this thing off."

The pilot stared at me for a long fifteen seconds. It seemed he couldn't figure out what to make of me. "All right. But any grief over this goes on you."

I gave him a broad smile. "Wouldn't have it any other way."

He found a level patch of dirt a little ways to the north to set the helicopter down. We hopped out onto solid ground. My ears rung long after the whine of the turbine had dissipated. The smell of fuel clung to my nose and throat.

"I'll keep trying to reach the other helicopter," the pilot said. "Get them to reroute out here. In the meantime, take this."

I grabbed the radio from his outstretched hand.

"Keep it on channel nine and listen out for me. If you need backup, let me know."

"That's it?" Sam asked. "Just gonna let two detectives from Philly take this?"

"One, I'm just a pilot," he said. "Two, we're out of our jurisdiction, so it doesn't matter who goes in there. From what I know, I figure this fella ain't coming out alive. So, go do what you gotta do."

Sam and I maintained silence as we picked our way through the dense forest. Poison ivy grew everywhere. Just a brush with the stuff would cause me weeks of pain. When I was a kid, I had it so bad they ended a Boy Scout camping trip two days early in order to get me to the hospital. My entire body had swollen so bad I must've had an inch of fluid under my skin. They said if we'd stayed in the woods any longer, I'd have died.

We reached the wood's edge and waited for a few minutes. The garage I'd seen from above was in fact a carport. Underneath was a rusted Dodge pickup truck. The grass all behind it was matted down. Someone had been in and out with the vehicle recently and regularly, judging by the path that extended across the clearing.

I watched the nearest greenhouse for a few minutes. The glass exterior appeared as though someone had covered the lower half with a film that allowed light in but made it impossible to see through. Of course, it could've been a thick layer of grime that had built up over the years.

"Ready?" Sam said.

"I'll go first," I said. "Watch my back."

"All right." But Sam took off before I could take a step. He hustled across the open field to the dilapidated carport. It looked like it was going to collapse as he reached out for the support pole and used it to break his sprint.

The truck shielded his body as he scouted the area up close. After a few seconds he opened the passenger side door and leaned in. I lost sight of him after he climbed into the cab and the door eased shut on its own.

I covered what was visible of the lot from my spot just inside the tree line. If someone had been watching, they had decided to remain in place. Can't blame them. If I saw Sam hauling ass in my direction, I'd get out of the way. Never understood why coach didn't let him line up at fullback in goal line situations. The other team would've created the holes themselves for him to run through.

Sam signaled over the top of the truck from the driver's side. That was my cue. I dashed across the open field to the waiting carport, refraining from using the support as a stop. It wouldn't survive a second collision. Instead, I jogged around the back of the truck and met Sam on the other side.

"Anything good in there?" I asked.

He held up a faded registration card. "Gotta be ten years old. Can't make out the letters anymore."

I wondered if anyone could. "Hang onto it. Someone might be able to help."

"And there was this." Sam held up a .357, pinching it between his thumb and forefinger. He glanced over his shoulder as though someone had called out his name. "Haven't checked to see if it's loaded. Might be some evidence on it."

"Let's leave it in the truck. Maybe we can find a bag inside the greenhouse to store it."

We didn't need the firearm. Cervantes had hooked us up with standard issue Glock 22s the afternoon before. The pistols offered plenty of stopping power. I was touched by the gesture. Of course, the bastard made us go to Wal-Mart to buy our own ammo.

"You ready for this?" Sam stood facing the nearest greenhouse. "Once we go in, there's no chance at turning back."

"There never was, bro."

CHAPTER SIXTY

Cassie had spent the better part of forty-eight hours strapped to her bed. That was her best guess. She'd lost all concept of time the moment she woke up in the horrid place. She'd freed herself from the restraint, but didn't risk spending much time untethered. Novak came and went at irregular intervals, and he rarely made much noise when he did so. Last night had been an aberration. His slurred words were all she needed to hear to know he was drunk or high. And he'd done the same to Alice. The young woman had actually laughed.

Cassie wondered whether she ever would again. There was nothing that could make her feel that way now. Maybe the sight of Novak's rigid body, his chest and head riddled with bullet holes. That, she thought, would elicit a joyous response.

She'd been ready for him last night. Her sweat-soaked body felt like forged steel as she lay there, waiting for him to enter her room. All he had to do was take eight staggered steps in her direction. She planned to feign resistance. And when he least expected it, she'd take him on.

But it wasn't meant to be. She could only hope Alice was okay now. Normally the two would communicate minimally throughout the day. It wasn't much. After all, Novak might be sitting outside their doors listening, so the women found ways to let the other know they weren't alone.

Cassie glanced at the shadow cowering in the corner of her room. She was never alone. Doubts crept into her mind as she watched the spirit. Was it really there? Were the things that had happened to her since that night in the graveyard really happening to her? All the evidence in the world pointed to the answer being yes. Hell, she'd converted non-believers with the information she'd gleaned from her helpers, passing it along to law enforcement agencies and family members. The NSA had even contacted her for help.

Where were they now?

She sunk her head into the pillow and stared at the dim overhead light.

Tell me you're out there, Mitch. I've heard your voice before. Talk to me again.

She waited for several seconds, studying the subtle movements of the shadow. There was no response from Mitch. Or anyone, for that matter.

A door beyond hers slammed shut. Cassie closed her eyes and tuned in to the dank environment. The smell of stale urine was strong. It was something she just couldn't get used to. She shook her head and ignored the odor.

Was Novak in Alice's room now? She counted the seconds. Novak rarely went more than a minute without speaking once he entered in a way that let them know he was present. It was as though he had the inability to do so, even when he knew the women would say nothing back to him.

More noise coming from outside her door caused her to

muscles to clench. What was he doing? Something was dragging on the floor. Not a body. She doubted she'd hear that. This sounded like metal scraping on the concrete. Chains, perhaps? Were the ropes not enough?

She tugged her left hand toward her waist.

No, the ropes were most certainly not enough.

Keep cool, Cass. Don't give it away too early. You've only got one shot at this.

And it was a shot she could not afford to screw up. Death would be the immediate and permanent response for doing so.

Several minutes passed with no activity in or outside of the room. The shadow had moved on to elsewhere. She hated when they came and observed without attempting to make contact with her. Who had sent it? What purpose did it have visiting her?

She heard faint humming. What was the tune? She couldn't quite place it. Something she'd heard before, though. The tempo was fast, upbeat. Maybe a song from the seventies.

What was taking him so long? Was he doing it on purpose? Novak never lingered in the background for long when he was deliberately making himself heard.

Then she realized, it might not be Novak. There was the other man. *"Hello, Detective."* At first she'd thought him to be a hallucination, but knew that was not the case. Was he going to become a frequent visitor? What did he want with them?

Her chest tightened, constricting her breaths. No panic, not now. She needed to have her wits about her. There could be no delay in her attack, either. Novak had developed a habit of sticking her with a needle anytime he got close. The drugs acted quickly enough that she would not be able to take him down if she were sedated.

The overhead light cut off and a moment later the door cracked open. A thin beam of light knifed across her stomach for a moment before it was blocked out by his body. He stood there for a minute, silent, unmoving. She resisted the urge to yell at him. She fought back the tears that tried to push through in waves. Hell no. She was too strong for that.

Cassie eased her left arm back. Her fingertips rested inches from the bedpost. A simple arch of her back would provide the necessary adjustment for her to wrap her hands around the hunk of broken wood.

Novak pushed the door open further, but he didn't advance. More light flooded in, scratching across the floor, up the bed, over her bare skin. His breathing was heavy, ragged. Had he been with Alice? This was unusual behavior, even for Novak. Something had happened. She felt the pressure in the room change, acknowledging her fears.

"I'll be back soon, my dear Cassie." Novak swung his arm around as he turned and slammed the door shut, casting Cassie into darkness once more.

CHAPTER SIXTY-ONE

The drum of the approaching helicopter drowned out the sounds I'd grown accustomed to while waiting outside. Cervantes had insisted we wait for them before investigating the greenhouses. Sam was right. I shouldn't have let the pilot call it in. But we couldn't keep our eyes on the man the entire time. He would have radioed them at some point.

The chopper crested over the trees and set down in the clearing. So much for the quiet approach. If someone was around, they knew full well we were outside.

Sam shook his sagging head and rubbed his eyes. "Amateurs."

"And it's their show. Nothing much we can do about it."

"No, there's something we shouldn't have done."

I waved him off. No point rehashing it now.

Gale force winds extended fifty feet out from the helicopter's spinning rotors. Cervantes hopped out, tucking his billowing shirt deep into his black tactical pants. Once he cleared the zone, the pilot lifted the bird and swung back over the trees. Silence returned within thirty seconds.

"Anything happen?" Cervantes glanced around the property. "I had him push it to get here as fast as possible."

"Where's Pennington?" I asked. "He take a different helicopter?"

"He received another lead. Felt it was best I take scouting duty today while he followed up on it."

An unusual request, I thought, but understandable given the circumstances. We had to spread ourselves thin if it led to finding Cassie.

"Place seems deserted," Sam said. "No signs of movement since we've been here. Looks like the truck's been in and out recently, though."

Cervantes followed Sam's gesture toward the rusted pickup. "I'll check it out in a minute. Think it's best we get inside those greenhouses."

He led the way. I wasn't sure what to even look for once inside. It was hard to imagine Novak would leave signs pointing to bodies buried in the dirt or the location of his captives. They wouldn't be inside, that much I knew for sure.

There were two long rows of weathered, wooden tables adorned with empty planters, dead leaves and branches, and a few garden tools. Weeds grew up through the concrete floor. The temperature and humidity were higher than outside. It hit me like stepping off a plane on the tarmac in Orlando in early August. The only thing the greenhouse had going for it was that it smelled like death.

"Not much going on in here," Sam said. "That supply store, they said he'd been purchasing, right?"

"Yeah." Cervantes had reached the other end. He pulled a table away from the wall and slipped behind it. Then he knelt down, out of sight.

"What's there?" I said.

He'd found something. Maybe something hidden.

Cervantes rose, holding a dead possum by the tail. Now we knew why the place stunk so badly.

We spent another five minutes looking over the greenhouse before moving on to the next. It was even easier to investigate. There was nothing but a crushed pad of gravel on the floor in there. Window panels had been knocked out. Glass mixed with the rocks on the floor. No signs of anything having grown in there for years.

"We should check out that house," Sam said.

"What house?" Cervantes asked.

"About a quarter-mile from here there's another clearing. House set on it looks like it might be related to this place. It's just as dilapidated."

"Maybe the supplies are there." Cervantes pushed past me toward the exit. "And the girls."

I got my bearings straight and led the way through the woods. We walked in silence, each of us scanning a different section of the forest. If this was where Novak was hiding, he had to know we were here. This was his territory. The guy could be perched in a tree, waiting with a rifle to pick us off one at a time.

The wound on my head ached a little. I still don't know what that little prick Seth was thinking. Pennington had said Seth thought I was involved and that I might've been out there to destroy or recover some evidence. His actions were the result of misplaced vengeance.

It was cooler under the woodland canopy, but without a breeze, it didn't matter much. It took five minutes to reach the clearing. Up close it was obvious the house had been abandoned long ago. Any inhabitants were sure to have four legs or wings. Maybe things that slept upside down. There were probably a few transients that called the place home over the years. Doubtful anyone would stay long, though.

We walked the perimeter looking for signs of life, then made our entry, clearing the place room by room. The floor bowed and sagged on the first level. Upstairs I thought it would collapse if Sam and I stood too close together. Every room had its own brand of character. Hard to imagine the furniture hadn't been taken years ago when it might've been in decent shape. Now it was rotten, covered with mold and feces.

The three of us huddled in the kitchen.

"This place got a basement?" Sam said.

Cervantes shook his head. "I checked every door on this level. Nothing but a couple of closets." He holstered his pistol. "We're just wasting time here, guys."

"My mind keeps going back to the other place," Sam said.

"What other place?" Cervantes asked.

"The one by the state line. Really secluded location with a couple of greenhouses and a run-down home. Kinda like this."

Cervantes shrugged. "You check it out?"

"You guys cleared it," Sam reminded him.

Cervantes crossed his arms and widened his stance. "What do you mean we cleared it?"

"The pilot," Sam said. "He talked to Pennington. He was already familiar with it. Said he had checked it out years ago when he was in narco after a tip from some teenagers about a large marijuana operation. People there were growing lilies, selling them on the roadside."

Cervantes's face turned three shades paler. "Pennington was never in narcotics here. He transferred into SCMPD twelve years or so ago as a homicide detective."

"Transferred from where?" I asked.

"Delaware. Not too far from where you guys are from. Figured that's why he cut you so much slack, Tanner."

I felt like I'd taken ten body blows while up against the ropes.

"So, he didn't tell you about the other place?" Sam took the information better than I had.

Cervantes wrapped his hands around the back of his head and stared up at the sky. "Ah, Christ. We gotta get over there." He pulled out his cellphone and called the pilot. "We'll ride together."

The situation, as they say, crystallized. There were no lily growers. No stand on the side of the road selling flowers. We'd found Novak's hideout.

And Pennington already knew the location.

CHAPTER SIXTY-TWO

Cassie had managed to drift to that place between sleep and wakefulness. She spent a lot of time there at home when dealing with her *visitors*. It hadn't been easy to achieve the state while confined to the cell Novak kept her in. It wasn't the same as eight hours of restful sleep, not that she knew what that was anymore. Since the attack in the graveyard, she hadn't managed more than four hours at a time. Still, every second she spent in that zone helped to re-center and recalibrate her mind and body.

There had been activity on the other side of the door. Heavy items dragged across the floor. Doors slamming shut. She wondered if Alice's time had come to an end and the sounds were her coffin being moved around. Would Novak even bother with a coffin? She figured he'd use a tarp or heavy plastic and duct tape. If he felt like taking his time, a nice six-foot hole would do the trick. If he was in a rush, a shallow creek would keep the body hidden for a while.

She saw herself in such a situation. The plastic wrapped so

tight her arms wouldn't move. Unable to draw a breath into her lungs. Stifled, yet alive, in an unending nightmare.

Wasn't she already in one?

She watched a shadow pass under the doorway. This one belonged to an earthly being. Why won't he just come in? The next opportunity would be the final one, she decided. Whatever was going on had the sense of panic and urgency about it. Perhaps Novak was getting ready to jump ship. He'd want to travel light, of course, and that meant Alice and Cassie were now expendable. *Maybe* he'd keep her around as a hostage, a negotiating piece. Hell, the psychological damage was done. Going forward, life would be a living hell, even more so than it had been.

The door banged open an inch. No one was there. No silhouette in the crack. No shadow under the door. Had it been intentional? Or had he slammed into it by accident?

Cassie closed her eyes and listened. A persistent hum she hadn't noticed before droned on in the background. What was it? She tried to place the sound. The closest she could guess was a power washer.

Alice.

She searched the corners of the room for a spirit who could confirm, but there were none present.

The door whipped open, crashing into the wall and bouncing back toward Novak. He extended his arm and stopped it. From his other hand, a needle dangled. A sedative? Or did he plan on putting her to sleep permanently? The latter could not be the case. Novak enjoyed killing too much. He'd stabbed her relentlessly in the graveyard all those years ago. A psychologist told her that Novak could build a story, a history, between two people in his mind in a matter of seconds. An entire history of him and Cassie existed solely in Novak's head. He didn't want to simply kill her. He was unleashing a torrent of passion and hate and fury upon her as though the two had been lovers for twenty years.

There was no doubt in Cassie's mind that he still felt the same way.

Novak took slow, deliberate steps toward her. His boots thumped on the floor. He set the syringe on the bottom corner of the bed. Cassie withdrew her foot as far as the rope would allow.

"You are my favorite," he said. "You know that, right? You are so damn special."

Cassie did not reply.

"When I found out that you were still alive, oh, man." He clasped his hands together while shaking his head. "A mental orgasm is the only way to describe it. I do have to say, it pissed me off quite considerably that they hid you in plain sight."

"No one hid me," she said. "I never feared you. I know what happens next, Novak. You can rid me of this fleshy shell, but I'll never go away. And I'll be sure to make you wish you had been the one to die."

The light washed over half of his face, casting the other side in darkness. His smile looked that much more sinister. He drew his right leg up and sat on the edge of the bed. "If none of the others have managed to do that, what makes you think you can?"

Cassie squirmed away from his touch, stifling her own smile. She hadn't needed to wait for him to advance upon her. She was now in reach. "Like you said, I'm special."

A soft laugh escaped Novak. He closed his eyes and lowered his chin to his chest. "Oh, Cassie, Cassie, Cass—"

With her hand wrapped tight around the post, she yanked it free and whipped it over her body in a high arc. Novak glanced up, placing his face in the path of the club. Cassie brought it down hard. His nose crunched as the post slammed into his face. He tumbled off the bed, leaving a tooth behind.

Cassie twisted and contorted her body to continue the attack. She landed two more blows as Novak clawed along the floor to get out of her way.

She had already loosened her bindings. Freeing herself took only a few seconds per limb. By the time she placed her wobbly legs on the ground, Novak had reached the walls and was using it to get to his feet.

The first two steps were not easy. Cassie felt as though she might collapse. She steadied herself, clinging to the post like a batter stepping up to the plate.

"You stupid bitch!" Novak leaned back against the wall. His face was darkened with blood. He wiped his eyes and shook his hands off. Crimson drops pelted her bare skin.

Cassie stepped forward, twisting at the waist. She drew the post back over her shoulder. The more range, the more torque. She didn't want to hurt him or knock him down. She wanted to kill him with the next blow.

As she started to swing the club around, Novak exploded off the wall. She side-stepped and short-armed her attack, bringing it down on his back with a loud crack. It had done some damage, but nowhere near what she had hoped. And it hadn't stopped him. Novak's momentum carried him through as he twisted toward her. His shoulder drove into her abdomen, sending her backward.

She collided with the mattress and lost her footing. The full weight of Novak came down on her legs and dragged her to the floor. He was reaching around his back, grunting in pain. Broken ribs, for sure. Maybe even a vertebra.

Cassie writhed her body in an attempt to free herself before Novak remembered what his main goal was. The pain he felt would dull, and if it did so soon, he had her right where he wanted.

She rested on her left elbow and managed to get her right leg free. Novak lifted his torso off her. He faced her. Light shone on half his blood-smeared face.

"I'm going to finish you now," he said.

She pulled her knees to her chest, then drove her feet into Novak. They deflected off his face, into his chest. He reared back on his knees, cursing in pain and reaching for his back again. The blow had only served to delay his attack. Novak threw himself forward, arms wide, fists clenched, mouth open.

Cassie fell to her left and flipped her hips. It was all she could do. Novak had her back. With one hand he clenched her hair near the skull and yanked back. The other pounded her shoulder, side, neck, and head. She drew her shoulders up tight to protect her neck. Novak now had both hands full of her hair, pulling up hard. She feared he was going to smash her face into the concrete floor, so she bucked hard, driving her hip into his groin.

Novak grunted and released his grip on her hair. Cassie dug her fingertips into the hard ground and pulled herself forward. She reached out to grab the bottom bedpost. Novak dug his hands into the bare skin of her waist and yanked her back. Her fingers, slick with his blood, grazed the post and slipped off, her palm slammed into the floor. Something sharp stuck her.

The syringe.

It had been left on the corner of the bed and had fallen to the floor.

She worked her fingers frantically to get a grip on the syringe. She feared plunging it prematurely and losing the powerful juice inside. Likewise, she had to be careful not to stick herself.

Novak was off of her. She looked back. He had turned and was going for the post. In the chaos it had skidded to the corner.

Cassie flipped over, twisting in the air, coming down hard on her back. Despite the pain and loss of air in her lungs, she planted her left foot, lifted her butt off the ground, and drove her right foot up, catching Novak from behind in the groin again.

He stopped and looked back at her. His lips looked comical, painted in red. His smile had tragedy written all over it. The kick had not had the intended effect. Novak drove his foot down on her knee. Cassie cried out in pain.

He turned and bent at the waist, hovering over her. Drops of blood splashed on her chest and face. "You gonna do something stupid like that again?"

She cried.

He reached out and slapped her on the face. "No, you're not, Cassie. Because in about two minutes, your brains are gonna be all over the floor."

"No, please." She forced a pained cry.

He leaned in closer. "Say that again?"

She licked her lips, coating her mouth with the metallic taste of his blood.

"Come on, girl," he said. "I don't have all day."

"I said, please." She stared into his eyes. A wide smile spread across his face. She matched it with her own.

"If only you would have done that from the start." He traced the tip of his index finger down the side of her face, over her lips, across her chin, skipped her neck, and settled on her chest.

She drew her hand over his, moved it closer to her breast.

"That's more like it," he said.

Cassie clenched down on his wrist, digging her nails into his flesh. She hooked her legs around the back of his knees and drew them in tight. He collapsed onto her. One of his knees drove into her stomach. She braced for the impact, but it hadn't been enough. Cassie gritted her teeth against the pain, while Novak worked to free his hand. With the other, he planted his palm under her chin and began driving it upward.

Cassie flipped the syringe in her hand. Her thumb hovered over the plunger. She lifted her arm. Light glinted off the needle. Eighteen inches, give or take, stood between the drugs and Novak's neck. Cassie let go of his arm and quickly wrapped it around the back of Novak's head, grabbing a fistful of hair. She brought her feet higher, crossed her legs at the ankle over his lower back, and pulled down tight. He was going nowhere. She yanked his head to the side, exposing his neck. The flesh and muscles protecting Novak's neck did little to stop the thin needle from penetrating two inches deep. Cassie drove the plunger down, filling the man with whatever he had planned using on her.

He pulled his head back. His eyes stared at nothing. "You..."

She pushed his chest away from her and brought her legs in to help keep him from buckling over on her. A few seconds later she worked herself out from underneath him. She felt for a pulse near where the needle hung from his neck. Her hands were too shaky to hold steady.

GET OUT!

Heed the voice, Cassie, she told herself. She struggled to her feet. Her knee ached where he had stomped on it, but it didn't prevent her from walking. She limped out of the room. The lights over the table blinded her at first. She shielded her eyes from the glare and shuffled her feet across the glinting floor. What the hell was that? Pain shot through her heel. Glass. The floor was covered in broken glass.

"Alice," she called out. "Alice, can you hear me?"

There was no response.

Cassie banged on the door before remembering she was standing on the outside. She grabbed the handle. It felt ice cold against her damp skin. She turned, but her hand slid off. It was locked. She looked for a latch on the door but there wasn't one.

"Come on, come on." She banged on the door again. "Alice,

I'm going to get you out of here. You hear me? Get your ass up, we're going home." Cassie placed her ear against the door.

A moan, slight as it was, filled her with a newfound sense of purpose.

Cassie hurried around the room in search of a key. There had to be something. Maybe it was on Novak. She reentered her room despite the voices telling her not to. Novak hadn't moved. She hoped he was dead. A quick search of his pockets revealed nothing.

Back in the grim foyer, she grabbed a round bowl on the table filled with dirt and flowers. Sitting on top of the dirt was a key. A moment later she pushed Alice's door open and all hope sank.

CHAPTER SIXTY-THREE

The pilot set the helicopter down a mile from the site. Couldn't risk getting any closer than that. If Pennington were there, he would know the moment he heard the rotors thumping that we'd figured out his game.

Cervantes was torn. He kept insisting his partner had nothing to do with this. Then he'd come up with a reason it was plausible. I studied Sam's reaction, wondering if he was thinking what I was. We'd been best friends for a long time. Was there a chance he harbored evil secrets like Pennington's?

Sam cut me a look that said something along the lines of *are you kidding me.*

Was it directed at me? Or the crap Cervantes espoused?

They'd arranged for a state trooper to transport us to a location about five hundred yards from the greenhouse. Sam and I crammed into the backseat with our knees practically pressed against our chests. I kept my gaze fixed on the woods. If I stared long and hard enough, I might just spot Cassie hiding in them.

"What's that?" Sam said.

I turned my head toward him as he tapped on his window.

"Hey, hey, stop the car." He grabbed the trooper's shoulder.

The statie didn't appreciate the gesture. He shrugged Sam's hand off, then hit the brakes. If I hadn't been wedged in so tight, I might've slammed into the back of Cervantes's head.

"What is it?" Cervantes said.

"Back up," Sam said. "I think I saw something."

The cruiser traveled in reverse for a few seconds.

"Stop here and let us out."

The trooper and Cervantes exited and then opened our doors. Sam had a hell of an eye. Driving by at forty-five miles per hour, he spotted two faint tire tracks in the knee-high grass leading into the woods.

"How far are we from the drop-off point?" Cervantes asked the trooper.

"Around the bend ahead, but this is probably just as close." He ducked back into the cruiser for a moment, then came back nodding his head. "Yeah, only thing between the road and the lot is these woods."

I moved to the trees and saw the path continued on for a while. "Feel like doing some off-roading?"

A few hundred feet later the trooper stopped near the wood's edge and we all exited the car again.

"I want you to stay here," Cervantes instructed the trooper. "I'll keep you updated with our movements, but if ten minutes pass without me checking in, you call in for backup."

The guy didn't seem to have a problem with that. Patrolling the highways was more his speed. He sat back down in his cruiser with one foot on the ground.

We made our way to the lot and waited in the shadows for a minute while surveying the grounds. They were eerily similar to the previous location. A run-down carport with a beat up pickup truck under it. Two greenhouses, though these appeared to be in better shape. The lot was more squared off than the last, and contained no additional permanent structures. I couldn't recall spotting a house nearby that might be on the same property.

"We do this my way." Cervantes had his Glock at the ready. "No one shoots unless threatened directly. If you come across Pennington, you keep him in place. He's my partner. I'll deal with him. Got it?"

Sam took a deep breath. He didn't like taking orders from anyone, let alone a detective from another state.

I grabbed his shoulder and leaned in. "You take the lead, Cerv. We'll follow."

Sam glanced at me out of the corner of his eye. He knew I hadn't meant what I said. Both Novak and Pennington had kill on sight written on their foreheads.

We dashed to the carport. The truck's hood felt warm. It had been running within the past hour. There was trash on the front seat, an empty pack of cigarettes, some energy drink bottles, receipts, and a few empty Budweiser twelve-packs. I checked the glove box for a registration and found a piece of yellow legal paper with an address scrawled on it.

"Look familiar?" I held it up for Cervantes to see.

He shrugged and took it from me. "I'll follow up on it afterward. Let's move to the greenhouse."

The humidity ratcheted up a notch inside the building. The place was alive with tomato plants, some other vegetables, and a section of flowers. Maybe Novak did sell floral arrangements. Two long rows of tables covered in dirt and green. At the far end were two large racks filled with empty planters, bags of dirt and fertilizer, and tools.

I headed to the other side while Sam and Cervantes moved the tables to check behind and underneath.

The ground was packed dirt in some places, gravel in others. I stopped every few feet and kicked at the ground for evidence of recent digging. The greenhouse would make a decent graveyard for someone intent on hiding the dead.

The other property popped into my thoughts once again. Was it possible that Novak had used that location as well before he had been caught? I dragged my heel across the ground in front of me. What if someone had paved over the ground to further conceal the contents underneath? I made a note to have Cervantes follow up on that. They could get a guy out to perform a sonar check and look for anything buried there.

"What do you have down there, Mitch?" Sam said.

I'd spent a couple minutes poking around the supplies and checking behind and underneath the racks. "Nothing, man."

"Let's move on to the next greenhouse," Cervantes said.

The second building was set up much the same as the first. Dirt and gravel floor. Two rows of tables topped with vegetables and flowers with a walkway down the middle. At the end was one supply rack and an empty space next to it.

Our assignments remained the same. Sam and Cervantes began sliding tables around, while I took my time walking to the other end, looking for anything that seemed out of place.

Sam came up with something right away. "Check this out."

I turned and saw him holding up a shotgun outfitted with a pistol grip and holders for additional rounds.

"Where was that?"

"Duct taped under the table." He checked the weapon. "And it is ready to go."

"Hang onto that," Cervantes said. "Might need it."

I had been focused before, but it reached a new level. We'd entered the hive. Time to figure out how to penetrate the core.

At the end of the path stood the single supply rack. It

contained some of the same items as the other greenhouse, but I also found lye. Now, I never had much of a green thumb. Momma did and kept it all to herself. But I couldn't think of any uses in a greenhouse for lye off the top of my head.

I moved around the side of the unit and pried my fingers between it and the wall while grabbing a shelf with my other hand. It took a few tries to move the unit six inches out. Other than a few cobwebs, only a shovel on the floor hid behind the shelving. Had it been placed there on purpose?

I took a few steps back and crouched down. My body teetered to the right as though I were off-center on a large balance board. I reached down and brushed the loose dirt aside. My hand grazed against something solid that led to a thin groove. The groove ran about eighteen inches in either direction, cornered, and went behind me. I moved to the side and worked my fingernails in the small gap until I could lift it high enough for my fingertips to grip underneath.

Dry, musky air rushed out. I eased the trapdoor up a few more inches and peered into the darkness. Enough light filtered through to illuminate what appeared to be a corridor. I set the top down and stood up.

"You guys might want to come check this out."

CHAPTER SIXTY-FOUR

"Alice!" Cassie lightly slapped the young woman's pale cheek. Her eyes opened to slits, revealing bloodshot whites. Drool trickled from the corner of her mouth. A puddle of vomit pooled on the floor near the bed. Cassie searched Alice's arm and found a small trickle of blood.

Novak had drugged her before he came in to do the same to Cassie. It had been strong enough to knock Novak out the moment she plunged the juice into him, and he was twice Alice's size. Cassie had felt the effects before, too. She feared the young woman had overdosed.

Normally she wouldn't hesitate to carry the other woman out of their prison, but Cassie was underfed and over-drugged. She felt weak and she feared for her life. Taking Alice with her reduced her own chances of escaping.

But what if the effects on Novak wore off too soon? What if the other guy showed up? Cassie leaving would mean they took their rage out on Alice.

She gave the room a once-over, looking for something to put on

Alice. Novak had left her nude except for dirt-stained panties. Cassie found a balled up dress in the corner of the room. She recognized it from the pictures she had seen of Alice early on in the investigation. Had it been what she wore when Novak killed her roommates and abducted her? Or had he returned to the house to retrieve it for her?

"I need you to sit up, Alice," Cassie said, threading her arm around the woman's back to assist her. "Come on, we don't have time to linger."

Alice groaned as Cassie lifted her back off the bed.

"That's a girl," Cassie said. "Keep talking to me."

Alice groaned again. Cassie's skin pricked and she swung her head around, expecting to see Novak in the doorway.

It was empty.

Alice's torso leaned forward. Cassie shifted her weight against the woman to hold her up. Alice's drool-soaked cheek slid down Cassie's shoulder and upper arm.

"Help me out, girl." Cassie worked Alice's arms through the bottom of the dress and out the arm holes with little assistance from the woman. Then she wrapped her arms around Alice and pulled her to her feet. "I need everything you've got, girl. I know you feel weak right now, like you're asleep, but you're with me, Alice. You and me, we can get out of here, but we have to work together. You hear me? You *can* do this."

Alice's eyelids fluttered open. Her eyes rolled forward, made contact with Cassie.

"I don't want to leave you here," Cassie said. "Please don't make me leave you."

Alice's grip on Cassie's arm was hard. Her words were slurred, but understandable. "Let's get out of here."

CHAPTER SIXTY-FIVE

Pennington stopped and leaned against the earthen wall. The first time he heard the tapping sound, he blew it off. But twice was a sign that something was wrong. Novak was supposed to be at the house. He had explicitly told the idiot to remain there until Pennington arrived. There was a chance of the operation being exposed. He needed everyone present to coordinate the next move.

Had Novak been stupid enough to ignore him?

Pennington unholstered his Smith and Wesson and turned back the way he had come. The tunnel snaked underneath the woods for a quarter-mile or so, running from the greenhouse to the old home. Nature had overtaken the house. It was impossible to spot it from the road or the air. You'd have to stumble into it to know it existed.

A few minutes passed. No noise. No breeze blowing past like he expected when the trap door opened. Just his imagination. It had been a long time since it had acted up like this. It had also been a long time since he was at risk of being outed as a psychopath. Not since he lived in Delaware when Novak had lost control. Relocating both of them had been a good thing.

He changed direction again and continued back to the house. How would Cassie take the news? He'd seen her in the cellar on more than one occasion. She had been so drugged that even when she looked him in the eye, she had no idea who he was. A twinge of guilt ate at him. His plan had been to free her. Be the hero. Maybe she'd thank him in more ways than one.

But now that he'd possibly been compromised, his plans had changed.

CHAPTER SIXTY-SIX

Cassie planted her foot on the next step and braced her arm against the wall. Alice's dead weight threatened to send them both tumbling down the steep concrete stairs. If Cassie didn't die on the way down, she'd be critically injured with nothing to do but wait for Novak to wake from his slumber.

The feeling that it was a mistake leaving him alive nagged at her. Every step she took she heard the voices telling her to finish the man. But it wasn't her place to decide his fate. She would be as bad as him if she took his life.

Cassie butted her thigh and knee against the back of Alice's leg and drove the woman up and forward. "Come on, Alice. Five more just like that."

Freedom existed beyond the splintered door at the top of the stairs. She had to believe it did or she wouldn't have the strength to move them any further.

Two more steps took close to two minutes of work. She wondered if she'd have the strength to make it to a road once they escaped the place. Out there, she could conceal Alice. At least she hoped so.

The wonder over what came next ate at her until she finally sat Alice down on a step, resting her head and torso against the wall and crossing her legs in a way to help prevent her from falling. Cassie climbed to the top and rested there with her ear against the door. She watched the bar of light that seeped from underneath. A minute passed. Then another. Was she frozen with fear, or being extra cautious? She could no longer tell the difference between the two feelings.

Alice moaned as she lifted her hand to her head. Cassie stepped down to her.

"It's okay. We're getting out of here. I need you to find every ounce of fight you have in you for the next step. You got it?"

Alice nodded, said, "Yeah, I can do this."

A good sign. The most Cassie had gotten out of the woman yet.

Emboldened by Alice's newfound strength, Cassie rediscovered her own. She marched up the steps and grabbed the door handle. It felt like ice on her hot skin. She twisted the knob and cracked the door. Daylight poured in through a dirty window. She shielded her eyes, allowing them to adjust. How long had it been since she'd seen sunlight? Days? Weeks? She had no idea if her sleep had lasted minutes or hours.

Cassie returned to help Alice the rest of the way up the stairs. The younger woman managed to climb them on all fours with Cassie's help. She plastered both hands on Alice's rear end and pushed. At the top, Alice managed to stand on her own. They emerged from the cellar into a dusty kitchen. Cobwebs hovered in the corners. The sink was piled high with pans. Dirty dishes lined the counters. She scanned the room and found two points of egress.

"Come with me." She grabbed Alice's hand and led her toward the hallway with more light. Turning a corner, a wide door with a large stained-glass window appeared. They were almost free.

A figure blocked out the vibrant reds and yellows and blues, turning them dull.

Cassie froze in place as the knob turned. Instincts took over. She spun on her heel and located a hall closet. With her hand on Alice's back, she shoved the girl toward the closet.

"Get in and don't come out no matter what you hear."

The front door creaked open.

Cassie felt a puff of wind as Alice pulled the closet door closed.

A breeze whipped down the hallway.

She spun around. Her knees went weak when she saw him. For a moment, she thought she was safe. But that illusion faded quickly.

"Hello, Detective."

Pennington's smile spread as he raised his pistol and aimed it at her.

"Hello, my dear Cassie."

CHAPTER SIXTY-SEVEN

We emerged from the earthen tunnel inside a structure. The smell of smoke didn't register until I spotted it seeping out of the overhead vent. I'd be lying if there wasn't a part of my brain saying, *fool, don't go in there.* It was no coincidence the house was on fire. Question was, who was inside?

Cervantes pushed past me and wasted no time barreling through the door, not bothering to stop as he kicked it in. Plates of stained glass broke free in sheets and shattered on the old pine floors. Shards skated across the room. Smoke wafted along the ceiling. The fire was in the walls, hopefully slowed by old plaster and lath and not accelerating through the hundred-year-old wood.

All three of us knew the risks being inside. The house could collapse at any moment. We ripped doors open with reckless abandon. I found the kitchen and reached for what I figured to be a closet.

"Found one!" Sam's deep voice tore through the room.

I followed it and saw him holding up Alice. The girl could

barely stand. She struggled to form words as Sam asked her simple questions.

I hurried back to the kitchen and pulled the door open. A set of concrete stairs descended into the darkness. Somebody was on the floor at the bottom.

"Cassie?" I yelled down into the chamber.

They didn't respond.

"Sam, I'm going down."

A loud bang erupted from the other end of the house.

"Christ!" Cervantes yelled as he ran into the kitchen. "It's coming down. We gotta get out of here."

"There's someone down there," I said, pointing down the staircase.

He craned his head to get a look, then glanced toward the front of the house. "Sam, get the girl out." He put his hand on my back and pushed lightly. "Come on, let's get them and go."

A light flicked on over my shoulder. The end of his large flashlight pushed past my face. Halfway down the stairs I knew the body was not Cassie's.

I hopped over it and squatted next to the man's head, grabbing hold of his hair and yanking his face off the floor.

"Where is she?" I yelled.

Novak looked worse-off than Alice. I slapped him across the face. Didn't even register with the guy.

"You drag him up," I said. "I'm gonna check the room. Give me your flashlight."

The floor overhead rattled, sending plumes of dust down.

He handed the light over. "I'm not coming back down, Tanner."

"I wouldn't expect you to." I spun and swung the light around, getting a lay of the land. There were four doors. Two were open and two were closed. The closed ones were closest, so I started with them. I kicked the first open and aimed the light inside to see a stripped-down bed and nothing else. Before moving on to the next, I shone the light up the stairs.

"Shit."

Smoke billowed in through the doorway. The kitchen was on fire now.

"Hurry up, Tanner!" Cervantes's voice barely reached me.

I pushed the next door open, found the room much like the first.

A large table dominated the foyer area. I hurried around it to the first open door. I gagged on the smell of human feces. It was strong enough to overpower the fire. Bedsheets covered the floor. Blood stained the mattress. The name Alice was written on the wall in blood or maybe something else. I had no intention of getting close enough to find out.

One more room. Not enough time to check it out. I ran into it anyhow.

The bed only had three posts. The fourth lay on the floor, the end of it coated in blood. The sheets were in disarray. Clothing was balled up and against the wall. It smelled awful as well, but I must've adjusted because I didn't feel like throwing up. I reached down for the bedpost and spotted a syringe on the floor, so I scooped that up, too.

By the time I reached the stairwell, orange glow filled the upper third. I closed my eyes and pictured the layout of the house. We'd come in from the right. The left had collapsed moments before I took my first step down toward the dungeon. There'd been a window somewhere in the kitchen.

I sprinted up the stairs like I'd just blasted past the left tackle and had a direct line to an unsuspecting quarterback with his back to me. Pain seared through my knee as I took the steps two at a time.

At the top, flames danced on the walls and ceiling. I knew the room to the left was a smoldering pile of rubble, so I darted to the right as soon as I emerged from the stairwell and stopped dead in my tracks. The wall had collapsed. I could see the front door wide open. But I couldn't get to it.

The intense heat burned my skin. The smoke thickened and threatened to choke me out. I saw the one way out. I grabbed a kitchen chair and placed it in front of the sink. Then I backed against the wall and made another dash forward. My foot hit the seat. I swung the bed post overhead and brought it down diagonally, smashing the window. Then I covered my face with my forearm and closed my eyes. It wasn't pretty. I sliced my arm, shoulder, and thigh. It felt like my wrist broke when I collided with the ground.

But goddammit I was alive and knew right then and there I would stay that way at least until I found Cassie.

CHAPTER SIXTY-EIGHT

The night went by in a blur. Pennington had injected Cassie with whatever Novak had been using. He had dragged her back down to the cellar where they found Novak stumbling around the room. Pennington snapped while confronting the man. He exploded into a fit of rage, pounding Novak in the face until he collapsed on the ground. Then he pulled Cassie back upstairs, where he injected her with the drug. The effects weren't as strong immediately, and she wondered if she had become immune to it.

Before leaving the house, Pennington lit the drapes on fire. It wouldn't take long for the blaze to take over. Cassie's legs grew heavier as they plodded through the woods. Pennington yanked on her arm, urging her to keep pace or he'd kill her right then and there. That was bullshit. But she couldn't call him out on it. Her mouth had lost the ability to form the words.

She remembered a van. Then a woman giving them her car. The lady stared into Cassie's eyes and asked if she was all right. Pennington answered for her, said she needed medical help right away. The woman tossed over her keys and that was that.

When Cassie woke again, the sun was coming up and they were traveling on a winding mountain road.

"Where are we?" she asked.

Pennington glanced over, smiled. "Almost to our final resting place, Cassie."

CHAPTER SIXTY-NINE

I returned to Philadelphia with Sam the following morning with thirty-seven stitches, a sprained wrist, and a heavy heart. Cervantes worked on Novak all day. He even brought in a couple heavy hitters known as ruthless interrogators. The FBI wanted a piece of the action, too. There'd be little he could do to stop them.

Before I left, Cervantes had asked me to promise to continue working the case. I'd never intended not to.

They found Pennington's car a couple miles from the property. A van that matched the description and partial plate as the one at the gas station turned up ten miles further. Late last night a woman reported her vehicle missing after a policeman flagged her down and said he needed to use her car to get his sick wife to the hospital. She remarked it was odd that his wife only had on a dirty nightgown. The vehicle he'd been traveling in? The same van. Around midnight, Cervantes interviewed the woman and showed her a picture of his partner. Exact match, not that there was any question.

The car was ditched in North Carolina, somewhere between interstates 85 and 95. The trail stopped there.

I stared out of the window from thirty-six-thousand feet, convinced I'd spot something below. It took my mind off the throbbing pain. The trip had been a rough one. I'd taken more than my share of lumps. Sam had come out all right physically. Pulling Alice from the closet, seeing the condition she was in, screwed up his head, though. He wasn't ready to talk about it during the flight, nor on the drive over to Momma's house.

The old faded-red Ford Galaxy with the rosary beads hanging from the mirror dominated the driveway. Just what I needed. A visit from God. Sam pulled up to the curb and left the engine idling.

"Coming in?" I asked.

"I'll come back around this evening," he said. "Take you out for a beer and try to work through some of this shit on my mind."

I knew he needed time. No problem there. I exited the car and made my way around the side of the house to the kitchen.

"Mitchy," Momma said as I pulled open the screen door. "What happened to you?"

I took a seat at the table and leaned back against the wall. "How about you pour me a cup of that coffee I'm smelling?"

She grabbed a mug and filled it without taking her eyes off me. "I'd ask how the other guy looks, but it appears you took on a truck."

"Pretty close." The steam from the mug opened up my sinuses. "It's still not over. He's got Cassie."

Father Reyes stepped into the kitchen holding a wine glass. I noticed Coltrane playing the sax in the background. He frowned as he looked me over. "Shame what I saw on the news. One girl rescued, another missing. I understand you worked with her?"

I nodded and said nothing.

"And Pennington." He shook his head. "I always knew he'd resurface again."

I set my mug down and asked, "Again?"

"He's from around here, you know."

"A homicide detective in Delaware, right?"

The chair scraped against the linoleum as Father Reyes pulled it away from the table. He sat down across from me. "He was part of a task force here, Mitch."

"How do you know this?"

"I was a police chaplain for years." He took a sip from his glass, licked the remnants of the merlot off his upper lip. "You really should come to mass sometime. I incorporate lessons from what I learned during my time with the force."

I didn't want to tell him I was a tad upset with God lately.

"Pennington was involved in that mess with O'Connell. He made a huge, huge error. One that got him removed from the team. If it hadn't been for the results he'd had previously in his career, he never would have worked again. Someone pulled a few strings and got him that job down south."

It took a few moments for the information to penetrate my thick skull. "This error he made, what was it?"

The priest stared down his torso and shook his head. "That I can't tell you."

"I get the feeling it wasn't a mistake, whatever it was." I took a moment to let a sharp pain in my chest subside. "He's been working with Novak all these years."

"What do you mean, working with Novak?"

"I don't have time to explain." I rose and grabbed my cell phone off the table. "Momma, kiss Ella Kate for me." I hesitated a second. "Better yet, don't let her know I was here."

"Mitch, where are you going?" She blocked the screen door

and put her hands on my chest. I winced in pain and she pulled them back as though she'd touched a power line.

I pulled up Sam's number and called. "Yeah, it's me. Get back over here. I think I got a lead for us to check out."

"On my way." The tires squealed over the line before he hung up.

I squeezed Momma's hand in my one good one and side-stepped her. "I'll call as soon as I can."

SAM PULLED to the corner five minutes later. I hadn't waited in front of Momma's house out of fear she and Father Reyes would have interrogated me. I didn't have the mental fortitude to deal with that at the moment.

"What you got?" Sam asked as I plopped down in the passenger seat.

I relayed the conversation with Father Reyes.

"You've gotta be kidding me," he said. "They've been doing this for a long time."

"What's worse, this whole 'screwed up big time' thing, my gut tells me that's how Novak got away. Pennington must've had some dirt on somebody that allowed him to be banished to Savannah instead of thrown in jail."

"Next move? Should we call Cervantes and bring him up to speed?"

I stared at an older couple walking toward us on the sidewalk. Hand in hand. The man using a cane.

"Let's get over to Sartini's house. He was involved in the hunt for Novak, or O'Connell, whatever you want to call him. Maybe he can tell us something about Pennington."

CHAPTER SEVENTY

Sartini cinched his robe a couple seconds too late and welcomed us in. "Didn't expect to see you guys so soon. Unfortunately, I haven't had any luck—"

"We got everything we needed on the van," Sam said.

Sartini shut the door behind us. "Oh, all right. Well is this just a social call then? I'll get the Maker's."

"I wish I could say it was," I said.

He narrowed his eyes as he studied my wounds. "The hell happened to you, Tanner?"

"Dove through a window to escape a burning house."

He arched an eyebrow and nodded. "I'm guessing your visit has something to do with that." His expression changed, lengthening his face as both eyes opened wide and his bottom lip dropped. "Did you get O'Connell?"

Sam placed his hand on Sartini's shoulder. "We did. He's in custody in Savannah. We've already provided them with the information you told us. Questioning will happen in due time."

Sartini sucked in a deep breath of air. His eyes misted over. I could almost see the weight rising off him.

"Excuse me, fellas. I think I need a minute. Why don't you head into my study."

Sam led the way down the hall and into the room. I tensed a little as he slid past the door opening. My mind always raced in an off-beat way. At that moment, I conceived the idea that Pennington had been working with Sartini the entire time, and was now waiting in there with Cassie.

"He's been working the old files." Sam pointed at the desk. Boxes were stacked on one end. Folders cluttered the rest of the surface. Other than that, it looked exactly as we'd left it.

"After you guys took off," Sartini said, "I couldn't sleep, so I started going through the cases we linked to O'Connell. I'd forgotten how many there were. Maybe it was necessary so I could rest easy. I swear, no other case ever left the task force so decimated."

Sam shot me a look. "Tell us about this task force. Who all was on it? Who led it?"

Sartini eased into his Herman Miller chair and swiveled to face us. "Well, it was a tristate setup where we had guys locally, and also from Delaware and Maryland. Actually, they had two detectives from D.C. as well. Some of the best narco, robbery, and homicide detectives. SWAT guys were pulled together and created a new unit. They ran with all the latest military gear. And then the tech guys. Everything from my expertise to surveillance and fraud experts. We had a lot of cases going at any one time. Might be homicide, suspected terrorists, and even high-end white collar and political stuff."

"This task force still in existence?" Sam asked.

"Why, you interested?" Sartini said.

"Maybe, but I'm mostly just curious."

"It is in some form or another. Not the incarnation I was a part of. It all changed after the O'Connell thing."

"You familiar with the name Pennington?" I said.

Sartini looked toward the window and nodded. "Yeah, I knew him. He took off around the same time we lost O'Connell."

"Anything in particular you remember about him?"

Sartini spun his chair and faced his desk. He flipped through a few of the files.

"I don't mean about a case," I said. "How well did you know the guy? Recall anything about his family, friends? That kind of stuff."

The silence in the room as he thought it over made me keenly aware of the high-pitched ringing in my ears. That was new. I worked my jaw open and closed a few times. The ringing faded.

"He was a funny guy," Sartini said. "Personable, but distant. I can't recall him ever speaking about his family. Never mentioned a wife, kids, parents, none of that. I guess he didn't want any of us to get close to him. He did his job, you know, and went about his private time, uh, privately."

I sighed and nodded, knowing the break we were looking for wouldn't be found here.

"Who else would have records regarding the task force?" Sam asked.

"I'm not even sure now." Sartini glanced toward the window again. He was holding something back.

"Give us a name to start with," I said. "We're detectives. We can figure it out from there."

Sartini scrawled something on a piece of scrap paper, folded it, and handed it to me. I stuffed it in my pocket.

"Make sure you tell him I put you in touch with him," he said. "Otherwise he'll hang up on you. Shit, he probably will anyway. Be persistent."

"What do you think about the Birds so far this season?" Sam asked, referring to our beloved Eagles.

"Not crazy about this new coach," Sartini said. "This ain't college football. You need more than three plays to succeed in this league."

The banter went on for twenty minutes as we discussed all the local teams and a few conspiracy theories behind why they all were doing so badly lately. I'd hoped it would lead to more revelations about what we were really there for. But it didn't.

Sartini escorted us out and shut the door before we hit the grass. I had one foot in the car when he flipped the outside light back on and whipped the door open.

I walked back toward the house. Sartini was out of breath, like he'd done his best Usain Bolt impersonation.

"What is it?"

"I remembered something," he said. "West Virginia. Pennington had a hunting cabin in West Virginia."

CHAPTER SEVENTY-ONE

It took less than twenty-four hours after telling Cervantes about Pennington's possible hideout for us to drill down to the exact location. We managed to keep it hush, too. No local authorities. No feds. This was personal to each of us in our own way.

Sam and I split up in Morgantown. He drove to Pittsburg to pick up Cervantes. I headed south to the cabin in a rental car with a mountain bike strapped to the back. Going alone wasn't ideal, but we couldn't afford to lose any more time. If he had taken Cassie there, they could move on at any moment.

A topographical map of the area helped me find the perfect spot to leave the car. The area behind an old diner that hadn't been open for at least a decade provided enough cover that no one could spot the vehicle unless they went around back. What were the chances of that happening? It would be at least a day or so before anyone grew suspicious of the vehicle.

I strapped a handheld Garmin to the handlebars and picked my way through the dense woods. The bike rode well over the mostly level land. An occasional hill mixed with a gradual descending slope. There was a chill in the air. The first snowfall in the mountains wasn't that far off.

I laid the bike down a thousand yards out. After catching my breath, I detected a hint of wood smoke. How many homes could there be here? The closest road was a couple miles to the south, with nothing for a while to the east, north, and west. The air had chilled since I left the car. I had on woodlands tactical pants and a matching compression shirt. I pulled a hood from the saddlebag and slipped it over my head. I'd also brought a .308 takedown rifle. If I had a visual on both Cassie and Pennington, I'd take him out from a distance. Rounding out my gear was a Glock 17 and a pair of binoculars.

A quick text message let Sam know I had arrived. He replied back that they were en route and should be in the area within five hours. All I had to do was get close and wait.

I worked my way toward the house, using the thick trees for cover. Growing up, I'd spent a lot of time camping. I'd hunted a handful of times. No one would accuse me of being an outdoorsman, but I could hold my own.

Every step brought with it the chance of being discovered. My gaze never rested. It bounced left to right, up and down, in search of cameras and tripwires. Pennington had a couple-days head start on us. He could have readied the place. It was only a matter of time before we tracked him down. No matter how safe and secure he felt upon arrival, he knew we would not rest. The thought had to eat at him, chipping away at his last strands of sanity.

The thick white mortar between the old pine logs came into view. Smoke rose from the stack on the roof. It dissipated among the red and golden leaves. I had a view of two sides of the house. There were two windows per wall, and a front door under a wide uncovered porch. A single dirty-white rocking chair sat at the edge of the porch.

I pulled out the binoculars and scanned the exterior. A small security camera was mounted under the corner of the roof overhang. I traced the eave, found two more at each end. Was I in view now?

I brushed aside the leaves on the ground and laid down. The sun had barely penetrated the thick canopy, leaving the ground cool.

I alternated between windows, which were covered with white curtains. I couldn't see behind them, so instead I watched for signs of their movement.

The urge to make a dash toward the house and burst in guns blazing was strong. A voice in my head repeated, "*Stay put, Mitch.*" It wasn't my voice, nor that of my internal monologue. Was Cassie reaching out to me? Did she know I was there?

A chainsaw revved in the distance. I craned my head to isolate the direction it had come from. The sound was too faded to have originated inside the house. Perhaps Pennington was out gathering some firewood. Hopefully he wasn't dismembering Cassie.

"Speak to me, Cassie," I whispered.

Two fingers appeared through the slit in the window curtains. They pulled the fabric back a foot or so. The glare on the glass combined with darkness on the other side prevented me from seeing who stood there. Had Pennington heard the disturbance in the forest and wondered who was cutting down trees nearby? Or had he thought he spotted me on camera and was watching for my movement?

The curtain fell shut again. It didn't dash my hopes. In fact, the opposite happened. We figured chances were fifty-fifty that Pennington would come here. And then another fifty-fifty that he'd remained for more than a day. Now we knew he was here.

We were close.

Here I come, Cassie. Here I come.

CHAPTER SEVENTY-TWO

The forest darkened as the sun hovered low in the western sky. The air felt crisp with a temperature drop of twenty degrees or so. Smoke continued to rise from the cabin's chimney. The smell, combined with the dead leaves on the ground, reminded me of playing football with the kids in the neighborhood when I was a young boy. Over the few hours I'd been laying there, someone had looked out the windows a number of times, and cracked the door twice. I never got a solid look at the person. Could've been Cassie. Probably was Pennington.

It was still now. No breeze, no animal movement, and nothing going on within the cabin. The chainsaw had stopped long ago. I considered making a move, but it was too quiet.

The urge to investigate rose. Bad idea, I told myself. Pennington was going nowhere. Best to wait for reinforcements rather than going in there solo with guns blazing. No point in getting myself killed. If Cassie was still alive, then Pennington planned on keeping her alive. A couple of hours wasn't changing anything.

A branch snapped a slight distance behind me. It sounded like a sledgehammer on concrete, it had been so quiet. I propped up on my elbows and drew my knees up, battling stiff hips.

"Don't move, Tanner."

I lowered my chin to my chest and stared at the raised pile of leaves where I'd hid a spare pistol. It was three feet away, almost within reach. Any movement to get it would be met with a bullet in my back. Things might be going that way now.

"All right," Pennington said. "Hands behind your head, you know the drill."

Indeed, I did. After I crossed my ankles, he grabbed me by the back of my shirt and yanked me up to my knees. He took a wide berth around me, remaining out of range should I decide to lunge at him.

"The hell are you doing out here?" He aimed the shotgun at my chest, flicked it up toward my head. "How did you find me?"

"Wasn't too hard," I said. "You're a stupid son of a bitch."

Pennington smiled. "We both know that's not true."

"What does it matter? I found you. You've lost. Let her go and she and I will be on our way. You can live out the rest of your pathetic life here in the woods."

"Shut up, Tanner." He took a few steps back, setting his feet down carefully. "Now get up."

I moved my hands a few inches.

"No, no, no." He pulled out a pair of handcuffs then tossed them at my knees. "Put them on, then get up."

He was content letting me cuff myself, so I kept my hands in front. A few moments later, I walked past him toward the house.

"How'd you get out here without me seeing?" I asked.

Pennington didn't reply.

"Didn't see a back door when I checked the place out."

"Yup," he said. "And just like you didn't see me, no one is ever going to find your bodies."

Was she dead already? I tightened my chest and arms, pulling the stitches tight. I ignored the pain. An outburst now solved nothing. I had to get inside and see for myself.

"When did you spot me?" I said.

"Almost right after you arrived," he said.

"Why'd you wait so long?"

"Had to make sure you were alone. I mean, I figured you were stupid enough to do this by yourself. Just had to verify."

I climbed the steps to the front door and waited.

"Do the honors," he said.

I reached out with my shackled hands and turned the knob. Warm, oak-laden air rushed through the crack. It went to work warming my chilled face. I hesitated on the threshold for a moment. Stepping in led to a new reality, one which I wasn't sure I was ready to face yet.

"Go, Tanner," he said. "There's nothing waiting there."

Did he mean Cassie?

I pushed the door aside and stepped into the dimly lit room, scanning from left to right. A small corner kitchen contained a stove, fridge, and coffee maker. A square table was placed nearby. An open door revealed a bedroom. I turned toward the fireplace where a couple of chairs and a sofa faced each other.

"Mitch." Cassie bit her bottom lip as she rose.

"Sit your ass down," Pennington said.

She wiped her eyes and lowered herself back into the chair. She had on a green mock-turtleneck sweater with the sleeves pulled up to her elbows and a pair of yoga pants. She looked pale, gaunt, and bruised in a few spots. I could only imagine what she had gone through in that dungeon. She had to live with that for the rest of her life, along with all the other shit she dealt with each day.

"Have a seat next to her, Mitch."

I glanced over my shoulder at Pennington and leveled as hard a stare as I could, given the current balance of power. He didn't seem impressed.

"Are you okay?" Cassie asked as I sat in the chair next to hers.

The rough fabric caught on my shirt. It smelled like a cat had inhabited the cushions for years.

"I'm all right." I smiled at her. "Glad to see you're alive."

"If you two don't shut up, neither of you will be alive." Pennington rested the shotgun on the wall and pulled two Smith & Wessons off the mantle. He sat on the couch opposite our chairs, keeping the pistols trained on us. "How'd you find me?"

"Dumb luck," I said.

Pennington smiled, shook his head, then fired a shot into the chair I was sitting in. The bullet entered between my legs. The singed fabric stunk worse than burning hair. I tried not to flinch, but the blast caught me by surprise. I clenched my jaw tight, felt my nostrils flare wide as my fingertips dug into the chair's arms.

"Do I need to ask again?" he said.

I thought about telling him Cassie's spirit friends had led me there, but figured that'd result in another round being fired. And that one might not miss its mark. I glanced around the room, taking inventory. Wasn't a whole lot to take in.

"The task force," I said.

He nodded slowly, realizing I'd figured out his secret. "So, who gave up this place?"

I recalled a name from the list and blurted it out. "Jamison."

Pennington stared at me for fifteen seconds. "Did Novak burn?"

"We assumed one of the bodies was his."

He rose and paced around the couch. He had the look of a man considering how many loose ends remained. Two were sitting right in front of him. We'd be the simplest, and would only remain alive as long as he needed information from me. I had to come up with a way to keep him asking questions.

"Why'd you keep Cassie alive?" I asked. "Couldn't bring yourself to kill her?"

He stopped and leveled the pistol at her. "You wanna find out?"

"Not particularly." I kept my demeanor level, refusing to give him the shock factor he begged for.

"She's a bargaining chip." He stood behind the couch, hands resting on the back, pistols aimed loosely at us. "I had a hunch you'd figure it out. Didn't see much point in staying around Savannah and finding out for sure. If you came calling and managed to surprise me, I had Cassie here to secure my release."

"Cool with me," I said. "Leave her here and go. I won't stop you."

Pennington's smile broadened. "I like you, Tanner. I really do. It's almost going to hurt when I kill you."

"Pretty sure it's going to hurt a little bit. At least for me."

He chuckled. "You got balls, my man." His smile faded. "How much does Cervantes know?"

"I assume all of it."

"Where's he now?"

I shrugged. "Back in Savannah, I suppose."

"He has nothing to do with this?"

"He's chasing his own leads. I told him he was looking in the wrong places. We had it out, and I was informed I was no longer welcome and would be charged with obstruction of justice if I set foot in Savannah again."

Pennington shook his head. "He really couldn't stand you. Probably blames you for this mess, too."

"I can live with that."

He lifted one of the pistols, wagged it, smiled. "Not for much longer."

A light on the mantle flickered red and a low beep sounded. Pennington glanced at the window, then back at me. He stiffened, held both pistols up. "The hell was that?"

I shrugged. "Your place, man. I don't know what you got rigged."

"Who's out there?" He kept his gaze and an S&W on me while he aimed the other at the window. It was the same one I'd seen him looking out of. Or maybe that had been Cassie. It appeared she was free to move about.

A second light turned red, and another alarm sounded. Pennington swung his head toward the door. Apparently, each light and tone matched a specific trigger he had outside of the cabin.

I could have sat there attempting to figure it out.

Instead I burst forward, planted a foot on the couch and jumped over it.

CHAPTER SEVENTY-THREE

The pistol wasn't the only thing I had left buried outside. My phone was hidden amongst the leaves as well. If they found the phone and not me, they'd know something had happened and they would split up. Pennington had the cabin for one purpose and this was it. A hideout. He was a smart guy and wouldn't leave himself blind should someone come after him. While I hadn't suspected he knew I was there the entire time, he'd know when we made our move. It was a calculated risk on our part. The three of us had the ability to take him out even if he knew we were there.

The plan hadn't gone accordingly. But Sam and Cervantes tripping the alarms had given me the moment I needed to make a move. I planted my foot firmly on the couch cushion and held my fists in front. Pennington caught sight of me out of the corner of his eyes and spun to brace himself. I drove my fists into his throat, let them slide around the sides, and then my fingers came together behind his neck. The handcuff chain dug in under his Adam's apple.

He'd dropped one of the pistols as we slammed into the wall. It thumped on the ground, and in our shuffling, skated across the floor after one of us kicked it. He drove his palm into my face. It caught on my nose and drove my head back. His thumb worked toward my eye socket. I'd once heard of a case where a woman gouged this old guy's eyes out and then shoved them into his mouth, causing him to choke to death. Hell if that was happening to me.

I had one of Pennington's arms trapped under mine. He slammed the other pistol into my back a few times. It wouldn't be long before he worked his arm around and shot me. I had to neutralize him. I grabbed a fistful of hair and pulled him close to me, then yanked back hard, driving his skull into the solid wall. There was no paneling or plaster here. Just solid wood beams. A couple times was all it took for his grip on my face to loosen. But he continued to slam the butt of the pistol into my back.

Cassie ran around the couch. I spotted her kneeling down, reaching for the pistol. Cannon fire erupted behind my back. Pennington had seen her, too, and turned his Smith & Wesson on her. I drove my knee into his groin three times, then head butted him until his body went limp.

"You okay?" I yelled, mostly so I could hear myself over the intense ringing.

She crawled from behind the couch and stared up at me. "I'm good."

I pulled my hands free from Pennington's head and let him collapse on the ground. But I was nowhere done despite the voice in my head telling me to gain control over the situation by securing the firearms. I dropped to a knee on his diaphragm. His face reddened as he struggled for air.

"You son of a bitch," I said. "You wore a badge, man. You wore a goddamn badge."

He strained to stare at me. I wondered what insults he wished to hurl at me. I didn't give him a chance. I drew both hands up, then smashed my fists into his mouth. I delivered blow after blow, like slamming a sledgehammer down on the guy's face, knocking his teeth into his throat. In the background, Cassie called my name, but I didn't stop. I wanted to kill this man with my bare hands.

Cassie darted toward the door and opened it. Sam and Cervantes rushed in.

I continued to pummel Pennington, ignoring the fire from broken bones in my hand.

Sam grabbed me and pulled me off. Five feet away I saw the damage I had done to the guy. His nose was split and driven to the left, eyes were swollen shut, blood poured from his mouth. Cervantes knelt down next to his former partner and felt for a pulse. He looked up at Sam with tightly drawn lips and shook his head. I almost missed that he then wrapped his thick hand around Pennington's neck. Cervantes's forearm muscles rippled as he finished the job.

Sam pulled me further away. Staring into my savage eyes, what did he think about what I had done? Would he have done the same? Did he wish it had been him in the room? I stared back at him while forcing ragged breaths through my lungs.

"It's done, Mitch." Sam squeezed my shoulders. "You finished it."

Cervantes stood over his partner's body. "We need to deal with this."

"What do you suggest?" Sam said.

"Burn it."

"Too much damage," Sam said. "Can't contain it and keep it from spreading."

"He got out of the house without me seeing," I said. "He's gotta have a trap door or something in here."

Cassie went to the kitchen and pushed the table out of the way. "It's here."

We all took a look at it. If she hadn't seen him open it, there's no way we would have found it.

"How?" Sam asked.

Cassie pulled a rod off the top of the refrigerator and lifted a cutout in the floorboard. Cervantes pulled the trap door open. We were hoping for a tunnel, but it just led under the house.

"We can dump him out here in the woods," Cervantes said. "Who's ever gonna come across it?"

"Never say never," I said. "I heard a chainsaw nearby earlier. There's people around."

In the end we buried him by moonlight a few hundred yards from the cabin. We cleaned the place up and removed any evidence that we'd been there. The look in Cervantes' eyes made me wonder if he'd return again to seek insight into how this had happened.

I knew I'd never return. In more ways than one, too.

CHAPTER SEVENTY-FOUR

The oversized rocker rolled over the decking with a rhythmic click-clack. The vodka and Mexican mineral water went down smooth. Didn't even need a lime. I'd already had a couple, and Cassie seemed willing to keep them coming.

We'd returned to Savannah that morning after finding a doctor who checked us out with no questions asked. I'd gathered my stuff from the old lady's apartment and thanked her for her hospitality. She told me I had a room there anytime I wanted to visit, and said with a wink she hoped that'd be often.

There was a time this past week when I thought that would be the case. Now I didn't know.

A cool breeze blew past. The skin on my arm pricked as the sun's final rays dissipated. The screen door slammed. I looked back and smiled at Cassie as she held out the drink to me. The wind whipped her dress and hair to the side. A smile formed behind the wayward auburn strands.

"You gonna be okay?" She eased into her seat and stared out at her overgrown lawn.

"Me?" I placed my drink on the table between us. "Aren't you the one who took the brunt in this ordeal?"

She held her glass close to her chest. "After dying, everything else seems so... ordinary."

"There's nothing ordinary about what you went through."

She shrugged. "I don't want to talk about it or think about it or relive it in any way. I still have everything going on around me. People need my help. Dwelling on this will squash any desire I have to be there for them."

"People?"

"Yeah, in a way. I don't know, Mitch. Call them whatever you want. They aren't going to leave me alone. I can't let what happened keep me from fulfilling what it is I need to do. This is my mission now."

"Do you have to do it here?"

She looked away. "The danger's gone. Pennington is dead, and there is no way Novak is ever getting out again. Maybe I'll move to another house, but I feel safe here. Savannah is my home."

"What about a place like Philly? Lots of folks needing help up there."

Cassie set her glass on the teal metal table between us. She rose and walked over to me. Leaning forward, she placed her hands on the rocker's arms. I let the chair come to a stop as she leaned in. Her hair tickled my cheek. Our lips met for a few seconds.

She bit her lip as she pulled back, shaking her head. "It's gone."

"It's gone," I repeated her words. Too much had happened. Her abduction had changed something within her. And it had changed my feelings toward her. We had worked together for so long, and the original spark that developed all those years ago smoldered over time until the flame erupted. But the pain she endured, and the anxiety I faced trying to find her, had stifled the fire. Might've put it out completely.

She fell into her chair and it rolled back almost to the tipping point. "I'm doomed, you know. I'll never find someone. It seems like they won't let me."

"They?"

"Someone, or something, knows that if I find peace and happiness, they won't get to use me anymore. And I guess, right now, I feel I need to be used."

We sat in silence as the orange and pink faded into the blue night sky. Stars spotted the darkness amid silver, wispy clouds.

"I'll be right back," she said.

I handed her my empty glass as she headed inside, then got up and leaned against the deck rail. A neighbor had fired up a grill. The smell of ribs hung thick in the air.

The screen door squeaked open.

"What do you say we order a pizza or something?" I said.

Cassie remained silent.

I turned and saw her standing in front of the door, clutching something to her chest. Her eyes glistened in the dim light.

"What is it?"

She moved one hand, revealing the postcard I had brought her. It seemed like ages ago when I asked her to see if she could gain any knowledge from it. I dropped it on the kitchen table after she invited me in earlier.

I reached for her hand and pulled her closer. "What do you know, Cassie?"

She took a deep breath and closed her eyes. A thin layer of tears spread between her eyelids. "He's in Denver with Marissa. She's messed up. I almost want to say she's brainwashed. Robbie feels like he's being held against his will in a... I guess you would call it a commune." She looked up at me with glassy eyes. "He's okay otherwise. He hasn't been hurt. They keep him separated from his mother a lot of the time. They keep him busy with work, and he's being told he has to think like they do if he wants to survive."

I searched her eyes for more, but that was all she had. "Denver. You're sure?"

The postcard had been postmarked from the Mile High city. Didn't make sense that Marissa would let him send it from there and then remain in place.

"He's there." She extended the postcard to me. "Trust me. As much as you ever have, Mitch, trust me."

I leaned in and kissed her on the cheek. "I have to go, Cassie. I have to go right now."

"I know. I already called for a cab to take you to the airport."

We retreated into the house. A few seconds later we heard the vehicle pull up to the house and honk. Cassie helped me gather my things and walked me to her front door.

I stared into her eyes for a moment. "Maybe, someday—"

She put her finger to my mouth. "Just go, Mitch. Call me if you need help."

I focused on a mole on the back of the driver's head for the entire ride. It kept me from rehashing everything I was trying to stifle. I dragged my carryon to the check-in counter and purchased a ticket for a flight to Atlanta leaving in less than an hour. The layover would be long, but by morning I'd be in Denver.

I found a quiet corner and called Sam, and then Momma, letting them know I wouldn't be home anytime soon. Then I dug through my contact list until I found another name. One I never thought I'd call again. Taking a deep breath, I hit the send button.

A man answered and spoke quick and gruff, identifying the FBI's Denver Field Office.

I cleared my throat. "Yeah, can you connect me with DSAC Bridget Dinapoli?"

The End

MITCH TANNER'S story continues soon in book three, *Deliver Us From Darkness.*

Sign up for L.T. Ryan's new release newsletter and be the first to find out when new Mitch Tanner and Jack Noble novels are published (and usually at a discount for the first 48 hours). To sign up, simply fill out the form on the following page:

http://ltryan.com/newsletter/

As a thank you for signing up, you'll receive a complimentary copy of *The Recruit: A Jack Noble Short Story.*

If you enjoyed reading *Into The Darkness,* I would appreciate it if you would help others enjoy this book, too.

Lend it. This e-book is lending-enabled on platforms that allow it, so please, share it with a friend.

Recommend it. Please help other readers find this book by recommending it to friends, readers' groups and discussion boards.

Review it. Please tell other readers why you liked this book by reviewing it at Amazon or Goodreads. If you do write a review, please send me an email at ltryan70@gmail.com so I can thank you with a personal email.

ALSO BY L.T. RYAN

Jack Noble Series

The Recruit (free)

Noble Beginnings

A Deadly Distance

Ripple Effect (Bear & Noble)

Thin Line

Noble Intentions

When Dead in Greece

Noble Retribution

Noble Betrayal

Never Go Home

Beyond Betrayal (Clarissa Abbot)

Noble Judgment

Never Cry Mercy

Deadline

End Game

Mitch Tanner Series

The Depth of Darkness

Mitch Tanner Book 2 - Late 2017

Affliction Z Series

Affliction Z: Patient Zero

Affliction Z: Abandoned Hope

Affliction Z: Descended in Blood

Affliction Z Book 4 Late Summer 2017

Printed in Great Britain
by Amazon

37195663R00199